Walking in Freedom

Truth=Freedom, Book 3

Julie Brown

35 Can anything ever separate us from Christ's love?
Does it mean he no longer loves us if we have trouble or calamity, or are persecuted, or hungry, or destitute, or in danger, or threatened with death?
37 No, despite all these things, overwhelming victory is ours through Christ, who loved us. 38 And I am convinced that nothing can ever separate us from God's love.
Neither death nor life, neither angels nor demons, neither our fears for today nor our worries about tomorrow—not even the powers of hell can separate us from God's love.
39 No power in the sky above or in the earth below—indeed, nothing in all creation will ever be able to separate us from the love of God that is revealed in Christ Jesus our Lord.
Romans 8:35, 37-39 NLT

Chapter One

"I lost him." Mark Bruens burst into the boys' bunkhouse at Shannah Ranch, slamming the door behind him. The vacuum of air fluttered posters on the wall. Large, screened windows cast shadows on the row of bunk beds around the perimeter of the room.

He was eye-to-eye with the top bunks and could see they were all empty. Empty. The uniformity of handmade blankets on one end of the beds with pillows lined up on the other, like he taught, and expected from the boys, rivaled the chaos in his head. Neatness meant order and order meant peacefulness. Mark was anything but peaceful.

"Billy, if you're in here, you need to come out right now." This was ridiculous. Searching, again, for the boy.

Mark rubbed his eyes. "Billy, I know this week's been hard and seeing your father pull up wasn't easy." He called into the empty room. He needed to put a stop to this behavior.

He strode over to the bathroom area and pulled the door open. Fog on the mirrors over the line of sinks greeted him from someone's recent shower. All of the stalls were empty.

Another closed door housed the mini-classroom he'd added several years ago and was locked. There was a back door which allowed people, namely female teachers, to come in without walking through the large, often smelly- they were boys, for Pete's sake- sleeping quarters. Mark pulled out his key ring and searched for the correct one. He fumbled through several, dropped the whole ring and scooped it up.

Come on, Mark. As the founder and director of the residential boys' home, he knew what all of the keys unlocked, but his brain would not connect with his fingers.

Of course, it was the last one on the ring.

"Billy!" The long table with stacks of books, science experiments on the windowsill, placards of the solar system, and grammatical sentence diagrams were all enveloped in silence. No lanky fourteen-year-old.

Mark relocked the door and trudged over to Billy's assigned bunk. He sank down on the neatly made bed and put his hands over his face.

Lord, this was supposed to be another routine Sunday with normal chores before leaving for church. After one of the boys had grumbled about not doing Billy's job again, Mark decided to go have a talk with the boy, remind him of the consequences for shirking his responsibilities. This wasn't the first time Billy had been upset in recent days. He'd hid for hours on Friday when Mark turned his father away from the ranch. Crazy old man thought he could just drop in at a court-appointed residential facility and pick up the son he hadn't cared two whits about for at least a year. How the guy found out where Billy was working out his probation, was still a mystery.

Mark spied the generic footlocker every kid was assigned, the combo lock dangling from the latch. Jumping up, narrowly missing the top bunk, he opened it and frowned. Not only were his toiletries missing, but so was Billy's baseball mitt. Why would he hide with his baseball mitt? If there was anything Billy got excited about, it was playing catch with Mark's brother, Colton. And the only time Billy responded without a smirk, snide comment, or glare from his dark, moody eyes.

He slammed the locker shut.

Mark looked up at the coat rack where the boys hung their jackets and backpacks. A space below Billy's name was devoid of the ragged hoodie he always wore or the newly purchased backpack.

What in the world? *Lord?*

Mark sprinted to the ranch house, the screen door bouncing back on its frame. Sweat ran down his back and froze in little nuggets of fear. The taste of anxiety gnawed at the back of his throat, acid moving up from his stomach.

"Mark, did you find him? I searched… what's wrong?" Colton trailed after him.

Mark ran to the back room where he'd set up his office. Switching on the computer, he scooted his chair up close to the monitor. Colton stood in the doorway. Mark frantically tapped a pen on the desk, waiting for the programs to boot up.

He raked fingers through his hair. Too slow. They had to invest in better equipment, a better security system. Click. Click. He chewed on a fingernail as one-by-one the images popped up on the screen. Mark struggled to gain some semblance of order in his head. White flashes of light were beginning to appear in his peripheral vision, a sure sign a migraine was lurking in the wings.

"Are you thinking he left the property?" Colton pulled up a chair next to him.

Mark started rewinding the security tape, carefully examining each clip. "His hoodie, his toiletries, everything is gone, even his baseball mitt."

"Hold on a minute. Billy knows what the consequences are. It's immediate jail time, his probation revoked. No one's ever left the ranch before." Colton gripped Mark's shoulder.

Mark shrugged him off. "Where is he, then? We've looked everywhere. Do you think he's hiding under his bed? No, because I looked there. How about in the goat pen like last time? Nope, not there either. Because you looked there. What about in the cellar where the monsters live?" Mark threw up air quotes. "Nope, because Aunt Eunice looked there, too. He's gone!"

"You need to calm down. Billy's pretty good at hiding."

Mark shook his head and continued to reverse the tape. One hour back, nothing. Two hours back, still nothing.

His anxiety rocketed every time there was motion detected on the security camera.

Then, a coyote or deer would pop into view,

eyes green in the camera.

"Take a breather. I'll look for a while." Colton shifted his chair, closer to the monitors.

Mark stood and looked out the window as Colton took over the search. Maybe he was wrong. Maybe Billy was hiding on the property and they'd yet to find him. It wasn't possible that he'd lost the boy, was it?

"Uh, Mark?" Colton narrowed in on a frame.

Mark looked over his shoulder, hands on hips, knowing it wouldn't be good news. Even a small bear or wildcat wouldn't have caused Colton's tone. It was laced with surprise, dread, and a little fear.

Mark felt it even before looking. Billy had left the ranch.

The screen showed the boy, hoodie and backpack in tow, climbing through the perimeter fence, unconcerned about the security camera catching the whole thing.

He slumped into the chair. "What's the time stamp?"

"4 am."

Mark looked at his watch, his Sunday best, the one he'd given himself for graduating from seminary. "He's been gone three hours." He pounded the desk with his fist.

"For the love of..." Colton blew out a breath. "What now?"

Mark hung his head. Thousands of thoughts swirled. Where was Billy going? Didn't he realize how much trouble he was in? No one had ever left the ranch, like Colton said. There hadn't even been any infractions since Mark opened the boys' home as an alternative to long-term detention.

He exploded out of the chair and entered the kitchen, Colton close behind. With a growl, he swiped all of the newspapers, unopened mail, and coupons neatly stacked off the counter onto the floor. His favorite mug, with untouched coffee from the morning, teetered on the edge before it crashed into a million pieces. Coffee splattered, narrowly missing Colton's boots. Mark closed his eyes and took a deep swallow of air.

"Oh, my goodness." Aunt Eunice rushed in, kneeling to pick up the shards.

Mark met his brother's gaze over their aunt's head. He wanted to break every single thing in the kitchen. How could he have let this happen? Billy was hurting and his normal mode of expressing pain was to hide, so this was a surprise? The boy had escalated from hiding to running away. Mark wasn't on top of it. Failed. Not doing his job. Since Billy's father's unannounced arrival at the ranch, Billy had already hidden once and was clearly distraught. After a call to Mrs. Jenkins, the case manager, it was confirmed his father had no legal authority or parental rights to visit or take Billy with him, despite the demand. Who was he kidding? Those comments were meant as threats, coercion.

But no pressure, Mark. You couldn't have known, Mark. Yes, he could. He'd failed.

"Leave it." Mark spoke harshly to his aunt.

Colton glared at him.

Aunt Eunice continued to pick up the pieces, and Mark bent down beside her.

"I'm sorry I yelled." Mark sniffed. A roller

coaster of emotions, but he didn't need to upset his aunt. He clenched and unclenched his jaw.

Colton pushed a trashcan in their direction.

"Thanks." Mark brushed the last of the mug pieces into a dustpan and dropped them in the trash. "I guess the next step is to call Billy's case manager."

What a fun conversation that would be.

She'd think he was an idiot, unable to control the boys he supervised. Failing. Unqualified. Maybe she'd recommend that the boys' home be closed down or have someone else run it. Someone more competent than him.

And what about the other boys? Would they see his ineptness? Doubt his ability to keep them safe? Or would they only see that Billy got away with breaking the law, and he was powerless to stop them from doing the same?

Finding Billy was paramount to Mark not losing what he'd worked hard to accomplish. His reputation was in jeopardy. He'd be done, no longer trusted by the courts or the boys he served. Not to mention the boy's own safety.

Sick to his stomach, Mark went back to the office where the image of Billy running away was still on the screen. He pulled up the file with Billy's court records and scanned for the case manager's number. Hopefully, a weekend number was listed. This couldn't wait until office hours.

~

Ellie Jenkins stepped out of her truck and pushed the button on the security post. The directions to the ranch had been easy and simple to follow, although she sensed Mr. Bruens hesitancy in her coming out. A heavy gate blocked the drive. The words 'SHANNAH RANCH' were etched into a metal sign, hanging on the gate.

Dust settled on her boots as the wind blew gusts of dirt across the property. She pushed tendrils of hair out of her face and waited for some type of response from the black speaker. This was not how she pictured her Sunday morning unfolding.

The box squawked. "Mrs. Jenkins?"

"Yes, that's me. I'm here to see Mark Bruens."

"This is Mark. When the gate opens, drive down the road, past the old farmhouse. I'll be waiting at the end."

"Ok, thanks." Ellie watched as the gate swung open. She chewed the inside of her cheek. His tone was curt, but that matched the image she remembered of him in court. No nonsense. A hint of military, a preciseness in his mannerisms, a solid man of values according to other professionals in the family court system. And he was a bit handsome. Tall, wide shoulders, perfectly manicured in a manly way. She'd only spoken to him briefly, but in that short time, he exuded confidence, structure, and safety.

Mr. Bruens's place, Shannah Ranch, was the perfect resolution for the juveniles placed in her care. She'd researched options for the boys she represented, if they were eligible, for places like this. Their website said 'Shannah' meant new beginnings and a change or redo. A perfect fit for a boy Ellie didn't believe needed jail time. More like an environment where he could flourish outside of an absent mother and an abusive father.

Ellie shook her head. In all her years of being a social worker, she'd never lost a boy before. As hopeful as she was about a positive outcome, it wasn't likely. Mr. Bruens stated facts, not theories. But boys didn't go missing. Not on her watch.

Ellie drove down the long drive. The ranch was well-maintained, something she expected from its stellar reputation.

The man standing out on the wide, wrap-around porch frowned as she stopped the truck. His shirt stretched across his chest, defining a muscular torso, a result of everyday farm work. Another time and place, she mused. She resisted the urge to check her appearance in the mirror, settling instead for a quick wipe of her hands on her jeans and a brush at the wrinkle in her shirt from the seatbelt.

"Hi." The man stepped down to meet her. He lowered his shoulders, his tension palpable.

"Hi." Ellie reached out to shake his hand. He clasped hers firmly and then stepped back, crossing his arms. He met her gaze and pursed his lips.

Apprehension spread like a cloak around them until he cleared his throat.

"Mrs. Jenkins…"

"Please. It's Ellie." He looked like he was about to throw up. She might, too.

He tore his gaze away from her. "I'm sorry to drag you out here on the weekend. I just didn't think it could wait. I clearly didn't think about a lot of things."

Ellie lifted troubled eyes to him and waited. People said unexpected things, silence was a great motivator.

"I really didn't think he'd leave the premises. I didn't. I was mistaken. He walked right off the property. By his own volition. Walked. Right. Off." Mark led the way up the steps, gripping the railing.

"Mr. Bruens," Ellie reached the top of the stairs, and standing on the porch next to him, she laid a hand on his arm. He was clearly shaken. She bit her lip and moved away from him. "Let's go look at the cameras. We can figure out what the next steps are. Together."

Mark opened the door for her, lips tight.

She stepped into the house, noting his height, his woodsy cologne. The police should be called and the agency notified that Billy was MIA. Her heart went out to both of them; to Billy for believing running away was the only option and for this gentle man who was responsible for Billy's well-being. She turned the wedding band on her finger.

Lord, give me wisdom.

A man and a woman stood in the doorway when they entered and Mark introduced them as his brother, Colton, and his aunt, Eunice. They turned down a long hallway where family pictures adorned the walls. The house had a neat, orderly feel with warm splotches of color, a mixture of Mark and maybe his aunt?

"This is my office, of sorts." Mark spun the office chair around for her to sit in front of the monitors. He sank into the folding chair next to the desk.

"You've got a lot of books." Ellie slid into the proffered chair after glancing at the wide bookshelves on two sides of the room. The third wall held a white-dusted brick fireplace that would warm up the room on a cold day. Mark's desk was covered with magazines and hard-bound books. Ellie picked up one of the smaller books, *Christianity has a Face*. Her eyebrows raised.

"Are you religious?" She glanced at Mark's face as he punched in passwords on the computer. His shoulder brushed hers as he leaned in. Ellie smelled his shampoo and resisted the urge to touch his curls to see if they were as soft as they looked. What was the matter with her? Under the desk, she twisted the gold band and let the question drop. "Tell me more about what happened prior to this morning."

Mark glanced at her and continued fiddling with the security system. "When I called you on Friday? About his dad stopping by?"

"Yes. And after that."

"I ran him off, the father, but he said he'd be back with the sheriff."

"You said when you called this morning that he wasn't hiding, that you'd looked everywhere first, before checking the security cameras. Did Dad come back? Is it possible Billy left with him?"

"No." Mark grunted. "Last time, he hid for a bit until Colton found him out with the goats. He said he was afraid his father would come for him again."

"Maybe he left so his father couldn't find him."

Images sprang to life in front of her. Four camera views moved through scenes.

"Right here." Mark pushed the stop button on one of the cameras. "See? He's going through the fence." Mark rubbed the stubble on his chin, making a scratchy noise. They watched as the boy split the barbed wire fencing and stepped outside the ranch perimeters. "I can't believe this is happening."

"What's the time stamp on this video?" Ellie squinted.

"4 am."

"Goodness, that's early."

"Another hour and everyone would be starting to move around."

"Don't you have an alarm that goes off when someone enters or leaves the property?

Mark cringed. "Yes, however, my aunt had friends over last night, and they kept setting it off. I muted it. Stupid, I know."

"Mark, that's not stupid. I know people with similar alarm systems, and the chimes can be very irritating."

"Well, I did it. Now what?" Mark sighed. "I'm worried about his safety. I'm worried about his state of mind. I'm concerned that he's either running from his dad or, Lord, have mercy, he's running to his dad. I know how messed up boys and their relationships with their dads can…." Mark hesitated. "I'm more than a little wary of what the other boys here are thinking. I don't know. I'm at a loss."

Mark looked at Ellie. She raised her blue eyes to study his brown ones. This close, she could see the flecks of green and gold. She studied his face. She wanted to believe they'd find Billy. He'd been gone only a couple of hours. Six, to be exact. She broke eye contact with him and steepled her fingers in front of her. If they waited, searched on their own, and something happened to Billy, they were liable for not telling the authorities. The guidelines clearly spelled out what type of response this line of behavior should receive. The case manager notified. Check. The police called. The guardian authority, her boss, contacted. Could she hold off on the second two? Without losing her job? But what if they found him? No harm, no foul? Nothing was that easy. Ellie frowned, reluctant to voice any of the other thoughts swirling. If they did find the boy, and he refused to come back to the home, the authorities would definitely get involved. And probably ask why they hadn't said anything early on. But what if they did find him, he returned on his own, would he run again?

Ellie looked back at him. Mark had an outstanding history with the court system, but she didn't know him. Was she willing to stake her career on their ability to find Billy and bring him home without harm? Just the two of them? Pretty big gamble. After all, the kid had walked away from Mark's property. Was she certain she could make this a win-win situation?

"Look, you don't know me, I get that," Mark leaned forward. "But I'm pretty sure I can convince him to come back if we can find him. I also know that my reputation is on the line, and I promise you, I'll do whatever it takes to keep it untarnished. Please don't close me down. I know other residential programs have been shut down for far less serious reasons, but I'm begging you. Please."

"Wow, that is some serious snowballing. Closing this place down?" Ellie and Mark turned to see Colton in the doorway. "Now that we know he's outside the boundaries, maybe we take a look first."

"Can you give us a few hours?" Mark pleaded with Ellie.

"This could cost a lot, Mark. Especially if we don't find him." She responded, acknowledging the fact that she said 'we'. "On one condition."

"Name it. I want to find him. Make sure he's alright. Bring him back." Mark pressed his fingertips to his forehead.

"I go with you. My reputation is at stake, too. I should have checked in more. Should have known the ripple effect his father showing up would have. If I'd done more on Friday, this might not have happened. First whiff of us being in over our heads, I'm calling the authorities, though. As much as you don't want to lose this place, I'm not ready to end my career either. Which means, I have to trust you, something I'm not likely to do a second time." Ellie could not believe her ears, her own voice saying those things. Saving one kid would be worth it, though. Billy's emotional state hung in the balance of how soon they found him. Or if his father found him first. She couldn't stop the small thought of what spending the next twenty-four hours with this man might look like. A tiny shiver went up her spine. Despite his attractiveness, she had to keep the goal of finding this kid as the most important thing. Had to.

Chapter 2

Mark put his head in his hands. The consequences were high on both sides. Billy could be in real trouble and he and Mrs. Jenkins could be as well. He wished he had more time to make a calculated response to the situation, but there wasn't time to spare. He hated making quick decisions, certainly more information would be helpful. If they called in the authorities like Ellie suggested, they'd probably shut him down until Billy was found and scatter the boys living at the ranch. He had an obligation to them, too. He and Ellie could go looking for Billy together, but if anything went wrong, she could lose her job and he, the ranch and the respect of the court. He didn't want that either.

Silence gathered. The dreaded ticking of the clock in the other room mocked his indecision. Six hours and counting.

When Mark looked up, Colton was still at the door and Ellie was still beside him, the computer monitor frozen on the image of Billy going through the fence. He looked out the window and rubbed a hand across his forehead.

"Okay, this is what we're going to do." Mark stood abruptly, startling Ellie. "We will look outside the perimeter until 6pm tonight and if we don't find him by then, we'll call in the authorities. Okay?"

Ellie nodded her head.

"I'll ride over by the fence he tripped through, but honestly, it's so close to the road, he's probably out of the brush and down several miles if he's still on foot." Colton chimed in.

"We'll go on the road, maybe stop at the neighbors, Selena and Brandon's." Mark added, looking at Ellie. "Are you still in this? Or would you rather be looped in if and when it's time to bring in the authorities?"

"I said I'd go. I think it's wise to set a time limit on finding him. He may be way out of our range or jurisdiction by now." Ellie looked at a wide-banded smart watch on her wrist.

Mark didn't miss the gold on her ring finger. She twisted it constantly. She was as anxious as he was. No surprise she was married. She was stunningly beautiful and had the maturity of a woman who was confident in her abilities and yet humble and compassionate in her tone and mannerisms. The whole package. Her husband was a lucky guy.

He couldn't have caught a woman like Mrs. Jenkins anyway. He wasn't magnetic like his brother or easy to talk to. He never saw the benefit in small talk, always jumping to the deep questions, which made people tuck tail and run. And where would he meet these women? Church? They were all married or divorced with families. He couldn't see himself with a ready-made family. The bars? Not hardly.

Maybe the grocery store or the library? Ha. That'd make for interesting conversation. He'd make a fool of himself, trying to say something of value.

What he found meaningful centered around raising boys in a safe environment. The hard ones. The ones who'd lived through what he'd lived through. Those he could relate to, those he could love and guide and take their well-being seriously. And be everything his dad wasn't. If he could. A niggling doubt surfaced often that said he'd never be good enough. His own demon voice. And what woman in her right mind would understand the dichotomy he lived?

"Let's go, then." Mark's tone was harsher than he'd meant it to be. Losing a kid was his fault only. No one else's. If he'd been more aware of how distraught Billy was, he could have checked in with him over the weekend. He should've thought Billy running away for real, not just hiding, was a possibility. But looking for Billy with Mrs. Jenkins? Made him feel better, like they could accomplish anything. Almost.

~

Ellie pushed her chair back and followed Mark out of the room. A quick glance at Colton's face told her a lot. Mark was beating himself up about Billy leaving and Colton was concerned. Who wouldn't be upset? She certainly was. She didn't know these two brothers at all, but they clearly had a tight relationship. Aunt Eunice patted her arm as they left the house.

"We'll take my ride." Mark opened the passenger door of his truck. "Colton, call me if you find anything."

"Yep." Colton answered.

Ellie walked to the extended door and then glanced up at Mark. His commanding attitude caused her to hesitate. He raised questioning eyebrows at her, shoved his hands in his pockets.

"I'd rather drive. I know the land and where the roads go." Mark's tone was soft, gentle, a complete opposite from his earlier gruffness. She could still feel the tension rolling off him, however, he was trying to be less curt.

"Yes, I'm sure. It's just that…" Ellie started.

"I'm not a crazy driver, Mrs. Jenkins. And we really need to find Billy." But…" She hadn't been alone with a man anywhere and certainly not crammed together in a truck. And a stranger to boot.

"Look, Mrs. Jenkins, I'm sure your husband would understand. As a case manager, you must meet with a lot of people, and I'm certain he's taught you to be safe. We need to get moving, unless you've changed your mind and want to stay here with Aunt Eunice?" Mark frowned.

Ellie shook her head and climbed into the cab. She could feel the tears filling her eyes, threatening to drop. Ellie turned away. *Get control of yourself. He's being nice and caring.* She couldn't cry at every handsome man's care and concern for her. She slid sunglasses from her purse over her eyes. She would not cry in front of this man.

She took a deep breath and surveyed the interior of the truck. Gum wrappers, hard candy, and Tootsie Pops littered the console. A half-drunk Diet Coke bottle rested in the cup holder. The cab had a faint earthy smell, the same she'd smelled on Mark when he bent next to her at the camera monitors.

She twisted the gold band. He thought she was married. She wasn't, not really, at least that's what people told her. Other opinions assailed her, too. Ones that said she had to wait a specific time before another relationship, or ones that suggested she would be forever married to her husband, ignoring the common vow 'till death do us part'. And what about the pictures in her house of them as a couple, when did she put them away? Or her rings? She wasn't ready to take them off yet. Her husband, Jason, had passed a year ago. Maybe she should. The thought of not wearing them after so many years of marriage, made her heart clench. Putting them away would mean it truly was final. Her rings were symbols of their union, of being committed to each other for life. However short that had been. People with good intentions would say, "he loved her for the rest of his life." Not long enough in her book. They were supposed to grow old together. Sit in rocking chairs and watch their grandchildren play in the backyard. Not live out her days as a widow.

Sorry, Lord. A touch, a kind word, all triggers for grief. When would she ever not be caught off guard? God was in control, and He was aware of every detail. He was also faithful and good. He'd taken better care of her than anyone and saw to needs she hadn't even voiced yet.

Ellie took a deep breath and refocused. She owed Mark no explanation or clarification. He could think what he wanted.

"The neighbors are over this hill. Billy's driven

cattle over there before, so maybe they've seen him." He glanced over at her, and she saw her reflection in his mirrored sunglasses.

Pick it up, girl. She looked so solemn. It was a serious situation, but the least she could do was be a little positive. And get out of her own head. "Ok." There you go, that's being encouraging, the sarcasm echoing in her thoughts.

Mark pulled into a lane with grass on either side. Brown cows and colored ponies roamed the pastures, grazing in the sun.

"Hey, neighbor." A muscled man rode up to the truck window. His big sorrel horse stuck its nose into the cab and snorted. "Sorry, he's obnoxious."

Ellie would have laughed out loud if they were there for a social visit.

"No problem. I think he's done that before on me." Mark stepped out of the truck.

Ellie stayed where she was.

"Hey, one of the boys got upset and took off. He left in the middle of the night, actually, early this morning. You haven't seen any of them, have you?"

"Wow. No, I haven't seen anyone. We went to the early church service, best way to start the day, and then Selena went to the store. I'll tell her, though."

"Colton is riding the fence where he went through, but I thought we'd stop here first."

"I can catch up with him, and we can search together." The man leaned down in the truck window to look at Ellie.

Ellie raised her hand, gave him a small wave.

"Brandon, this is Mrs. Jenkins, the boy's case

manager. Brandon used to be a Texas Ranger, like in law enforcement, not baseball."

"Nice to meet you, Ma'am."

"Likewise."

"How long has the boy been gone now?" Brandon asked.

Mark looked at his watch. "Almost seven hours now."

"I'll send Selena and the ranch foreman a text in case he does show up here." Brandon turned his horse. "We'll do our best to find him, Mark."

"Thanks." Mark threw his arm up over the seat, behind Ellie's head, and backed the truck up so he could turn around.

Ellie stared ahead, willing herself to not respond to his arm so close. She was a hot mess. Her little world consisted of courtroom hearings, her office cubicle, and her small, cozy home. Not the company of a good-looking man. Jason had been attractive, too. And a charmer. She was not prepared for the desires of having another man look after her, really see her, want to be in her company. She was doing fine by herself, thank you very much. And yet, when grief washed over her occasionally, male attention was a gift. Any interest thrown her way since Jason died, halted when they noticed her rings. Besides, no one could fill Jason's shoes.

You're being ridiculous. This man is a stranger. The fact that you got in the truck with him was foreign enough. Maybe you need to get out more. Ellie chided herself.

She cleared her throat. "What now?"

"We can intercept Colton where Billy left the

property. Or close to it." Mark put the truck in drive and pulled out of the driveway.

"Wouldn't he have called if he'd found Billy?"

"Yeah." Mark took a deep breath. "I don't know what to do."

Ellie gazed out the window, willing Colton to call or for Billy to materialize in front of her eyes.

Silence filled the cab, along with an undeniable whiff of fear and trepidation.

As they rounded the corner, they saw Colton and his big horse standing at the side of the road. He looked as dejected as Ellie felt.

"Anything?" Mark rolled down Ellie's window and leaned across her to talk to Colton.

"No. Some brush was knocked down, but the ground is too dry to see much."

"We're going to drive down the road a bit," Mark looked at Ellie for confirmation, who nodded her head. "We stopped at Brandon and Selena's. Brandon's planning to meet up with you along here."

"Ok, I'll watch for him. I think we'll ride the ditch for a ways."

Ellie sucked in a breath. Riding the ditch meant the possibility that harm could have come to Billy, and he was lying somewhere alone. Not a prospect she was willing to entertain.

"Colton was always closer to Billy, because of baseball." Mark left the truck in park.

"Baseball?"

"Yeah, they connected over baseball. Colton was almost drafted into college ball, but..." Mark drifted off. "Anyway, Billy liked baseball, so they started tossing the ball around. It was interesting to watch, my little brother connecting with Billy. He never wanted anything to do with any of the boys. Probably brought back too many memories for him." Mark's jaw tightened. "Now, he's putting Billy in this nice, little box called a J-O-B and disconnecting from Billy as a kid."

"I'm not sure I know what that means." Ellie probed.

"Colton's military through and through. He disengages emotionally when there's a job to be done."

Ellie heard admiration and a little envy from Mark as he talked about his younger brother. She suspected Mark didn't disengage as easily.

"We're not doing any good sitting here." He pulled the truck onto the pavement. They drove down the road in silence. Ten minutes passed with only pastures on either side. The countryside was beautiful with its rocky terrain and the wildflowers standing tall by the road. The beauty was overshadowed by the growing uneasiness in the truck. Farmhouses began to show up with dusty, gravel driveways.

"This is a little town outside of Dallas. He could have come this way as it's our normal route to church. He would have been familiar with it, at least."

Ellie watched as the town materialized before her eyes, complete with a four-way stop on Main Street. A mechanic's shop, a small grocery store, a six-room motel added to the charm.

"Of all things holy…" Mark exclaimed, pulling into the parking lot of an old barn-turned- flea market building.

"What? Do you see him?" Ellie craned her neck at the windshield. She might hug Billy before the case manager side of her yelled at him. What a relief to find him alive and unharmed.

"No, sorry." Mark dashed her hopes. "But that's his father's car parked over at the motel. I didn't think he'd stay around."

Ellie blanched. Blood was always thicker than water. Billy's father may be a co-conspirer in Billy's absence. Or worse.

Chapter 3

"Let's watch for a minute. If he's in there with his dad…" Mark clenched the steering wheel. He wanted to bust the door down and knock the guy out for disrupting all of their lives. Why Billy felt the need to meet up with a father that hadn't cared about him before now, was a mystery.

"What if Billy's being held against his will?" Ellie put a hand on Mark's upper arm.

He stiffened and she retracted it. Not acceptable even though his arm tingled where her fingertips touched. Ellie might be okay with a simple touch, Mark was not. She was married. She shouldn't have touched him, despite his insane desire for her to do it again.

"He left of his own accord, so I have to believe he was planning to somehow meet up with his dad. What I don't know is how they could have planned it. Or how Billy knew where to find him. Or why. He seemed pretty scared of him when he was found the first time." Mark stared at the motel.

Ellie side-glanced at him.

"I'm going over there. Are you going to be

okay?" Mark questioned. "Are you ready to confront him?"

Ellie looked out the side window and then turned to him. "I'm ready. Are you?"

Mark nodded. She was tenacious, that was for sure. "Yes."

He pulled out of the lot and entered the motel parking area. Driving past the entrance, they both could see the front desk and the hotel clerk hovering over a magazine.

Ellie grimaced.

Mark raised his eyebrows at the broken-down motel. Chips of paint were flaking off the door frames and the whole place could use a new coat, something besides its current institutional gray. In two of the windows, cats appeared, blinking in the sunlight. People must have permanent residency in the motel. Or at least, a more long-term contract. Parking two spots up from Billy's dad's car, Mark paused before getting out.

"I don't know what we're going to walk into." He glanced at Ellie. No telling. Angry kid? Angrier dad? She twisted a lock of golden hair around her finger. An ominous cloud hung over them, threatening rain. A breeze picked up and blew stormy clouds to their north. "Should we call the cops?" An uncomfortable feeling washed over him.

"That would jeopardize you…and Billy…and the other boys." Ellie shivered. "No, let's check this out."

Mark gave her a slight smile as his gut turned over. He glanced at the dusty car he'd seen twice now in a few days. Took a deep breath. As he scanned the length of the motel, his eyes rested on the door in front of Billy's dad's car. Was it ajar? It didn't line up with the door frame. Mark's mind spun. "The door's not closed," he whispered, breaking his own cardinal rule and touching her arm.

"What?" Ellie's face belied her concern.

"The door, it's not closed."

"Mark, I've got a bad feeling about this." She put her hand over his.

"Me, too."

"What if he's got a gun?"

"These are the times when I wish Colton was here." Mark withdrew his hand. Dang it. Her skin had been so soft. And still married. "Stay in the car. I'll go check it out."

"No way. I'm going with you."

"Please, Mrs. Jenkins. Ellie…" Mark quietly tried to convince her, but she was already out of the car, shutting the door softly. "Crap."

Mark followed her to the walkway in front of the rooms. Clinging to the fake brick, Mark stepped in front of Ellie and led her past the window. Putting his foot at the base of the door, he slowly pushed the door open wider. No shotgun loading, no voices, only silence. Sweat rolled down his back.

"Hello?" Mark cautiously knocked on the door. The breeze rifled the papers on the bed. "I don't think anyone's here."

"What is that smell?" Ellie wrinkled her nose.

Mark stepped into the room. The bathroom door was open, and he could see the toilet and sink, like any normal hotel room. Turning towards Ellie, his eyes adjusted to the dim light in the room. "Oh, holy mother of …"

"What? What are you looking at?" Ellie's head popped around the corner.

"No!" Mark threw himself in front of her, blocking her view. In a chair inside the door, a man sat, his throat slashed and his shirt, blood soaked. The scene was violent and horrendous.

Ellie ran out of the room and threw up in the gravel by the car.

Mark followed her out, turning his head while she vomited, giving her as much space as he could. Opening the driver's door to his truck, he pulled a napkin out of the console and handed it to her.

Ellie wiped her mouth off. "That guy, he's too big to be Billy. Is he Billy's father?"

"No. I don't know who that is." He wanted to puke himself. "We've got to call the cops now. Tell them everything."

"I agree." Ellie looked at Mark, mascara staining her cheeks, brow furrowed. "Where's Billy, Mark?"

~

"Mark?" Ellie dabbed her mouth, face, stepping over the vomit. She'd never thrown up in public before, nor had she ever seen a body with its neck slashed. Only in the movies. And this was definitely not the movies. Her stomach continued to churn, threatening another wave of puking. Kind of Mark to try to block her view, however, she'd been insistent to see what he saw. The image was horrific and forever burned in her brain. Ellie watched as Mark, ashen-faced, pulled out his phone.

"Colton, I need you here. Bring Brandon with

you." Mark turned away from her. The breeze caught the rest of the conversation and swept it away.

This was not good at all. Not only did they stumble onto a murder scene, but they still hadn't found Billy. What were the chances that Billy had been there, seeing his father? Saw the murder of the guy in the chair? And neither of them were there in the motel room, so they'd be Subject #1 and #2. Could he have been? Truth be told, she didn't know Billy that well. Maybe he was capable of …

"Where are you going?" Mark caught her arm.

"The motel needs to know." She turned to face him.

"Colton said to call the police first. The motel manager should be the second one notified. Let the police question him." Mark let go of her.

"I know he's your brother, but why should I listen to his advice? I'm the one ultimately responsible for Billy." Tears gathered in the corner of her eyes, threatening to fall again.

"I am, too." Mark glanced at her hands, spinning the rings around her slender finger. "We don't know that this has anything to do with Billy yet. And Colton is ex-military, and Brandon is still connected with the FBI. That's why I wanted their advice."

"So, they are coming here."

"They were still riding the ditches, but they'll come as soon as they can." Mark pulled out his phone again. "I'm calling 911 and then we can talk about what to do next. Do you want to go sit in the truck?"

"Yes. I'll do that." She started to shake, the grizzly scene displayed in vivid color. The weather blowing in had nothing to do with the chill she felt to her bones. In all of her time in social work, doing home visits, listening to gruesome stories from clients, she'd never encountered anything like this. Ellie watched as Mark spoke into his phone, one hand in his pocket. She was thankful she was on this case with him, his presence was as strong and confident as his jawline.

Her thoughts were cut short when Mark got in the truck next to her, slamming the door.

"Well?"

"The police will be here soon. We're supposed to hang tight until they've interviewed us." Mark looked at her, his brown eyes cloudy. "They're gonna want to know why we are here."

"I know. We'll just have to tell the truth." She liked the sound of 'we', reminding her she wasn't alone. "Then we can go back to looking for Billy. This is going to set us back even further."

"Yeah."

Ellie didn't want to think about the possibility of Billy being involved. What if he was? "Mark, what if …?

"Billy couldn't have done that. And the guy was not his father. His father was big, but not in the same way as the dead body. Taller, more linebacker shaped, not heavy-set like that guy. I don't know if Billy had anything to do with this, where he is, or where his dad is. I have no answers." Mark put his head on the steering wheel.

Lord, give us direction and wherever Billy is, show us how to reach him. Protect him while we look.

When the police car rolled in, lights and siren blaring, Mark stepped out of the truck, hands raised.

Chapter 4

"I'm the one who called it in." Mark stayed by the truck, keeping his arms up. The cops didn't know him from Adam. What was the old adage about the perpetrator sticking around the crime scene to see what the cops were going to do? Mark could be the one who murdered the guy in the hotel room for all they knew.

"Stay where you are." One cop rushed into the open motel door, his partner locking his weapon on Mark.

"Mrs. Jenkins, put your hands on the dashboard, slowly." Mark whispered. Ellie did as she was told. He could read the fear on her face. It mimicked his own.

"Passenger! Get out of the truck and keep your hands up." The officer moved to the back of Mark's truck, switching his gun sights from Mark to Ellie and back. "Passenger, walk backwards to me."

Mark watched as the officer shouted directions at Ellie. She was terrified now, for sure. Why hadn't he made her stay at the ranch? Or go to her office? Neither expected to be in this situation. Only about how angry he was at Billy for pulling a stunt like this. And, honestly, the consequences that would befall the ranch. Not dead bodies. Certainly not dead bodies.

Once Ellie was back near the officer and patted down for weapons, it was his turn. He followed the directives and stood next to Ellie. He knew it was necessary to secure the scene, but so humiliating.

"We called it in, sir." Mark pointed his statement to the officer in charge.

"Ok," the big man stated. "Let's start at the beginning. Who are you?"

Mark glanced at Ellie. "Mark Bruens. I own a ranch outside of town for juvenile boys. This is Mrs. Ellie Jenkins, one of the boys' case managers. A boy ran away from the ranch early this morning. We were trying to track him down."

"And he led you to this motel?" The officer jotted notes in his small notebook.

"Not exactly. Sort of." Way to sound wishy-washy. "His father tried to pick him up on Friday without authorization, so when we realized the boy had left the grounds, we went looking for him. That's his father's car over there."

"Left the grounds? Like run away?"

Mark winced.

"And you happened to knock down a door with a dead body behind it?"

Even to Mark's own ears, their story sounded made-up.

"No, sir. The door in front of Billy's father's car was ajar, so we decided to ask the father if he'd seen Billy."

"You didn't expect foul play? Kidnapping? Coercion?" The officer squinted at him.

"No, sir. The boy left on his own. We don't know if he was meeting up with his father or exactly what happened, except for the fact that he's not allowed to leave the premises. And he did."

Ellie shifted next to him. "I don't know what happened to that man," she pointed at the motel room, "but I do not believe Billy could do something like that."

"Why is that?" The officer turned his attention to Ellie. "What was he under your authority for? What crime?"

Ellie hesitated. Mark couldn't recall the details of Billy's case at the moment, only that he had no custodian to be released to and Mrs. Jenkins referred the ranch to the court for Billy. There was obviously a crime somewhere for the state to be involved in the first place.

"It was a domestic violence case. The initial one."

"Like as in between the parents? Or between this kid and his parents? And the initial one?" The officer pushed.

"Both, I believe." Ellie looked at the ground.

Explained why Billy was so angry all of the time. And why he connected with Colton. They were kindred spirits, rebellious, ready for a fight, anger brewing.

"Stay here. I may have more questions for you."

Mark stepped closer to Ellie. "I'm sorry about all of this."

"You couldn't have known Billy would take

off." She held Mark's gaze. "I do not believe Billy had anything to do with this. It may have something to do with Billy's father, but not Billy."

"I wish I could be as certain."

"We don't even know if Billy came this way or not."

Mark pointed at a black hoodie one of the officers held in his hand. "Now we do. That's the hoodie he was wearing when he went through the fence."

Ellie put a hand over her mouth. "Oh no."

Mark and Ellie watched the motel manager join the officers.

"Took him long enough to realize something was going on in his own motel parking lot." Mark observed.

Ellie nodded. Apprehension was all over her face, her tone, her sad blue eyes. He couldn't do anything to help alleviate the stress. It was radiating off him, too.

The coroner's van pulled up, rolled equipment along the asphalt parking lot, avoiding the wheels dropping into holes from poor upkeep.

Billy still needed to be found, but was he a suspect? Or a kid caught up in his father's foolishness? Pretty serious with the dead body. Mark watched as a stretcher was brought out of the room, plastic covering the body.

He heard Ellie's sharp intake of breath.

"Mark, we have to find Billy."

"I think we need to wait and find out what happened here."

"Mark? Is that…?" Ellie grabbed his arm as a

second body was brought out.

Mark groaned. He hadn't seen anyone else, dead or alive, in the motel room, but he hadn't gone into the bathroom. What if the body was Billy's? What if he'd checked the bathroom and Billy was still alive and he'd left him there? No, that wasn't possible. Mark tried to slow his racing heart. Whoever that was, had been dead longer than a couple of minutes or the police would have called for an ambulance. Right? Mark's hands shook.

The officer walked back over to them. "Know either of these guys? Robert Townsend or Lawrence Parleigh? We found wallets on both of them. The murderer could have switched out their identities, but we'll start with those names."

It wasn't Billy in either of the body bags.

"I don't know the first one. The second one is Billy's father." Ellie dropped her hand and stepped away from Mark. "Neither of them are Billy, then."

That wasn't a good thing. Especially if the authorities determined Billy had been with his father at the motel. Mark turned to see Brandon's truck pull alongside his. Colton jumped out of the passenger side and grabbed Mark's shirt.

"Is that Billy?" He pointed at the coroner's van.

"No. We still don't know where he is." Mark let out a breath. "Brandon, do you know any of these officers? It would really help us find him if we knew more about what went on in that hotel room."

"Let me see what I can do." Brandon headed to the knot of officers outside the room.

"Colton, Billy's hoodie was found in the room. The one he left in." Mark watched Ellie. She was quiet, hands clasped in front of her.

"Doesn't mean anything, does it?" Colton questioned.

"Doesn't look good. Two dead bodies and a missing kid's hoodie." Mark's hair was a wreck, curls looser from running his fingers through it so many times in frustration.

~

Ellie stepped in front of Mark and drew herself up so she could look him in the eye. "Do you really believe he's capable of killing two grown men? Mark, really?"

"No. We have to look at the facts, though." Mark pleaded.

"I think we're wasting our time here. We could be out looking for him." She wanted to yell at him. At least yelling would be doing something. He looked as horrible as she felt. Pain radiated through her head.

"So, they're not saying a whole lot because the missing kid is a juvenile, coupled with the crime scene, but I did overhear a few things." Brandon rejoined the group around Mark's truck. "There's a receipt from a local casino. Someone won a lot of money. I mean, a lot."

"Billy wasn't old enough to gamble." Ellie interjected.

"But his dad was. And the money is missing." Brandon tossed out the fact.

Ellie shook her head. "Now he's a murderer and a thief?"

"We don't know anything." Mark contradicted her.

She knew what they were thinking. Bad father, bad kid. Billy was used to violence in the home, therefore, he was capable of stepping over the line and killing people? And why not just steal money, too? She knew he was an angry kid, knew he didn't make the best decisions, but murder? Did *she* believe it was possible for a kid to lose it like that? She'd heard unimaginable stories in her line of work, but Billy? God, where are you?

"How about we find Billy and let him tell the story? He was clearly here at one point. That's a fact." Ellie ticked off points on her fingers. "Second fact, Billy's father is now dead along with some other guy that we know nothing about. How's this for a scenario? Billy finds his dad at the motel, dead, someone else is here with the other dead guy, grabs Billy and the money and Billy manages to leave his hoodie for us to find."

"Like a bread crumb?" Mark stood up straighter and then let the air out of her sails. "Mrs. Jenkins, I'm sorry. I think that's a little over the top."

"It's Ellie. And why not?" All of the men were staring at her as if she'd grown a third eye.

"Ellie,…" Brandon started. "I know this is incredibly difficult to believe."

She didn't mean to be sharp with any of them. She shook her head again and wet her lips. Brandon was the least likely to believe her, and she quite frankly didn't need him to. She did, however, expect Mark to see her side if they were going to continue to look for Billy.

"Mrs. Jenkins, Brandon's being realistic. I know you're upset, so am I. We'll figure this out together."

Mark kicked a loose rock in the asphalt.

"I know. I'm sorry I snapped, Brandon. I just don't believe he killed these men, especially his own father." Ellie saw a shadow cross Mark's face. Colton turned and walked away. Whatever happened in these two brothers' lives, it clearly resonated with Billy's actions. "And I think if we don't find Billy first, these cops are going after him with their own preconceived ideas."

"I agree." Mark looked at the ground.

"So, what now? Where do we look for him now?" Ellie questioned.

"Can we look at his file? Maybe that would give us some type of clue?" Brandon suggested.

"You can't, but I certainly can." It was something to do and the best idea so far. "Do you want to follow us to my office? Or, Mark, should we go back and get my truck?"

"We can take mine." Mark shuffled his toe, sending the loose gravel into the weeds.

"We'll follow." Brandon agreed.

Colton returned to the group as an officer approached.

"We're going to check out some leads. I have all of your information. We'll be in touch if we need anything." The policeman handed Ellie his card.

"Thank you, sir." Ellie stuffed it into her back pocket.

The four of them loaded into the trucks, and Ellie gave directions to her office in Dallas.

Lord, please help us find Billy. And protect him, too.

Chapter 5

Mark whistled as he stepped into Ellie's shoebox-sized office. Comfy chairs, colorful art, a little feminine, a little farmhouse-y. Impressive, making the tiny space welcoming.

"It's not very big, but it's mine and where I spend a great deal of time." Ellie shuffled books off of the seating opposite her desk.

Mark wandered around, looking at the pictures on the bookcase and the things hanging on the wall.

"I have to go get the file from the file room. Make yourself comfortable." She indicated the chairs with a sweep of her hand.

Ellie maneuvered around him in the narrow space and Mark didn't dislike the fact that she was required to brush past him to get out. Her nearness unnerved him. He shook his head and homed in on the pictures again. She was stunning in a wedding gown with an equally attractive groom by her side. Their gaze held so much love, it was difficult to look at. No one had ever looked at him like that. He was a horrible person for admiring someone else's wife. Shameful, really. He'd fight to the death if he caught someone having those types of thoughts about his wife. Mark moved on to a wall hanging, a brightly colored piece of crochet or knitting or whatever it was called.

"I made that. Isn't it beautiful?" Ellie re-entered the room, file in hand.

"How? Is it crocheted?"

Ellie laughed, and Mark shut his thoughts down to anything other than the melodic sound. This was not going to be easy. The more he was around her, the greater the draw to know her better. What started out as a physical attraction to her beauty was quickly becoming secondary to other things, like her laughter. Or her compassion for the same boys he cared for. At least Billy. And the way she handled the horrific scene in the motel room. Sure, she'd thrown up, he'd wanted to as well, but she kept it together and defended Billy to the cops and to Brandon. He glanced back at their wedding photo. Oh, to keep that image foremost in his mind.

"Finger crocheted, of sorts. They used to call it macrame and made with a brown jute. I updated the look with a variety of yarn and scraps of multi-colored rope."

"It's very pretty." And very you. Watch yourself, Mark, she's married. He released a breath as his brother knocked on the glass door of the office. Mark tried to keep his eyes off her as Ellie crossed the room to let Colton in but failed miserably.

He remained standing as his brother followed Ellie back to the office. Colton caught his gaze and raised his eyebrows. With a slight shake of his head and a warning look, Mark took one of the chairs, leaving the other for Colton.

He could feel his brother's eyes still on him, eyebrows even higher. Colton was 'reading his mail' as people liked to say. His looks and facial expressions were obviously giving away his attraction to Ellie, and Colton picked up on it. Hopefully, Ellie didn't.

"Can you give us a brief synopsis without going against any policy?" Mark tried to still his hammering heart, clasped his hands in his lap.

"I've already mentioned the domestic violence." Ellie flipped pages in the fairly thin file. "He was in foster care prior to your place."

"Any mention of involvement by either parent?"

"You met the dad. He went to jail for almost a year and was recently released. Not much mention of Mom. She was picked up for prostitution in downtown Dallas a couple years back." Ellie sucked in a breath. "Billy's been bounced around the system quite a bit."

"Explains the attitude." Colton commented.

"Can we get in touch with the last foster family? Are they local?" Mark added, studying her face.

"Yes. I have an address. Let me call first." Ellie grabbed her phone, stepped around Mark's chair and went out into the hallway.

Mark glanced at Colton. "What?"

"You're a little smitten with Mrs. Jenkins." Colton watched him.

"What do you take me for? Look around. She's married. There's her wedding picture." Mark protested.

"I know. I can see," Colton frowned. "I know

you, and I know that you would never act on those feelings. I'm just saying, I can tell you're attracted to her."

"She is beautiful."

~

He thinks I'm beautiful? Ellie walked back into the office and tucked her phone in her purse. She'd been called pretty before, and Jason always said she was hot. She smiled at the memory. Jason always responded with that comment when she would refer to her internal thermostat. He'd say, "I know, that's why I married you." Their bantering was one of the things she missed most. That and their conversations and his touch and… her thoughts were taking a turn for the worst. She missed Jason's touch, his reassuring "you've got this" with a pat on the back, his hugs where she could cry if she wanted, his slender fingers in hers. Runaway train, her thoughts. She never knew what would trigger the grief. Here was a flesh and blood guy paying her a compliment, and she reverted back to the past easily. Life wasn't fair. She should still be happily married, yearning for children. Instead, she was trying to make it through the day, wrestling with grief, wanting to get back to normal. Impossible. People encouraged her to plan for a new normal. She didn't want a new normal. She wanted the dreams back.

"The foster family said we could stop in for a short visit tomorrow." Ellie stood behind her chair and looked at Colton and then Mark. Re-reading Billy's file, being reminded of his mother's occupation, all cut too close. Flashbacks of her days as a dancer hit her. Not the same as prostitution, but the lasting effects of feeling dirty, numb, and unseen by normal people assaulted her, and she blinked slowly, pushing them back into the deep recesses of her heart. "It's been a long day, and I know we set a deadline, but it's 5:45 pm now, and we can't go any further until morning."

Mark frowned but agreed with a slight nod of his head.

Ellie picked up her purse and headed for the door, choosing to go around Colton's chair this time, leaving a wide margin around Mark. "Can I ride back with you?"

"Of course." Mark opened the door of the building and followed her out into the crisp air. The streetlights were coming on, and they had a clear walk to the parking lot. Calling a car service would have been the best route if she was trying to squelch the crazy, unexpected feelings she had with Mark. The feeling of safety, of being seen and heard, and treated with respect. But what the heck? They would find Billy together. Where was the harm? His company was fresh air to her stagnant life, even when he frowned.

"Mark, I'll meet you at home." Colton clasped Mark on the shoulder. "We'll find him."

Ellie couldn't meet his eyes as he opened the truck door for her. He was such a gentleman.

"Are you okay?" Mark asked, starting the vehicle.

"Yes, why?" Did her face give away her growing feelings for this kind man she'd just met?

"It's been a long day." He gently smiled at her.

Ellie twisted her rings. "Mark, should we let the

police handle this? If Billy is involved with his dad's death or at the very least, stealing the money, this is way over our heads."

"You know as well as I do that Billy is quickly becoming the main suspect."

"How is that even possible?"

"He was there in that hotel room at some point. If we don't find him before the police do, I don't know what will happen to him. I don't know what to do, but I have to do something. He was under my care."

Ellie winced at the pain she heard in Mark's voice. They were both responsible for Billy. His leaving of his own accord complicated things, and she knew Mark wanted to help him out of this situation as much as she did. "I know, mine too."

They arrived at the ranch much sooner than she would have liked. Ellie slid out of his truck and into her own. The moonlight was beautiful, casting a silvery sheen over the barn and lawn. Mark got out of his truck, too, and leaned up against it. She rolled down her window. Better to keep the truck door between them. His wistful look spoke more than she suspected he wanted it to. She felt that tug, too, that they could be in a much different place if they weren't on the search for a lost boy. Of course, they might not have ever met if it hadn't been for Billy.

"The stars are thick tonight." Mark said, hooking his thumbs in his jean pockets.

Was he prolonging her leaving? The moon shining brightly on Mark's face told her to stay in her truck, don't step out. If she did, she might do something foolish and be carried away by the magical ambience of standing out in the glimmery starlight.

"Bye, Mark." Ellie smiled at him. What a handsome man.

They said their goodbyes and made arrangements to meet again in the morning to talk with the foster family. At home, in the quiet of her home, Ellie fixed a simple dinner and relaxed on the couch. She put her feet up on the edge and stared blankly at the dark TV.

Mark stirred up feelings in her that she'd put away, she thought for good. But, maybe not.

Chapter 6

The next morning, Ellie woke a little earlier than normal for a Monday, showered and contemplated her attire for the day.

The blue or coral shirt? She turned to Magic, her very large, very hairy dog, for direction. His tail wagged. Lot of help he was.

She patted him on his massive head and looked him in the eye. "You don't care, do you? And neither should I."

What difference did it make? Two squirts of her favorite perfume told the story. It did matter. After spending the day with Mark, albeit dire circumstances and gruesome discoveries, she wanted him to see her. Maybe even be caught off guard by the delicious… no, hot… no… good grief. She just wanted to be… liked.

His truck wasn't yet in the parking lot when she pulled in, so she had time to run to her office and confirm the address. Thankfully, her boss was out of town for a couple days, so she sidestepped the other employees at the office, left word with the receptionist that she'd be unavailable for the day, and went back to her truck.

Lord, this is getting complicated. If her boss had been there, he would have pounced on her absence and whereabouts for the day. Not that she minded someone from work being aware of where she was. Most people didn't know how dangerous social work was with mental illness and easy access to drugs a common thread with the population. But she was with Mark and he…

Ellie shook her head. What was she thinking? First, she didn't know him that well, and second, she could handle her own life, thank you very much.

"Hi." Ellie re-locked her truck and climbed into the cab of his.

"Hi." Mark glanced at her, and her toes curled a little in the warmth she saw in his eyes.

"Loaded up on Tootsie Pops, I see." Ellie smiled shyly at him and pointed to the cup holder full of lollipops. Stop it. This wasn't a middle school crush. She couldn't help her grin, though, he was so attractive with his cinnamon-colored curls peeking out from his broad cowboy hat.

He nodded and offered her a lollipop. "Do you have the address?"

"Thanks." She chose a purple one, unwrapped it, and stuck it in her mouth.

He raised his eyebrows at her. Quit staring and answer his question.

"Yes, the address." She handed over the Post-it note, and Mark put it in his truck's GPS. The closer they got to their destination, the more she doubted this was the right thing to do. They rode in silence as tension mounted. What if they should have just called the police and not super-sleuthed on their own? If today was anything like yesterday, it was going to be a long one with surprises.

"Do you know what you are going to say?" Mark pulled down an oak-lined street.

"I can't say much. Probably that we're trying to connect with Billy and any information they can provide would be helpful?"

"That sounds okay. It's not like we can blurt out that we don't know where he is, especially if the police aren't far behind us."

"True." Ellie ran cold fingers across her forehead. The police could be close. It was so important for her and Mark to find Billy first. They might be the only ones with his best interest at heart.

Mark turned into a large driveway that led to a two-story house, complete with a picket fence. Ellie looked at him, squared her shoulders and got out of the truck.

After ringing the doorbell and hearing the chimes inside, an older man opened the glass door. While not elderly, he and his wife, just steps behind him, were definitely older than she or Mark. Ellie hoped this was one of the good foster homes. So many of them were, but a few were not. The couple looked sweet and capable.

"Good afternoon. I called earlier? I'm Ellie Jenkins."

"I don't mean to be rude, but can we see some identification? We're usually not allowed to talk about anyone that stays at our house, but I actually remember you from the courtroom. And you, too."

"Oh sure." Ellie reached into her purse and

brought out her ID badge. Mark handed him a business card.

The man shook Mark's hand and then took Ellie's hand in his own. Her fingers were ice cold in his warm ones.

"Thank you." The man broke into a smile and ushered them in. The room was lovely and held a mixture of modern and vintage. They smelled amazing, too. A brown sugar concoction sat on the kitchen counter, fresh from the oven.

"Freshly made coffee cake?" The wife offered.

"Thank you, but no. We don't want to take up much of your time." Ellie started and sat next to Mark on a flowered sofa.

"Billy Kramer is under my supervision, and also my friend's," Ellie gestured to Mark. "We're trying to connect with the boy and wondered if you could share with us anything you can remember about when he stayed with you?" She glossed over the boys' ranch or Billy's current undetermined location.

"Billy was an angry kid. He got the short end of the family stick, if you know what I mean." The man looked at his wife, who nodded her agreement. "Quiet, although he'd jump at the chance to beat the tar out of someone. We were never afraid of him, per se, but we always knew he had it in him to rage against authority."

"We were pretty careful in how we spoke to him." The woman clasped and unclasped her hands. "It was like he respected us but didn't know how to express any emotion except anger."

"Typical of any kid that came from a home life like his." The man pulled his wife's hand into his.

Moisture formed in his eyes, threatening to spill.

"Can you tell me what you know of his family history?" Ellie moved to the edge of the couch. The information they provided next might be a clue to where Billy was located.

"You probably know more than we do."

"Remind me."

"When he first came to us, he had all of his belongings in a grocery sack. So sad." The wife wiped her face. "He had so many physical needs, his clothing didn't fit, his shoes had holes in them, and he needed medical attention."

"We bought all of that for him and took him to a doctor for a physical. Apparently, he'd been hit so many times in the head that he needed hearing aids. He was ten years old. Ten." The man sighed. "We're not trained to deal with the emotional things, of which he needed help with, too. They have counselors for that, but he never saw one. He was on the list, but it kinda fell through the cracks."

Ellie sucked in a breath. She knew Billy had a rough go of it, but not to this extent.

"I know his dad went to jail for violence in the home." The man continued. "Not only did he try to stand up to his dad and got clocked for it, but Billy was a tall kid and ridiculed at school for everything from his pants that never seemed long enough to his hearing aids to his living with us. It was an uphill climb for that boy."

Ellie felt Mark's foot start to bounce. He wiped his hands on his jeans and then locked them on his knees.

"I know he came to my ranch through the court

system after an incident at school." Mark recounted the courtroom documents without divulging too much.

"Yes, he hit a teacher. After several detentions, suspensions, and general rebellion towards authority, the school had enough of him. The teacher wasn't seriously injured, and I firmly believe Billy was fighting with some older boys, and the teacher was trying to pull them apart. He got caught in the fray, but hitting a teacher is hitting a teacher no matter how you look at it. The school was obligated to press charges, and in my opinion, Billy wouldn't have made it there much longer."

"What about Mom?" Ellie asked. With Billy's dad dead in the motel, maybe Billy took off to his mom's?

"She was a mess herself, from what we heard. Whether it was from the abuse in the home or before that, we don't know. Rumor was, Mom was a prostitute downtown. I'm sorry, maybe she was a stripper. I can't remember. We heard stories that she would take Billy to work with her, so he wasn't left alone with Dad. How sad, is that?"

Ellie remembered reading those stories. Surreal. She'd prayed it wasn't true, but this kind couple had just confirmed it. Made her sick to her stomach. She wanted to put her hands over her ears. Her breaths became shallow as the memories flashing before her. She needed to get out of there. Take a break. Ellie jumped up, startling Mark and the couple. "May I borrow your restroom?"

"Of course, dear." The lady rose and showed her down the hall to the restroom.

~

Mark watched Ellie follow the wife out of the room. What was that all about? Billy's story was incredibly sad and made Mark angry, but he couldn't read what was going on with Ellie. Yesterday had been a lot. He figured she'd gotten as much sleep as he had, which was none. Her emotions had to be spiraling like his. From losing Billy to the dead bodies in the motel to this horrific story, and they still did not know where Billy was.

When Ellie returned, he could see the slight smudge of mascara. From tears? Surely, she'd heard stories of abuse and neglect before as a social worker. And didn't she know some of the back story already? Maybe this one hit harder because they didn't have Billy in front of them to talk to face-to-face. What if Billy lost his temper on his dad and it escalated too far? That story would collaborate with what the foster family said about the domestic violence in the home. Why would Billy want to even see his father? Maybe Billy thought he was protecting his mom? But what about the other dead body? And the money?

"Thank you for your time." Ellie shook both of the couple's hands.

Apparently, she had all of the information she needed.

"We hope we've been helpful." The wife locked eyes with Ellie. "We'll be praying for you."

"Thank you." Mark ushered Ellie out, opened the passenger side door and waited until she was settled before closing it.

Not sure where to go from here. Ellie was lost in thought. He sat quietly for a moment and then started the truck. He drove around the corner and pulled in front of a mom-and-pop coffee shop.

"Do you want to get some coffee and maybe something to eat?" Mark watched her spin her rings. "Or I can go get it and you can call your husband? Give you some privacy."

Mark swallowed hard when she turned impossibly-blue eyes toward him. He was unable to tear his gaze away from her. "Mrs. Jenkins…"

She held up a slender hand, stopping him. "I'm fine. Coffee would be nice. Mocha with two sugars and a bunch of cream, please."

Baffled, Mark got out of the truck. She hit a switch, instantly regained control of her emotions, and schooled her face to the 'I'm fine' status. She was quickly becoming the most intriguing female he'd ever met. One hundred percent all womanly soft, two hundred percent business, and three hundred percent attractive. He sighed as he opened the coffee shop door and heard the tingling of the bell above, announcing his entrance.

They needed to get this incident with Billy squared away in a hurry so he could put Ellie behind him. He was four hundred percent falling for a married woman. He had never in his life been so captivated by a person as he was with Ellie. He looked at his watch. And their togetherness was only a day old. He was sure if they spent much more time together, he would say or do something morally wrong. Mark was breaking half a dozen commandments right now by coveting another man's wife. He was already morally failing.

Opening the truck door with one hand and

balancing the cup holder with the other, Mark slipped behind the steering wheel. Careful to not allow their fingers to touch, he pulled one coffee out of the holder and handed it to her.

"One mocha with two sugars and a bunch of creamers."

"Thank you." Ellie said, her voice and face controlled.

"What now?" Mark sipped his coffee. Black and free from any additions, he enjoyed the robust flavor of the freshly-ground liquid.

Ellie chewed on her lip. "I'm not sure I learned anything new. Nothing they said will lead us to Billy. Maybe we should let the police handle it from here."

"Really? You know what will happen. Billy will be blamed for two deaths and stealing the money."

"Maybe the police will find out something different at the casino."

"That won't explain what happened in the motel room." Mark countered.

"No." Ellie took a sip of her coffee. "This is good. Thanks again."

Mark glanced at her. She was closed off, distant. "This is a long shot, but we could see if we could find Mom. Confirm he's not with her. It's not nighttime, and she wouldn't be out yet, but maybe…"

"No." Ellie exploded. "I'm not going to look for a mom that cares more about making money than she does about her own child." Ellie struggled to get out of her seat belt and finally, hopped from the truck.

"Hey. We're looking for Billy, but what if he's looking for his mom? Then, we're looking for both of them." Mark got out of the truck and came around to Ellie's side. "Listen, I don't like what Mom's doing…"

"If she still is," Ellie interrupted. "You're assuming. Once a prostitute, always a prostitute."

That was left field. Now she was defending Mom? Mark pursed his lips. His head was spinning, trying to keep up with her shifting emotions.

"My training suggests…" he tried again.

"What training? Your religious beliefs?"

"Seminary school."

"Well, that explains your haughtiness towards someone trying to survive."

"Trying to survive? What are we talking about? Billy's mom?" Mark took a step toward her, bridging the gap between them. "You don't have to tell me anything, but I saw how visibly shaken you were about what they were telling us. Surely, you've heard worse stories."

"And I saw how disturbed you were by the domestic violence."

Tit for tat.

Mark shrugged off her comments. He would not discuss his life with her, regardless of how similar it was. They were talking about Billy's mom. Weren't they?

~

Ellie took a step back, leaning on the truck. Mark was getting too close for comfort, both physically and emotionally. Her husband would never have cornered her like this. Of course, he knew her background and how close this was hitting. Mark did not.

How she wished Jason was here to help guide

her. So frustrating. She was spiraling, defending Billy's mom, and lashing out at Mark. None of what was happening with Billy was in her control. It was these times that made her angry. Angry that she was left to go on emotional journeys by herself, with no one to talk through and rationalize her thoughts. She was learning, but she didn't like it. Not one bit.

"Let's back up. The only possibility we have is that Billy may have gone to find his mother. There are no other options on the table, correct?" Ellie moved around to Mark's other side, allowing herself out of the semi-trapped position against the truck.

"As far as I can see. The foster family said Billy was always wanting to know about his mom, so they tried to keep tabs on her to some degree." Mark turned to her. "Look, I'm sorry if I seemed insensitive to Mom. I just don't understand selling your body. Everyone knows it's morally wrong, and I find it incredibly disgusting."

Ellie flinched. Looked at him, long and hard. He had no idea. She'd struggled for years, knowing the bad choices she'd made, choices that led her to the same job her mother held, and feeling judged for those wrong decisions for the right reasons. She kept her face still, non-committal, and resisted the urge to yell at him. He just didn't know. He'd probably spent his childhood growing up in a nice, polite family with no real life-altering problems. Mark hinted at some earlier issues with Colton, however, she doubted either of them had survival on the brain like she had when she was younger. People with a history like hers were usually a little more compassionate towards others in the same lot. A general understanding between equally tormented human beings.

He had no idea how his words cut. Of course, prostitution was wrong. Would he equate dancing in a strip club as a form of prostitution? Would his high and mighty religious training preclude him from helping her find Billy? Shouldn't, but she'd known people who wouldn't rub elbows with the likes of her, even if she hadn't danced in years and was free from that world. After leaving dancing, she was often afraid to venture out into the light of day for fear someone would recognize her. Shun her. Judge.

Discouragement filled her face. "Look, we don't even know where to look for Mom. We could drive the streets until Jesus comes back and never find her," Ellie paused. "Or Billy for that matter."

"Don't you want to try?" Mark ran fingers through his hair.

"I don't know that *you* do." Ellie snapped at him. Her thoughts chased around in her head, battling. He was so repulsed by Billy's mom's choices, would he be respectful if they did find her? And what if Ellie belied her past in their search? He would judge her in the same way.

"Are you kidding? If finding Mom means finding Billy, then I'm going to find Mom." Mark stomped over to the driver's door. "With or without you."

"Oh, really?" Ellie grabbed the door handle of his truck and jumped in. "You're not going anywhere without me." Why hadn't she brought her own vehicle? She'd broken a cardinal rule- always meet a person at the specified location, so she wasn't dependent on a ride home. She could leave anytime she chose. She was attracted to Mark, that's why. She wanted to test the waters. She wanted more time with him. And it backfired. Now, she was stuck riding with him when they clearly disagreed.

"Mrs. Jenkins, Ellie, please. We want the same thing. For Billy to return safe. My home, the ranch." Mark turned to her. "I'm worried sick."

Ellie saw that in his eyes, his slumped shoulders. So, they disagreed about their thoughts on Billy's mom. They weren't after his mom. They were looking for Billy. A conversation about Mom could wait. And, this wasn't about her, her history, or her past mistakes. She needed to keep her personal feelings out of it.

"Let's go and come back out later when it's dark." Mark didn't need to mention that dark was also Billy's mom's work hours.

"Okay." Ellie looked out the window as he drove her home, contemplating where to search now. It was an impossible task, but worth it if they found Billy before the police did.

Chapter 7

"Anything?" Colton met Mark on the porch.

"No. Here?" At the silent response, Mark hung his head. He sat heavily in one of the chairs. "We're going out tonight…"

"You and Mrs. Jenkins?"

"Let me finish, will ya?" Mark let out an exasperated sigh. "The foster family felt like Billy was consumed with his mom, so we're going out to look for her." Nothing else. This was all business. Despite his increasing attraction to her, this could only be business.

"Where is she?"

"Mom? Well, we don't know. We're guessing at this point. She was a prostitute." Ellie's words reverberated in his ears. Once a prostitute, always a prostitute. That's what she thought he believed. Did he?

"Is she still?" Colton asked the obvious.

"We don't know."

"So, you're just going to drive around Dallas looking for a prostitute that looks like Billy?" Colton snorted.

Mark glared at his brother. Sounded like a stupid idea. "We really don't know what else to do. The police are after Billy, and we need to find him before they do or he's toast. If we find him first, at least he'll have two people on his side."

"Three."

"Yes, sorry, three." He knew Colton was just as concerned as he and Ellie were.

"Do you know her name?"

"Just that she goes by Kitty."

"Which includes 90% of most prostitutes."

"I know." He didn't know, but it was a viable assumption.

The men sat in silence. The wind kicked up dust and whisked it away. Fall was descending on Texas with its comfortable days and cooler evenings.

"Be careful, Mark." Colton stood.

"Of the prostitutes?" Mark looked up at him.

"No. With Mrs. Jenkins."

"What's that supposed to mean?"

"You know what I mean."

Yeah, he did. He'd tried numerous times to think of someone else. Anyone other than the blue-eyed case manager. Every time she snuck into his thoughts, he mentally replaced it with the picture of her and her husband in her office. Better to keep that in the foreground.

Walking out to the goat pen, Mark checked to see if chores were still being done and to pass the time until he was with Ellie again. Mrs. Jenkins, he corrected.

Was he insensitive to Billy's mom's occupation

because of his training? He'd told Ellie, Mrs. Jenkins, he didn't understand why she would become a prostitute. It was morally wrong. He'd said so and added even if for the right reasons. Were there right reasons? No, there weren't right reasons. She'd mentioned survival, but was that a good reason? There were tons of other options to provide for a family beyond prostituting. He remembered a conversation with another seminary student, a friend, who worked with the homeless. His eyes were opened when he heard the stories he was told about the doctors, lawyers, successful businessmen who'd become homeless after a series of unfortunate events. His immediate thought had been their situation was a result of bad decisions and choices. He quickly learned most didn't choose that lifestyle but were rather forced into it. The cycle was much harder to get out of than the slippery slope leading to their homelessness had been, his friend shared with him. Maybe prostitution was the same way? From the foster parents, it sounded as if Billy's mom was trying to protect Billy from more harm by Dad. Was that enough of a reason? After graduation, Mark still talked to his friend occasionally, but hadn't seen Toby in a decade.

Wonder if he would know where to look for Billy's mom? It was worth a shot.

Mark went in the house to look for Toby's contact number, a renewed energy in his step.

"Mark? Will you be here for dinner tonight?" Aunt Eunice called from the kitchen.

Mark stepped into the room and answered, "Yes, if it's early."

"Will Ms. Jenkins be joining us?"

"It's Mrs., Aunt Eunice, and no, she won't be joining us." Mark turned away.

His aunt reached out and caught his elbow. "Mrs?"

Mark sighed. "Yes."

"Oh. I'm sorry, I thought maybe…" She trailed off.

He did, too.

~

Ellie lay on her couch, hand trailing over the edge, ruffling Magic's fur. Magic was her constant companion in the small house. No replacement for Jason, but a warm, loving creature, none-the-less. With two bedrooms, one used as an office, and two bathrooms, the home was the perfect size for Ellie and a hundred-pound dog. Buying a house had been an accomplishment after the cramped apartment she and Jason lived in. Still a hard decision to leave behind the memories she'd shared with him. Almost like she was leaving him behind. No harder, though, than any other decision she'd had to make without him.

When she'd moved, she gave several things away to thrift stores that catered to transitional housing programs or shelters. Helping others, Jason's legacy, continued on. Jason loved people. All people. His heart was so big, and his actions supported it. He was an all-or-nothing person who would give his shoes right off his feet if he felt they were needed. Nothing he did or said was wasted on trivial concerns. It didn't matter what a person's background was, Jason loved equally and unconditionally. He was the first person to ever truly represent Jesus' love for Ellie, and she thought Jason walked on water. She'd known of Jesus, but her world gave no indication that he was a real person until Jason. Jason always gave God the glory, for the good and the bad, for the challenges and the triumphs. Ellie elevated him above what a normal person should be, but, in her eyes, Jason was so pure and unlike anyone she'd ever met. He'd shown her what grace was. It was incomprehensible that Jesus could still love her, despite everything. How could she ever repay Jason for showing her such an amazing gift? Or Jesus? She couldn't. She'd tried, though. Jason repeatedly told her that repayment wasn't required, either for him or Jesus. Just that she continued to grow in her love for Him. So, she'd done that and prayed Jason would recognize her efforts and always be proud of her. When he chose her, in the infancy of her Christian walk, she'd been shocked. How could she ever equal up to his expectations?

"Still don't believe it always," Ellie said to Magic. He wagged the tip of his tail. "Mark is so different. I don't even know what is attractive about him. I'm just drawn to him. Sure, he's good looking and all that, but he also has a soft edge for people and a hard edge that, I suppose, keeps everything in line. He's well-liked, has a solid reputation, motivation and drive to change young mens' lives..." Ellie laughed as Magic sprawled on his back so she could reach his tummy. "I don't know, Magic. I'm not ready to give up Jason yet."

Magic jumped up and left the room, as if he

really didn't care.

Was she betraying Jason by entertaining thoughts of another man? Jason had been gone for over a year now. She still felt married. It was impossible to think of being attached to anyone else as amazing as Jason. At her age, being alone forever wasn't the dream, either. She was far too young to be single for long. She just couldn't imagine anyone else in her life.

Mark. He was nothing like Jason. Oh, there were some things. Mark was compassionate towards the boys on his ranch, the same as Jason was passionate. Mark was tender towards her in the short time they'd interacted, and he'd been protective of her when they found the grisly scene at the motel. But where Jason freely expressed his emotions, Mark was brooding and cautious. His seminary training left him a little short in the grace department- the opposite of what she thought seminary training should do- or maybe he hadn't had enough life experience to see the hurt his assumptions could cause. Or she could be totally off the mark on who Mark was. She was physically attracted to his broad shoulders, deep brown eyes, and his work-calloused hands, but she needed to see more of his heart. That was where the real attraction began. His actions and responses would speak louder to her if she knew his heart.

And there she was again, thinking about Mark. The man was invading her every thought. Once they'd found Billy, they could go their separate ways and she wouldn't be in this conundrum. Ellie looked at the ceiling and let the tears flow down her cheeks into her hairline. A wave of grief settled over her. If

Jason hadn't died…

She wiped her nose and sat up to the phone ringing. Mark.

"Hello?" Ellie tried to calm her racing heart. If he knew she'd been thinking about him…

"Hi, it's Mark. I realized we didn't set up a time to meet tonight."

They hadn't discussed a specific time. Could she really wander all over the city with this man and not give away her growing attraction?

"True." She hesitated. "I'm not sure this is a good idea. Or one that will even pan out. We could drive for hours and never see anyone, let alone Billy or his mother, not that we know what she looks like."

"What are you saying? That you don't want to go out tonight looking for him?"

Ellie could hear the defeat in his voice. She was torn. If they spent more time together, would her growing attraction be evident? Or would she be more conflicted? Nothing was easy. Nothing.

"So, we just sit and wait to hear something?"
Silence.

"Hello? Do we wait for Billy to come back? Or how about this… maybe it will be on the news 'Juvenile Runaway Kills Two, Steals Their Money.'" Mark's tone held a desperate note.

"Mark…"

"I'm sorry, Mrs. Jenkins. I can't eat or sleep until I know he's ok."

They were holding with formalities… and his assumption that she was married. What would he think if she told him she was a widow who had allowed him to believe something different?

Sounded deceptive. But was she ready to be not married? Ellie put her face in her hand. She hated her situation and wished she could talk to Jason one last time, find out what she should do.

"I understand. Mark, I need to pray about this before we proceed." Maybe God would speak to her directly. When Jason was alive, he was usually her guiding factor, but now she had to go it alone. Part of her didn't want to speak to the God who took her husband, the other part knew that God had proven faithful to Jason and in turn, would her as well. She hoped. She needed to hold on to the truths that she knew.

"That's a good idea. I'll do the same. Please call me if you hear anything." Mark responded, curtly.

Chapter 8

Mark shook himself awake. He adjusted his seat. He'd fallen asleep in the recliner again, unable to rest in the bed. He could hear Aunt Eunice in the kitchen and the smell of coffee and bacon.

Colton came in the front door and seeing Mark, stopped in the doorway. "Sleep there?"

"Part of the night. I cannot believe this is happening." Mark stood and stretched.

"Yeah. The worst part is we've done everything we can do."

"Have we, though? I keep thinking I could do more. Something. Anything."

"What does Ms. Jenkins think?" Colton adjusted his pants.

"Mrs."

"Ok, Mrs. Jenkins."

"She's praying about it." Mark blinked at Colton. He should have been the first to suggest praying. He was the one with the seminary background. All he'd done was worry. Some Christian he was.

"Good for her." Aunt Eunice met them in the

hallway and announced breakfast.

The boys filed past Mark, not looking at him, concern etched on their faces. Were they wondering if they could get away with leaving, too? A domino effect where one person could get away with it, the next one could, too? Did they want to leave? They had to be concerned about Billy's absence, although their worry was probably how it would affect them and not so much what was happening to Billy. Many of them had been abandoned or rejected and coped with that reality as best they knew how.

Mark looked at each boy closely as they passed. He'd missed the signs of Billy planning to leave, if there were any. Maybe they didn't want to leave, but were taking non-verbal cues from Mark? Projecting his disappointment, his fear?

He had to be honest with them, needed to continue being their alpha, directing, mentoring. That's what he offered them at the onset of their stay at the ranch, a consistent, stable, God-fearing man who cared about each of them. As the director of the program and founder of the ranch, he'd promised to be upfront, transparent as much as possible, and a constant in their everyday lives, their spiritual growth, whether they liked it or not, and their emotional health. He had a responsibility that he fully intended to keep, despite his worry about Billy or the future of the ranch.

"Listen boys," Mark waited until he had their full attention. All eyes on him. "I know this situation with Billy is unnerving. I made each of you a promise when you were assigned to this ranch that I would keep you informed of anything related to the ranch that I thought you should know and that I would always treat you like mature young men." He paused and put his hand on the shoulder of the youngest of the group. Only eleven years old, the boy had been there half a year already, but still showed signs of fear any time Mark turned his attention to him. "We are actively searching for Billy, to make sure he's safe and to find out how to best help him. He, however, as do you, know the consequences for leaving the ranch without authorization. The courts will reverse his assignment here, and Billy will most likely spend his remaining probation time in juvenile detention. That is not the ideal outcome. I would rather you serve your time here, prove to everyone that you can make mature decisions and that you're living for Jesus, but I also know life is hard, and we make bad decisions sometimes. I've been short with some of you and I'm sorry. We are all worried. But what do we do with that worry?"

A boy the same age as Billy looked at Aunt Eunice and back to Mark, "Pray."

"That's right. Let's do that now." Mark prayed over the meal, over Billy for protection, himself for wisdom, and the entire lot of them for peace.

After grace, Colton picked up the conversation again in the kitchen out of earshot of the boys. "I thought you were going to go look for Mom."

"I have no idea where to start. Dallas is big and the areas with that type of activity are even bigger."

"Why don't you start with some of the ministries that cater to the downtown area, like the homeless shelters or the human trafficking ministries?" Colton suggested.

Mark frowned. He'd been thinking about Toby, his friend from seminary. Maybe God was pointing him towards his friend. Colton never knew Toby; it was odd that his friend should come up twice in the span of twelve hours. "I actually know someone from university who was involved with the homeless. Great idea, Colton." Mark shot a heart-felt prayer up to the heavens. "I'll see if Ellie is on board."

"You mean, Mrs. Jenkins?"

Mark shot his brother a hard look. "You know what I meant."

"I did. I think you're throwing caution to the wind." Colton licked his knife.

"What do you mean?" Heat on the back of Mark's neck intensified.

"I mean, if she were my wife, I wouldn't allow the two of you to go looking for a boy who may not want to be found at night in that part of town."

"Mrs. Jenkins is safe with me." Mark blurted.

Colton quirked an eyebrow at him. "Safe physically, maybe." Colton goaded.

"Thanks for breakfast, Aunt Eunice." Mark placed his plate and silverware in the sink with a clank. He would not be pushed into a discussion about Mrs. Jenkins' safety. He would never approach another man's wife. He stopped in the hallway and leaned against the wall. Colton was right. He was buying as much time as he could with Mrs. Jenkins' under legit reasons, but what would happen when Billy was found or captured and their reason for spending time together was no longer legit? He'd cross that bridge later. He needed to be careful that he didn't blow up the bridge in the process.

He found Toby's number in an old notebook he kept from seminary days. He'd be surprised if Toby still had the same number.

"Hello?" a voice on the other end spoke.

"Toby? Toby Marsh?"

"Yes. Who's calling, please?"

"Toby, it's me, Mark Bruens from seminary."

"Well, how are you? Long time, stranger. You doing okay?"

"I am…sort of…I've got a situation that I'm hoping you can help with. It's a long shot, but here goes. Of course, this is a hypothetical case." Mark told him about Billy without breaking any laws. "You were always involved with the homeless back in the day. I'm not saying Billy's mom is homeless, but you'd know the areas we should start looking in, I think."

"I might, yeah." Toby paused. "Can you give me a couple of hours? I need to finish up with some things, and then I could meet you and talk some more. That would give me time to process and help with a game plan."

"Sure. That would be great." Mark wrote the name of the ministry headquarters and the address. "I'll see you this afternoon." Mark hung up. A lead. *Thanks, God.*

He waited until a decent time of the morning to call Ellie. Mrs. Jenkins. Ugh. Get that straight in your head, man.

"Mrs. Jenkins? Sorry to bother you again, but I think I have a lead."

"Mark, you're not a bother. What do you have?"

She sounded like he felt, raspy and in need of

sleep.

"I know someone who is familiar with downtown and the areas Billy's mom might frequent. He said he could meet us at 3 p.m. today." Careful, don't be pushy. He really wanted her with him and last night, she'd sounded like she was done. Let the police handle it was her response.

"I don't know, Mark." Ellie hesitated. "Hey, I'm going to put you on hold for a minute, someone is trying to call me."

"Okay." Mark tapped his fingers on the desk as she picked up the other call.

"Mark, it's actually the police on the other line. I'll call you back."

That could not be good news.

~

"Yes, officer?" Ellie held her breath. She knew they would call at some point, but she'd hoped she and Mark would find Billy before then.

"Ma'am, we picked up a real character outside of Dallas who's telling us a pretty big tale about what might have happened in that motel room with your runaway juvenile."

"Yes?"

"We marked this guy from the security cameras at the casino who was seen with one of the dead bodies in the motel."

"Billy's dad?"

"No, the other one. Billy's dad hit the jackpot and these two goons followed him out of the casino." The officer paused. "His story is they followed Billy's dad back to the motel and tried to rob him for the money."

"Okay. That doesn't implicate Billy."

"This guy said when they got there, Billy's dad was already dead on the bed and he said this kid came out of the bathroom and fired on them, killing the partner."

"That doesn't make sense. The man's throat was cut, not killed by a bullet." Ellie jumped up, shouting into the phone. "There was only the dead body in the chair, no one on the bed. He's lying. We didn't even know there was a second body until you all showed up and loaded him in the coroner's van. That was Billy's dad and he had to be killed in the bathroom, because we didn't see him in the room."

"I hear ya, Mrs. Jenkins, and we want to hear Billy's side of the story. We do. Right now, all we have is a missing kid who was in the motel room at some point, two dead bodies, and a lot of money missing."

"That guy is lying." She shouted again.

"You've got to calm down. We're going to need to see his file now. Can we meet you at your office?"

"Yes, yes, of course. Sir, I know it wasn't Billy."

"Help us figure that out, the details aren't matching up. But ma'am? It doesn't look good for him, right now."

"I understand. I'll meet you there at 11 a.m." Ellie hung up the phone and dialed Mark. "Mark, they caught another guy who says he was partners with the dead guy in the room."

"Mrs. Jenkins, slow down. Now, who did they catch?"

Ellie liked 'ma'am' better than the 'Mrs' reminder that she was being deceptive to the whole, wide world. "For Pete's sake, will you please call me Ellie?"

"Okay, okay. just slow down. This is a mess."

Ellie put the phone on speaker and collapsed in the closest chair. She repeated what the police said to her. "I know it's not Billy, and this guy's story is way off."

"That is not the scene we saw." Mark agreed.

"Mark, I know what I said earlier about letting the police handle Billy's situation, but I think we're the only ones who believe he is not guilty. We have to find him before they do." Ellie paused, willing her emotions under control. "The officers want to meet me at the office to look at his file. They're going to want to meet you, too. Did you say you knew a guy who might be able to help find Billy?"

"What time are you meeting them?"

"11 a.m."

"I haven't heard from the police yet, but I suppose I'll be the next visit after your office. And yes, but we can't meet with my guy until 3 p.m. Can you stall them? They'll be one step behind us and may have more information than they are letting on, but it's worth a shot."

"I can't leave out information. That's obstruction."

"I don't mean obstructing, I mean moving a little slow to open the file, offering them water, you know, stall."

"I can try."

"Do you want me to meet the police with you? Then they can talk to both of us at the same time?"

She'd like nothing more. His quiet strength and

logical thinking was what she needed. And the width of his shoulders and how his eyes would lock on hers. Good grief.

"Ellie?"

Mark saying her name, minus the 'Mrs' brought her back to the here and now. And the way he said it. She shivered slightly.

"Sorry, I was thinking. No, no, I'll do fine by myself. I can call you when they're heading your way," she decided. "However, I will meet up with you later and talk to your seminary buddy, and then we can go look for Billy."

She hung up and stayed in the chair, cheek on the soft fabric, legs curled under her until Magic came over to check on her.

Jason made her feel safe…she meant Mark. She sucked in a breath. Before, she compared the two men, now she was interchanging them. No, Mark could never be what Jason was to her. But in a twisted way, she looked forward to spending more time with Mark, even if it was in the pursuit of finding a lost boy.

Her eyes landed on a plaque, given to her by a friend, hanging on the wall. I trust the next chapter because I know the Author. The next chapter. What was that, really? If she had to say what grieving stage she was in, she'd say the one above being utterly and completely devastated. Was that the next chapter? Or maybe the next chapter came after she'd stumbled her way through the entire process. She couldn't ever imagine not feeling overwhelmed and sad when she thought of Jason. The tidal waves of grief that used to leave her sobbing in bed for hours at night came less often. She was learning how to walk on her own, make her own wise decisions, know who she could ask help from when she knew nothing about what needed to be fixed, and trust her own instincts without relying on another soul. Was that the next chapter? Did the next chapter after this one involve another relationship? She was not ready to share any of her new-found freedom with anyone. But somewhere down the line? Maybe. Could Mark be a part of the next chapter?

Ellie looked at her rings, light glinting off the diamonds. Maybe it was time to take them off. Not to show she was available, but rather a reminder that she was an independent, strong woman and could stand on her own two feet.

Ellie patted Magic and then stood by her jewelry box. Was there a ceremony of sorts when you took off your wedding rings? Something significant to say or do? She took out Jason's ring and wandered back to their wedding day. He'd wanted a gold band with distinguishable etchings on the face of it. Although slightly worn, she could still read the engraved inscription. *Jason and Ellie. Love you forever.* His fingers had been so cold when she put the ring on his finger.

"Jason? Is this okay?" Tears clouded her vision. Every time she thought of him, more times a day than she could count, she pictured him in Heaven, rejoicing with the angels at the foot of the throne. She wouldn't wish him back to this earth… who was she kidding… of course, she'd wish him back if she could. Before that fateful day. Before their argument. She'd been petty and selfish and in return, she'd lost the very thing that helped put her life together. She couldn't bring him back, but, occasionally, she wished for a sign…a glimmer of his approval. She would love Jason until the day she died, but the rings were symbols to others that they were united, committed to each other. They no longer meant that to her.

Slowly, Ellie twisted the wedding band and diamond engagement ring off her finger, tears flowing freely. She placed both alongside Jason's ring. Taking off the rings didn't need to be a forever thing; she could always put them back on. For now, it seemed like the right thing to do.

Chapter 9

Mark beat Ellie to their agreed upon spot, a small diner north of the ranch.

"How did it go with the police?" Mark approached Ellie's truck. He opened her door, allowing her enough space to wriggle out between the car parked next to her. And close enough to smell a light, floral scent on the breeze. Shampoo? Lotion? Didn't matter, she smelled amazing.

Mark saw the smudges under her eyes, she wasn't sleeping, either. Wished they'd met under other circumstances. This was a nightmare and wasn't looking to get better anytime soon. Nothing about this entire thing fit into his safely controlled world. Not Billy, and certainly not Ellie. Numerous times, he had to get on his knees, figuratively, and plead with God to make things normal again. Normal, boring, never changing he could handle, relish even. This, he had absolutely no control over. Maybe if he prayed harder or longer. There's got to be something, anything, he could do to turn this around.

Ellie shrugged. "If they know anything different

than we do, I didn't hear it. They are one hundred percent certain Billy is their only suspect, despite that guy they picked up. I don't think they believed what he said, either."

"I agree. Have you eaten? This place has great coffee, and the fries are limitless." Mark waved for her to enter the little mom-and-pop diner ahead of him. An old-fashioned, but clean, interior greeted them. Several of the patrons turned to look.

"I haven't. I just keep thinking that the more time we waste doing mundane things and not actively searching for Billy, the police are going to get ahead of us."

"You have to eat. And we've got some time to spare before we go see my friend. We're doing everything we know to do." Mark ordered fries from the waitress. "Coffee or Coke?"

"Diet Coke, for now." Ellie gave him a tiny smile. "The later it gets, though, coffee will be needed."

"No doubt." Mark glanced at her. She was so beautiful, even when exhausted. Tension settled in his shoulders and neck, and he rolled his head, trying to release it.

"I feel that, too." She mimicked his movement.

Silence hung between them until the fries were brought to their table, piping hot.

"Ketchup?" He shook the ketchup bottle.

"No. Don't laugh." Ellie squirted mustard on a small, round plate and dumped pepper over the pile. Swiping a French fry through the mixture, Mark watched as she popped it into her mouth.

"Umm... that is not attractive at all."

Picking out another fry, her hand paused. "Is eating fries supposed to be attractive?"

Wow, he'd stuck his fist in his mouth. He hadn't meant to say attractive. The mustard slash pepper mixture was not appealing, that was the word. He laughed. "No, no, of course not. Mustard and pepper, though?"

She shrugged her shoulders. "I like it."

"Well, then, when in Rome," Mark took a small plate, mixed the same concoction and winked at her.

What are you doing, man? Like cramming toothpaste back into the tube was futile, he wished he could take back the wink. Completely inappropriate.

"So, the police took a quick look at the security footage of Billy leaving the ranch, asked a few questions and then left. I have no idea where the investigation is or what steps they'll take now." Mark filled her in.

"They got precious little from me as well." Ellie wiped her fingers on a napkin. "Tell me about your seminary friend."

"Toby? We were both students then. He went on to teach at that same college." He took a quick sip of his Coke. "Toby was always the humanitarian, loved people, had connections to help, organized food drives, that sort of thing."

"And you?"

"I was not nearly as good as Toby. He was as close to sainthood as anyone I knew. I was more into the history side of theology, studying human behavior based on past actions and decisions. Toby was about the here and now."

"Sounds more like psychology, rather than

studying to be a pastor."

"That is not what I wanted, to be a pastor. Far from it. I guess I wanted to help people, juveniles mostly, by studying past mistakes and changing their futures so the cycle didn't continue."

"What cycle?"

"The one where kids are thrown into adult problems, expected to survive, and those kids grow up to be adults who bring their kids into their problems because it was normal. A cycle. You've got to break it somewhere." He'd hinted at too much. No one needed to hear his background or why he was passionate about juvenile offenders. He hadn't been a delinquent growing up, but he'd learned how to Play the game, to stay out of his father's way, to lock his lips shut at risk of getting beat himself. His brother, on the other hand, was angry and determined to confront with his fists, not his words. Mark carefully used words and a tightly controlled personality to lock away emotionally charged interactions. Easier to leave them guessing what he was thinking than have to explain why he was thinking the way he did.

Losing a boy was his undoing. Billy had taken all control out of his hands. And caused Mark to doubt whether or not he was capable of running a home for boys. Or just trying to right the wrongs in his own childhood.

"How can Toby help us?"

"When I called him earlier..." Mark started.

"Wait, did you call him before or after I agreed to keep searching for Billy?"

"Before. I was going after him regardless if..."

"I was going or not." She interrupted again.

"I- yes. I wasn't sure how much you could be involved with you being his case manager." Mark glanced at her. Was she mad? "I just wasn't sure." Plus you're married. And I'm super crazy attracted to you.

"I said I was in this boat with you. We need to stick together as partners if we're going to find him." Ellie dusted her hands off on a napkin.

Partners. He liked that idea. No, wait, they could never be partners. Get that through your head, buddy.

~

Why had she said that? Ellie stepped outside and watched Mark pay for their fries. They weren't partners. Working the same case, but not partners. He was friendly with the old man at the cashier, on a first name basis it appeared. Both of the men glanced her way, and Mark caught her gaze and smiled, which didn't quite reach his eyes. Mark turned back to the man, shook his head. The older man clasped Mark's hand and patted him on the back with the other. Had she done something wrong? Were they talking about her mustard and pepper concoction?

Ellie started to twist the rings that were no longer there. She didn't realize how much she fidgeted with them. She looked down at her hands, devoid of anything sparkly or gold. Very strange. Like she forgot to put something on and walked out of the house like that. Naked. Maybe she needed to get another ring, one she picked out for herself. One that meant nothing other than a pretty bauble on her finger.

"Can we take my truck?" At her nod, Mark led

her to his truck and opened the passenger door for her. "You okay?"

Jason used to open the door for her, too, despite ribbings from his friends that he was being old-fashioned. She was comparing again. There was no comparison, Jason was the love of her life. Mark, a colleague of sorts, together trying to find a lost boy. And here she was for the second time, in his truck, breaking her rule to always have the upper hand in her own vehicle.

"Anxious to get going." She hopped into the truck cab. His smelled way different than hers. Not an unpleasant one, it smelled of manly things, outdoorsy scents. Minus a few lollipops.

"Sure." He glanced at her.

Kind of him to notice something was off, that her mood changed since her defense of the mustard and pepper fries. Nice that he'd asked. She felt a stirring in her gut. Mark was probably a great guy, but he wasn't Jason.

He drummed his fingers on the steering wheel and hummed to a Christian song on the radio. "Mind if I take the long way around? Downtown is always crazy, and we're not in a big hurry." He added, "Yet."

"That's fine." Ellie chewed on her lip. Better than chewing her fingernails to the quick or spinning her no-longer-there rings. "What do you hope Toby can help us with?"

"He said he was running one of the shelters north of Dallas, and people drop in and out of there all the time. He can also point us to areas of the city that are known for prostitution."

"You still feel she's in the business, don't you?" Ellie took a gulp of air. The word, prostitution, brought up so many heavy feelings. She deeply wanted to believe Billy's mom had found a way out. A cruel lifestyle. Surely, Billy wasn't trying to buy her way out with the money he stole. Wait, did she believe what went down in the motel room really happened? No. Maybe. Maybe parts of it, like snatching the money and running from the horrific scene, but not the murders. He was a kid. Those were adults, twice his size, albeit probably drunk.

Mark shrugged his shoulders. "I don't know. She's our only lead, though."

He glanced over at her. The gut stirring was back. Sometimes when he looked at her, she felt a slight nudge. A poke that said she was safe with him. A bigger prod that suggested she might want to be more than partners. And then he'd do something so-Jason-like she'd pull back and refocus. He was not Jason. What if all the good things in Jason were also in Mark? What if this spark of interest she was feeling could develop into more? That'd be okay, right? Jason? That'd be okay?

Ellie turned and looked past Mark's profile at the setting sun. Or pretended to. With small laugh lines at the corner of his eyes and a shadow of whiskers, she wanted to explore his face with her fingertips. Good grief. It was going to be a long night if she couldn't get her hormones under control.

He must have sensed her scrutiny because he turned and gave her a warm smile. This time it reached his eyes. Whoa girl. He could not, should not, do that very often.

"What?" he asked, resting his arm on the console between them.

"The sunset is stunning." His hand was not very far away, she could close the gap if she wanted. Little hairs on his forearm glinted in the sun bouncing off the windshield. His forearm looked strong and capable, tapering to his slender fingers. She turned farther in her seat, adjusting the belt so she could see more of the orange globe, now painting pinks and purples across the sky. And more of him.

"Hmm…"

Ellie wasn't sure he bought her story. Although it truly was a beautiful sight, looking at Mark was just as pleasing to the eye. If this was a relaxing trip through the countryside…she could wish, couldn't she?

An hour down the road, Mark turned into the large parking lot of a brick building that had weathered the test of time, based on its slightly eroded front and the peeling paint on the door. It had seen the wear and tear of the neighborhood, settled in for the long haul. A sign read St. Christopher Catholic Church est.1921. Over a hundred years old. The stories this building could tell.

Ellie sat, stone still. She could feel the past pushing around her, gathering steam. She'd spent some time in a building exactly like this, minus the doors with the welcoming wreaths hanging from hooks. Of course, the doors she was accustomed to were in the back, hidden from the niceties of the world. No one wanted to see the riff raff coming and going from the old church.

"Ellie?"

"Yes?" She shook off the hesitancy and jumped out of the truck before Mark could open the door for her. His arched eyebrow said he'd noticed that, too. "Let's go meet your friend."

Mark opened one of the heavy doors with bars welded to the frame. The pretty wreath covered the bars as if to say "You're welcome to come in, but I protect those who enter."

Signing their names in the open book in the vestibule, Mark dialed Toby's number. "Hi, we're here."

Within minutes, the infamous Toby stood in front of them. "Ah, friend. It's so good to see you." Mark pulled the man into an embrace.

Toby punched Mark lightly in the bicep. "Still lifting weights, I see."

Ellie saw, too. His long-sleeved shirt fit him like a glove and rolled up to the elbows, he looked, well…Ellie shouldn't even be thinking those kinds of things in church. Or anywhere. His muscular frame was hard to miss. She should be concentrating on other things. Like finding a boy.

Chapter 9

"Still hanging around the seedy parts of town, I see." Mark slapped Toby on the back.

"It's where my joy is." Toby motioned for them to follow him down a hallway, past a grand sanctuary where its solid wood pews stood through generations and the stained-glass windows painted multi-colored shadows on the red carpet. Down some steps, and the basement opened before them.

"Good grief, this is huge." Mark looked around at the floor-to-ceiling bookcases with everything from hymn books to weather-worn Bibles to more contemporary novels scattered in piles.

"Remind you of anything?" Toby asked, a light in his eyes.

"Yeah, the basement of that old church on campus. They had the best selection of teas and coffees. We studied down there often." Mark smiled.

"We have coffee down here, but the books can't be checked out. In the other rooms," Toby pointed down a long hallway, "we have a food pantry, a clothing pantry, and a gymnasium the kids can come play in when the weather's bad or they just need to be away from home for a bit. It's a pretty cool setup."

"I thought you managed a shelter." Mark pulled a book off the shelf.

"I do, a couple of streets over. I was here today, so I thought it'd be easier to meet here."

"This is great, Toby. Something you always dreamed of doing. Good job, man."

"Not me. I just put the dreams out there and God worked the only way He can. Perfect."

"Let's hope He sees fit to help us." Mark sat down on a sofa that had seen better days. He sunk into the cushions, readjusted, and finally gave in to a not-so-graceful sprawling, which, honestly, was the only option.

Toby laughed at him, and Ellie sat in an adjacent chair that looked far more sturdy than the couch.

"So, tell me a little more about this boy. Hypothetically." Toby pulled a small pocket notebook and sat, pen poised, to take notes. "Oh, first, tell me how you all met." He looked at Ellie and back to Mark.

"Mrs. Jenkins is the boy's hypothetical case manager," Mark started.

"Oh, this is Ellie? He told me about you on the phone, but he didn't mention your full name." Toby turned to Ellie.

A slight hesitation, and then Ellie smiled at him.

Why the hesitation? Because he introduced her as Mrs. Jenkins? Wasn't that professional? Or because he'd already talked about her to Toby? Ellie wouldn't meet his eyes. "Like I said earlier on the phone, the boy left my property," Mark explained.

"I really need to get down there and see what

you've done with the old homestead." Toby interrupted.

"Yes, you do." Mark sped on, hoping to get the rest of the story out before Toby had another thought. "He left on his own, although we're not sure if he had help or was coerced. Anyway, we found his father, or rather his father's car, at a seedy motel down the road. When we went into the room to ask his father if he'd seen him, we found a dead body. Not Billy or his dad."

"Holy Moses." Toby exclaimed under his breath.

Mark looked at Ellie, who was as white as a sheet. "Is it okay to go on?"

"Yes, he needs to know, and if he can help." Ellie raised tired eyes to him.

He hated to have to relive the grisly scene in front of her. He would likely have to recount it again for others, but he hated that she was taking it so hard. He could feel the weight of responsibility in her gaze. He was at fault, too.

"We called the police who discovered a second dead person, which *did* happen to be the boy's dad."

"Poor kid."

"It gets worse. The police found the boy's jacket in the room and a lot of money was missing."

Toby whistled. "Oh. The police suspect the kid for two dead bodies and robbery?"

"They do, or at least they are saying he's a person of interest."

"How do I fit into this mix?"

Ellie jumped in. "We think the boy may try to find his mother. The foster family he stayed with, before Mark, mentioned he always talked about his mother. She works the streets here in the city, we think."

Toby put away his notebook and rubbed his hands together. "This is a pretty large territory to canvas. Do you know her name?"

"She goes by Kitty." Mark pursed his lips at Toby's eye roll.

"So do the majority of prostitutes in the northern hemisphere." Toby stood. Ellie stood with him while Mark tried to extract himself from the cushions, springs, and any other thing that was holding him to the couch.

Mark pointed, "I think that couch needs a new place to live. Like a dumpster."

Ellie ducked her head, but not before Mark caught her smile. If nothing else, he was good for laughter. He enjoyed seeing her smile, a twinkle added to her normally serious look. Warmed his heart.

Argh. He didn't need to be warming his heart over someone else's wife.

Toby led them over to a large map on the wall. "This is the area I serve." He drew an imaginary circle around the map. "This whole northern section is where you'll find the strip clubs, the street walkers, and plenty of unsavory characters. I'm not sure what you hope to accomplish by driving up and down the road. You said the mom was a prostitute? Not a strip club dancer?"

Mark paled. "We keep hearing the word 'prostitute'."

Ellie shifted next to him, and he glanced at her.

"Both were mentioned," Mark explained. He heard Ellie breathe in through her nose. "I know it's a long shot. We've got to try, though."

He tried to memorize the map. There wouldn't be any stopping to ask directions or pulling over to look at the GPS. It'd simply be cruising the street on the lookout. Preferably for Billy. They had no concept about what his mother looked like, only her name and possible vocation.

"Visiting the strip clubs would be easier, although not pleasant." Toby sighed. "It's not like there's one spot where all of the prostitutes congregate. I can contact some of the other ministries around. It's just doubtful there's only one 'Kitty' out there."

"May I use a restroom before we go?" Ellie interjected.

"Sure. Let's go to the employee one." Toby led them back upstairs.

The two men waited outside the ladies' room.

"She's pretty fantastic." Toby commented.

"She is. She only said, like two words, though. How did you come to that conclusion?" Mark raised his eyebrows at Toby.

"She's hanging with you, for one." Toby punched him lightly in the arm. "I don't know. A feeling I get. And the looks between you."

"What looks?" Mark blanched. Toby thought he was making eyes at a married woman? Good grief. He was in deeper than he thought, if he couldn't conceal his attraction better than that. Toby was perceptive, or had been, but they'd been here for a total of twenty minutes and there were *looks*?

"Relax, dude. She's pretty."

"And married."

"Yes, you said that. Are you sure, though? I don't see any wedding rings." Toby stretched his arm across Mark's shoulders in a side hug. "Take care, buddy, and let me know what you find out." Toby winked at him.

What? He'd seen her twist the rings around her slender fingers, and she never corrected him when he'd said her married name. Actually, she had. Anytime he'd said 'Mrs', she'd ask him to call her Ellie. Maybe? Mark felt his heart pound a little faster when she came out of the restroom. She was very pretty. Heart-stoppingly pretty. He tried to get a look at her hand, but she was saying goodbye to Toby and ready to leave. What in the world?

~

Ellie got in the truck and pulled her seatbelt on. "Do you think it's late enough to start looking?"

When Mark didn't answer immediately, she turned to him. He looked baffled. Or something. She couldn't quite put her finger on it. He'd been pensive, upset, even angry, in front of her, but never whatever this was. Maybe seeing his friend stirred up old feelings. She stayed quiet, not asking any more questions or trying to make conversation, while he was lost in thought.

Flashy lights and neon signs began lighting up the cab of the truck as they drove closer to the strip. Still, Mark said nothing. She wasn't about to be the one to break into that train. He'd tell her when he was ready. She hoped.

Old insecurities flooded her being, her hands

trembled as she sat on them, willing them to stop. Had she done something wrong? That had to be it. People didn't flip a switch and be someone different. False, Ellie. Mother did it all the time. Or at least when she was around. And not entertaining guests. Ellie was always doing something wrong. She ran people off when she did wrong things. Whoa, slow down the wagon. That's a bad line of thinking. She'd clawed her way out of the deep dungeon of negative self-talk, certainly not with her mother's help. Her counselor said it was natural to move inward when the outward was not controllable. She also suggested Ellie's coping mechanism, the self-loathing negative talk, may be her own perception, a way to punish herself. Truth and reality could be very different.

She'd said very little, enjoying watching the interaction between Mark and Toby. It couldn't have been something she'd said for Mark to suddenly go radio silence. And now, she was stuck in his truck. Why hadn't she driven herself? Breaking the rules was a no-no, and she'd done it twice now, both with Mark. She felt safe with him, that's why. The two of them on the same mission, yes, partners. Like they could tackle the world.

Mark pulled onto the strip, driving incredibly slow, keeping pace with the other cars. She guessed the vehicle passengers were scanning the clubs, tattoo shops, and weed stores for where they wanted to stop. She and Mark were there for a completely different reason.

At a stop light, Mark looked over at her and smiled. A genuine one. His eyes took on a warm glow from the flashing sign behind her, but the warmth was really, truly there. Maybe all was right with the world, and she'd jumped off the train too early. And for no reason.

She wanted to scoot closer to him, put her hand in his. They didn't need to talk. She missed the power of a touch. Reassuring, complete, supportive. A touch could calm even the most ignited anger.

She watched intently on her side of the truck as they crept past sleazy signs and ugly offerings. She looked into the faces of the heavily painted, scantily dressed women on the corners. Scanned the throngs of people on the sidewalk for a boy who would be taller than most. Nothing. It was a long shot.

The sounds and sights made her skin crawl. From the inside out. She struggled to breathe, cracking her window added to the pressure in her head. Ghosts from her past were shifting in her peripheral, taunting her, daring her to come closer. She shivered. Stay focused, Ellie. You're with Mark. *They can't get you, nor can they hurt you. God? This is almost too much.* Praying silently, she eased farther back into her seat and looked intently for Billy. Too often, she thought she saw the face of her own mother. Which was impossible. Her mother had been dead for a long time.

Ellie's phone rang, startling them both.

He smiled at her again. "That's your ringtone?"

"Law and Order? Yeah." Ellie looked at the caller ID. Her boss. Calling after business hours. "Hi, this is Ellie." She nodded and "uh-huh-ed" her way through the conversation. "Yes sir, see you in the morning."

Mark raised his eyebrows at her.

"My boss. He wanted to know if I'd be there tomorrow. I wasn't in the office for very long with the cops this morning. He was out of town yesterday, so I don't think he realized I was gone."

"Does he know? About Billy?"

"No, not yet. I don't know how much longer I can keep it from him, though, especially if the cops keep stopping by.." Ellie looked at her hands in her lap.

"I don't want you to get in trouble. This was my fault."

"It's Billy's fault, not yours. I should probably get home, though. I'll sidestep my boss for as long as I can." Ellie sighed.

Mark took a vacant side street and headed back the way they'd come. He reached across the seat and offered his hand. "We'll find him. I promise. And we'll get him out of this together."

Ellie glanced at his hand and bit her lip. Slid hers into his. Just a handshake on the promise. That's all it was. He didn't intertwine fingers, a business handshake. That's all. One that made her blush. Not a handshake, more of a promise.

His palm was warm and felt right in hers. Jason always rubbed his thumb on the back of her hand, but this was different. At the thought of Jason, she pulled her hand away.

"Can we come back out tomorrow night?" She bit the inside of her cheek. Run away, girl. You're getting too close to tearing down the self-constructed rock wall around your heart. They had to find Billy or his mother. And soon. She had a lot to lose either way this played out. The more time she spent with

Mark, the more likely she was to share the growing conflict in her gut.

Mark's face was blank. She couldn't read his thoughts. Had she screwed up again? Her emotions were all over the map.

"Sure. I'll pick you up around 8 p.m.?"

"At the same diner? Maybe some more fries?"

"Not for me. Especially not drenched in mustard and pepper." He laughed and all was right again.

Sheesh. She needed to get this under control.

Chapter 11

That night Mark slept fitfully, tossing his bed covers off his feet and onto the floor. Crazily painted ladies and tall boys haunted his dreams. He was awake most of the night.

After watching Ellie drive away, he'd sat there for a long time, head down on the steering wheel. She wasn't wearing her rings. When he'd put his hand out to her, he hadn't expected her cool fingers to be void of the diamond rings she normally sported. They were bare, like his. No warm metal on either hand. What did that mean? She hadn't put them on for the day? They were getting cleaned? Maybe, it was like Toby said, that she wasn't married. But why wear the rings to start with? Women wore cocktail rings and such on their left ring finger, didn't they still? These were clearly a wedding band and an engagement diamond.

And then there was the guilt. He purposefully offered her his hand to find out if she was wearing the rings. He didn't want to examine that thought too closely, but it was out of character for him to be manipulative. He was trying to calm her and let her know they were in this together. Right? She seemed pensive and he wasn't exactly thrilled to be taking her down into the belly of the beast. But if they were trying to find Billy's mother, they had to start there. Against his better judgment and his desire to protect her from the depravity they saw.

He shuffled out to the kitchen, smelling coffee and hotcakes.

"You were out late." Aunt Eunice handed him a cup of the dark, hot liquid.

"Mrs…Ellie and I," Mark corrected himself, "were out looking for Billy in a pretty raunchy neighborhood."

"You think he's out there? Living in such a place?" Aunt Eunice loaded a plate full of pancakes, bacon, and two heaps of scrambled eggs.

"His mom, probably."

"Hey, bro. Any news?" Colton sat heavily next to him at the wide table that could hold twelve.

"No, we're going back out tonight, but after that, I think we'll have to wait on the police." Mark shoveled in food.

"We as in you and Mrs. Jenkins?" Colton asked.

Mark didn't correct him. For all Mark knew, she *was* married and didn't have her rings on yesterday. His gut turned. Wishful thinking would get him nowhere. Facts were facts. "I'll pick her up tonight at 8 p.m. One more night."

"Be careful, bro." Colton sipped his coffee, reiterating his earlier warning.

Mark finished his breakfast, kissed Aunt Eunice on the cheek, and stepped into his office. And he thought last night was long, the day would prove to be longer as he waited until he could see Ellie again. Correction, until they could look for Billy's mom and hopefully find Billy.

After hours of watching the clock, piddling around the house, getting on Aunt Eunice's nerves, and doing odd chores around the ranch that needed fixing a long time ago, it was time to get ready for the evening. Finally. What did one wear when with a beautiful lady searching for a teenage runaway?

"Stop it. Wear your normal." His inside voice chided. Mark pulled on a worn pair of jeans, his dress boots, and a comfortable cotton t-shirt under a long sleeved button-down. He looked like an average Joe driving his lady friend down the strip. Through the strip club neighborhood, just for fun.

Pulling into a parking spot in front of the diner, Ellie waved at him from a window seat. The fluorescent lights bounced off her golden hair, forming a halo. His heart drummed faster. He took a deep breath. *Calm down. This isn't a date. The pretty lady in the window isn't excited to see you, she's ready for this drama to be over.* The convincing thoughts didn't stick. He tried to wipe the grin off his face and remind himself of what they were doing.

Would she have her rings on tonight?

~

Put your hand down, girl. You're not a schoolgirl waiting for her boyfriend to arrive. Ellie twisted a lock of hair around her fingers and then sat on her hands, willing herself not to pull her hair out of place. She'd spent an hour getting it into shape, not to pull it out in nervousness. Sure, she was anxious about going back down on the strip, but more so to see Mark. He undeniably messed with her head and convoluted most of her thoughts in the last couple of days. Abnormal for anyone, but Jason, to be in her ponderings. And yet, there Mark was, invading her dreams with his hand in hers. She contemplated what a hug from him would feel like. Safety, cared for, warm…for Pete's sake. Stop.

"Hey. Long day for you." Mark sat across from her.

The smell of soap, bacon, and a hint of aftershave wafted over her.

She would not let that schoolgirl get shy. She was not that schoolgirl. Right. He smelled good, bottom line.

"Yeah, but anxious to go out again." To search for Billy, she should have added. This temporary partner of hers was certainly distracting.

"Did your boss say anything about Billy?" He ordered coffee for himself. "Diet Coke or coffee for you?"

"Coffee, lots of creamer, please."

"Fries?"

"With coffee? No thanks." She wrinkled her nose. Gross. "He didn't. We had some repeat cases come through that needed to be dealt with."

Mark frowned. "I don't suppose you'll ever use my ranch again."

"Mark. This is not your fault."

"I know that and yet," he let the sentence hang as his phone rang. "It's Toby. Hello? Hey. No way. Of all the 'Kittys' in the northern hemisphere? Really. Okay, thanks."

"Toby from yesterday?" Ellie asked as Mark put

his phone down on the table.

"Yeah. He said he'd put out some calls and one of the pastors who works with a ministry in that area called him back. Said he had a worker that knew a dancer named Kitty. It's a long shot, but worth a try."

"Come on, let's grab those coffees to go." Ellie pushed out of the bench seat.

Mark signaled to the waitress and met her at the cashier counter. "I'll take care of this."

"No, it's my turn."

"Sorry, but I'm not going to let a lady pay for my coffee."

Gentlemanly thing to do. She'd have to repay the favor next time…what next time? After they found Billy and cleared him of the murders, she may never see Mark again. "Then let me pay for mine."

Mark let out an exasperated breath. "No."

"I should have ordered fries and a steak dinner." Ellie said, under her breath. She snuck a quick look at Mark who acknowledged her joke with a slight smile. That's better.

"Okay to take my truck again?"

For Pete's sake. The feeling of being taken care of washed over her. She was so used to doing things for herself. This felt good, though. As if they weren't on the hunt for a runaway boy and about to dive into the depths of Dallas. She could almost imagine…

"Sure."

He opened the passenger door for her, and she slipped in. The cab felt smaller than it did last night, probably because she was even more aware of the man driving. He put his arm behind her and backed out of the space. She braced herself. Control, control,

control. Ellie closed her eyes and tried to slow her heart rate down. She loved having his arm around her, even just reversing his truck. She shut her mind to any thoughts that contained Mark, not an easy feat when she could still smell his aftershave and concentrated on the scenery out her window.

"Toby didn't get an exact location, just the west side of the strip." Mark flipped to an easy worship station on the radio.

Ellie let the notes and words flow over her, calming spaces with rough edges. Peace was what she needed. Exactly what she didn't have.

As they entered the line of clubs, their windows plastered with naked women silhouettes, Ellie breathed deep. Her hands shook. She wiped at the sheen on her forehead. The place made her jittery as if she'd loaded her coffee with espresso. Seeing this side, from the outside in, she cringed at how ugly this world looked. And she'd been in its abyss. Ellie cleared her throat as they drove past clubs that were all too familiar to her.

"Hey, would it be corny to have a name like Kitty and work in a place called CATS?" Mark slowed down and pointed to a stand alone building sandwiched in between a tattoo shop and a bar with metal spikes on the window. CATS in neon letters lit up its roof.

Ellie swallowed. A lump the size of Texas gathered in her chest. She licked her lips and stared at the sign. Bile edged its way up in her throat, threatening to bust out. She wiped sweaty hands on her jeans.

"Ellie, you don't have to go in." Mark looked at

her, concern in his brown eyes.

They watched two men stumble from the club, one leering at her in the truck. "I think I do. I'm not staying out here by myself."

"I don't know what to expect when we go in, I've never been in one of these." Mark came around to her side, helped her out, and tucked her hand in the crook of his arm.

She had. And it was not going to be pretty. Even though several years had passed, the ugliness never changed. The neon lights outside were inside, too, with spotlights on the stage where the women performed and vulgar men, young and old, wasted time and money on the depravity.

"Hey cutie." An older woman, scantily clothed, wrapped herself around Mark as soon as they opened the door. Ellie felt him shudder.

"A table, please." Mark cleared his throat.

"Aren't you polite?" She led them to a booth in the shadows.

Mark let Ellie sit on the inside, facing away from the dancers. The woman scooted in next to Mark.

"So, what can I get you and your girlfriend here?" The fake cat ears woven through her grayish-yellow hair threatened to fall off when she rubbed a chalky cheek on Mark's shoulder.

Mark turned ashen.

"She's not my girlfriend," he started.

"Well, she ain't got no rings on, so your lady friend, then." The woman purred.

Ellie's eyes widened and she pinched her lips together. Mark sucked in a breath.

"Is there someone who works here named

Kitty?" Mark kept his eyes on the table.

The woman laughed, which abruptly turned into a coughing fit. "You'd think there was more than one in here, wouldn't ya? But, we don't. I'll be right back." With a bop on Mark's nose, the woman left them and shifted through a curtain to the right of the stage.

Was it possible that they'd found Billy's mom at their first stop? Ellie's eyes skipped around, avoiding the stage where a new girl started her routine.

"I am so sorry. This is a nightmare." Mark wiped his nose with his hand.

"I'll know for certain that God is in this, if the first place we stop has Billy's mom working in it."

"I don't think I can do this again, so, I pray you're right." Mark looked up at her.

"You'all lookin' for me?" A younger version of the first lady approached their table, her leopard-skinned bikini leaving little to the imagination. She had a contagious smile which Ellie was certain caused many men to ask for her. Plus, the scant clothing.

After glancing at Mark, Ellie looked at the table. Mark was carefully keeping his eyes above the woman's chin.

"I'm not sure. Is Kitty your real name?"

She smirked. "There's lots of Kitty's in this room. You can call me Kitty or KK, whatever you'd like, sweetie."

"Do you have a son named Billy?" Mark asked.

The woman narrowed her eyes as she looked around. "Who's askin'?"

Mark shifted in the seat and pulled out his wallet. He slid her a fifty-dollar bill along with a business card. "We are."

She stuffed the cash in her bikini top and palmed the card.

"We think Billy's in trouble, actually we know he is, and we thought he might try to find you." Mark glanced at the bouncer heading their way.

Kitty looked where he was looking and whispered in Mark's ear.

Oh my word. Ellie shut her eyes. The woman was close enough to stick her finger up his nose. Ellie slid out of the booth, wondering what filth she was sitting in, and stood by the edge of the tabletop. "It's time to go." She could barely hear her own voice over the bass-pumping music.

Kitty eyed her as she stood up next to her, and then strolled over to another table full of men. She blew a kiss over her shoulder at them.

Mark took Ellie's arm and led her through the throng of men, now standing on their feet, whistling at the stage. Ellie was sobbing by the time they reached the truck. The whole thing was too much. CATS, Kitty, the looks on the men around them, the pulsating music.

As she rounded the front of the truck, the bouncer from the club raced out and grabbed Mark's shoulder. Spinning him around, the man put a meaty fist in Mark's face and growled at him.

"Reason for you to come after one of my girls?"

"Um…" Mark swallowed.

"Didn't buy anything. Didn't drink nothing, neither."

Ellie raced back to Mark and the big bouncer. "I couldn't handle being in there. It's his birthday, and I...I … I thought I could handle it, but," Ellie threw up inches from the bouncer's shoes. The big man jumped out of the way, let out a string of expletives along with a hard look, and returned to the club. Mark took her by the arm and led her to the passenger seat.

He leaned over and grabbed the half-drunk bottle from the console. "I don't have anything, but a couple drops of this Diet Coke. Are you okay?"

"That's fine." Ellie leaned her head on the headrest, eyes closed. She used the back of her hand to wipe off the spittle she could feel drying on her face. What a freaking mess. At least she'd had the forethought to close in on the bouncer's boots, versus Mark's. Who was she kidding? She could have just as likely thrown up on her own shoes. And the second time she'd thrown up in public. With Mark present, no less. She took a swig of the warm Diet Coke.

"Are you okay?" Mark repeated, concern in his eyes. He continued to stand in the open door, just inches from her.

Images of the woman whispering in his ear had her undone. There was an overtly sexual tension in the room already and she knew how disgusted Mark was, just by his shudder when they first entered the place. Had she been like that? And then the memories. Assaulting her from the first step in the club. The writhing bodies on stage, the smell of sinful desires, the vacant look in the women's eyes. All crashed in on her until she had to escape. Had to get out into fresh air. The last straw was the bouncer coming out and grabbing Mark. Bile leapt from her gut up into her mouth. What Mark must think…with his theology background and his lack of experience of true depravity in the world.

She knew what it looked like. Experiences she wanted to forget. A box of hopes and dreams buried in the backyard, crushed under the dirt and slime of choices and circumstances. She'd almost dug that box up and shared them with Jason. He wouldn't have judged. He would have told her that she needed to put the box at the feet of Jesus. And she'd tried. Some things were too painful to share with anyone. Pieces of her that no one could know about. Parts that were too disgusting to say out loud.

Chapter 12

Mark gently shut her door and quietly got in the driver's seat. "Ellie…Mrs. Jenkins?" She was clearly shaken. Whether it was from the strip club itself, the bouncer grabbing him, or throwing up in public, he didn't know. A combination of all?

"Yes?"

Mark sighed. He'd hoped she'd correct him, hoped she'd tell him she wasn't married anymore. She didn't have her rings on, even the woman in the club noticed. Maybe…? How could he even be thinking about that after what happened? Mark felt more and more like David in the Bible, pining after Bathsheba until he could stand it no longer and ordered her husband killed. Not quite that dramatic, but what did the Bible say about sinning in your heart? Even if you never acted on your thoughts, you were still sinning. Hope against hope there was a legit reason for Ellie to not be wearing her rings. His thoughts were runaway trains on tracks that would lead to destruction if he didn't shut them down. Lord, let this be over before I do something stupid and disappoint you, me, and Ellie.

"Are you alright?" Mark wavered. If he knew her better, he'd joke that she had impeccable aim, but one look at her solemn face and he knew she was upset. just not why.

"Yes, I'm fine."

Mark's thoughts turned over and over, creasing into each other, at times, overlapping, at others, fully disengaged. Frustrating.

"Do you think that was Billy's mom?" He shifted into Drive and left the strip.

"You could always go back and ask her."

Mark glanced away from the street. "What?"

Ellie's head was up against the window, face obscured from his view. Was she being sarcastic?

"What did she say to you at the end? When she was all up in your ear?"

All up in his ear? It was horrible. Mark's thoughts tumbled.

"She said she was Billy's mom and wants us, both of us, to meet her for coffee tomorrow. She said she couldn't talk there." Ellie turned to look at him, and Mark nearly stopped the truck when he saw relief flood her face. Relief that they'd found Billy's mom and wouldn't have to go into any more clubs? Mark plunged ahead. "Look, Mrs. Jenkins, if you don't want to meet her tomorrow, I can do it without you."

Her mouth dropped open.

"I'd bring Colton or Brandon with me, of course." He hastily added.

Ellie closed her eyes for the briefest of seconds. Not long enough for a blink, but a subtle shift in her body language. He'd made the right move.

"No, I'll come. We're in this together." Taking

a deep breath, she spread her hands out in front of her. "About the Mrs. Jenkins…"

Here it comes. "Wait, this feels like a big conversation, and I want to give you my full attention. Can we talk when we get to the diner? We're only about ten minutes out."

Ellie nodded her head and laid it back on the seat. Closed her eyes.

Oh boy. He had no idea what to expect. He flipped the radio on and attempted to quell the nervousness that was gaining speed in his body.

As they rounded the corner where her truck sat, Mark pulled in next to it, rolled down the windows, and turned off the engine. A perfect summer's night. Maybe not for long? The night air was filled with the smell of greasy hamburgers from the diner and a hint of a bonfire somewhere close by. Would have been nice to enjoy an evening out without heavy conversation. That didn't seem to be their track record, though. He braced himself for whatever was about to come.

"So, the first…um… lady that greeted us? She pointed out that I wasn't wearing my wedding rings." She displayed her hands again.

Long and shapely fingers, nails perfect. They were hands he wouldn't mind tucking into his. Without the rings.

Ellie traced her left ring finger where the rings used to reside.

"I guess… I… I." Ellie chewed on her lip.

Mark watched her struggle to get words out. "Listen, you don't need to tell me anything." Really? Is that so? It wasn't the truth, but he also didn't want her to be any more upset than she already was.

She gave him a slight smile, and then in a rush of words, said, "I'm not Mrs. Jenkins anymore."

What? Since when? Mark watched tears flow down her beautiful face. Hauntingly beautiful. She covered her eyes with her non-ringed hands. What was he supposed to do? He wanted to gather her up in his arms and stop the tears. Inappropriate? Maybe. His heart went out to her. So vulnerable, so open, so fragile and yet, he knew she was anything but. He sat still and waited.

After a minute of silence, Ellie lifted her head and looked at him, mascara pooling under her lashes.

Mark watched as tears continued to course down her cheeks and onto her jeans. "Ellie, please don't cry."

"Mark, I'm a w... a widow." She covered her face again. "I hate that word."

A widow?

~

She *did* hate that word. It put her in a club she never dreamed she'd be in, one that separated her from the singles or marrieds, one that left her in the gray area. She couldn't stop the tears once they'd begun rolling down her face. Dripping off her chin and onto her pants. She needed to reign it in, get control over herself. She could only leak the grief out every so often, and never for any length of time. Letting herself cry was dangerous. If she didn't push the grief back in, it might overwhelm her and tug her down in its undertow, something she could not afford.

The parking lot lights shone in her window,

backlighting her and putting Mark half in, half out of the shadows. She sat up, back straight, hands in her lap. Get it under control, girl. She squeaked a glance at Mark, who turned his head to meet her eyes. His compassion and desire to sit quietly next to her, let her take the lead, almost undid her.

"I'm sorry, I didn't know." Mark said, softly.

"I know. It's not something I share with everybody." Ellie spread her fingers out again. "It's a very strange place to be in. I, honestly, haven't figured it out myself."

"Is there anything I can do?"

Ellie shook her head.

Mark leaned over the console and put her hand in the two of his. "I'm so sorry."

His gesture was so sweet and kind, she wanted to bawl her eyes out.

Get it together before you do something truly ridiculous. They had work to do.

The silence in the truck lasted less than a minute and yet, during that quiet moment, a shift happened between them. One that she wasn't sure she was ready for.

Mark cleared his throat, returned to his serious tone. "Do you want to meet here again tomorrow? Or can I pick you up closer to home? The office?"

It was easier to respond to this Mark, versus the kind one who made her want to scoot closer to him if she could. The one she wanted to know better, the one who reminded her of Jason. Mark's theological background and upbringing separated him from who Jason had been. Mark was careful and cautious while Jason had been passionate and 'all in' regardless of what he was doing or who he was involved with. The first time she and Jason met, she was skeptical of his hundred percent 'in' attitude. In her book, it didn't pay to go full throttle into anything, there were calculated risks, backgrounds to check, history to examine, motives to guess. Jason ran headlong into everything, including his pursuit of her. It wasn't love at first sight, but Jason wore her down with kindness, his steadfastness, and integrity. She hadn't known Mark long enough to determine any of those things. The look in his eyes, however, made her question whether or not tucking her feelings and emotions away was a good idea. A rational one, for certain. A protective one. But what if…

"The office would be good. I can get some work done." No way was he picking her up at her home. Rule #2. "That'll make the boss happy."

"Tomorrow, it is, then. Nine o'clock?"

"Sounds good." Ellie got out of the truck and into her own, rolling down the window. "Until tomorrow."

"Careful going home." He called out as she backed out.

She waved and drove out onto the main road. Yes, until tomorrow, Mark Bruens.

Chapter 13

Tread lightly, my friend.

When he'd picked up Ellie earlier, Mark didn't know if her revelation about being a widow would change anything for them. It certainly had for him, but her? Her vulnerability to share something so deeply intimate, personal, opened up unexpected possibilities, positive ones. He didn't need to feel guilty over his attraction to her, but he couldn't rush in and scare her, either. Finesse was in order, along with a healthy dose of wisdom and consideration for her feelings. Mark didn't know the first thing about widows, except they, as a church, were commanded to take care of them. Which he would happily oblige, if she let him. Mark's heart skipped a beat.

Mark opened the door to the diner, ushering her in ahead of him. His desire to protect and care for Ellie had grown in leaps since hearing she was a widow.

"I think she's over there." Mark pointed to a woman sitting by herself with her back to them. They criss-crossed through the restaurant until they were beside the woman.

They both froze when the woman looked up at them. She hurriedly pulled sunglasses from her hair, but not before they saw the black eye.

"Oh my word." Mark whispered.

Ellie gulped. "Good morning."

Mark offered the inside seat to Ellie, across from Billy's mom. Sadness etched wrinkles in Kitty's face.

Billy's mom had already ordered her coffee and dumped multiple creamers in it, from the looks of the empty cups on the table. "You've already seen it, I guess." She pushed the sunglasses back on top of her head, revealing dark bruising that no makeup could cover.

"Kitty, what happened?" Ellie reached across the table, just shy of touching the woman.

"The boss was suspicious until I showed him the 'Grant' you gave me."

Ellie looked at Mark, a quizzical look on her face.

"Grant." Mark repeated. "Fifty-dollar bill."

"Oh."

"The boss didn't think it was enough." Kitty shrugged her shoulders.

"Enough for what?"

"Whatever I was sellin'." Kitty glanced at Ellie and then Mark. "You two a couple or what?"

"No." Mark stammered.

Kitty sat back and smiled.

Mark groaned inwardly. Why would she say that? Was it written on his face? Maybe etched on his sleeve? And if they weren't a couple, would Kitty take that as an opportunity to conquer and divide them? She was, after all, a stripper, and someone who looked like she knew her way around a street hustle.

"Do you know why we're here?" If Ellie noticed his uncomfortableness, she didn't show it.

"You wanna buy me breakfast?" Kitty reached out and touched Ellie's hand. "That's so nice of you." At a sly glance at Ellie, she added, "Just kidding, sweetie. You want to talk about my boy, Billy."

Careful, she's smart, devious, and a little desperate looking with the swollen cheekbone and scantily covered bruise.

"Yes. Billy." Ellie said, quietly.

"Why should I tell you anything anyhow? I don't know you."

True.

Ellie pulled out her badge for the second time in as many days. Mark crossed his arms. "He's with me."

"How do we know you're his mom?" Mark ordered coffee from the waitress.

"You found me, remember?"

"Look, we're not here to play games. He could be in a lot of trouble. Again, how do we know you are his mother?" Mark hated the way 'mother' rolled off his tongue. This one was no one's mother. Or at least hadn't been for awhile. Maybe never. Who would give up their kid like she had?

"Billy's in trouble? What kind of trouble?" Kitty sat up straighter on the heavy plastic bench.

Mark squinted at her. Really? Motherly concern now? He looked down at his hands as he added sugar to his coffee. Ellie was taking her time sweetening hers as well. Seconds of silence ticked by.

"Ain't ya going to tell me?"

"Are you his mother?" Mark looked her full in the face. Ellie placed a hand on his arm, a gentle warning. He leaned back, catching her shoulder behind his, relaxing into her. This is what it was supposed to be like, working together, a relationship. He did not take his eyes off Kitty, although his thoughts were spinning in a totally different direction.

"Yes. That is," Kitty broke eye contact and swept some eggs into her mouth, "if you are talking about my Billy. He was taken from me when he was about eight years old, loved baseball, brown hair, brown eyes."

Mark ignored the 'taken from me' comment. More like Billy was removed from Mom, in all her spectacular, upright citizen glory, because she couldn't take care of him appropriately.

"Is your real name Kitty or is it a stage name?" Stage name. A foreign concept to him.

"It's really Kitty." She rolled her eyes and shoveled in a forkful of hashbrowns.

"Billy talked about you a lot with the foster family he was staying with." Ellie cocked her head at Kitty. "Kitty, I think he really missed you."

Leave it to Ellie to be all soft and concerning. He was trying to wrap his head around Kitty actually being a mother. No wonder Billy was so angry if he was always fighting to get his mom's attention.

"You think?" Kitty looked wistful for half a second. "So, what's he in trouble for?" Her face regained its hardened look.

"Well, kinda a long story," Mark started. "His

father stopped by…"

"What?" Kitty put a hand over her mouth and then slammed it down on the table. "You let his father near him? What are you, crazy?"

"Kitty, calm down. Everyone's looking at us." Ellie's quiet voice commanded attention and Kitty folded herself back into the seat, crammed against the window.

"We didn't know the man was his father, until Billy saw him. He hid from me at the ranch for several hours until my brother coaxed him out. And then he ran away." Mark schooled his tone to an even, calm sound. Blowing out a breath, he continued, "We went looking for him and found his dad at a local motel, dead."

Kitty raised her eyes to his. A haunted look huddled just behind her tight smile. "He's dead? Billy's father?"

"Yes." Ellie nodded at him. "Billy was at the motel with his dad, he left his jacket, and to the police it appeared that Billy killed his father."

"That's not possible. You don't know my Billy." Kitty exclaimed.

Ellie handed her a napkin. Kitty looked at her breaking point, tears threatening to fall.

"Actually, we do. And we don't believe Billy could, or would, do anything that violent." Ellie pursed her lips. "We do need to find Billy, though."

"Before anyone else does," Kitty finished Ellie's sentence.

Mark arched an eyebrow at Kitty.

"Someone killed his father. If it wasn't Billy, then who?" Kitty pushed her empty plate out of the way and rested the palm of her hand on her cheek, elbow on the table. "The cops? The guys following you?"

Mark and Ellie looked at each other.

"What?" Mark questioned. They were followed to the club? By cops?

"They came in after you. I was heading their way, next up for the paying customers," Kitty's shoulders slumped. "Then I was told that you two were asking for me, so I switched direction."

"Did they talk to you after we left? How did you know they were cops? Or that they were following us?" Mark gave Ellie a worried glance. The cops were merely steps behind them. "And why did you act surprised when we said Billy was in trouble? You obviously already knew."

"Lots of questions." Kitty slyly looked at him.

It took a second for Mark to understand. Pulling out his wallet, he laid a $50 bill on the table. At her fingernail tap on the formica, he put a twenty on top of the fifty. Ellie kept her head down. How uncomfortable. "That's all the cash I have. What else do you know?"

"One of them had his badge tucked in his shirt, but I saw it."

"It could have been anything." Mark groaned.

"Dude, ya think I don't know what a cop badge looks and feels like?"

"No, I'm sure you do." A caustic tone crept into his words. She'd shown her cards, readily admitting she really didn't care what was happening with Billy as long as cash was involved.

"They warned me not to talk to anyone else."

Kitty moved her hair off her neck. Bruises the size of fingerprints were visible on her skin.

Ellie sucked in a breath.

Mark put his hand on his forehead, elbow on the table. Not only a black eye, but someone had choked her as well. No wonder she wanted payment for information, constantly weighing the physical punishment over the need to make money.

Mark thought about the bouncer who'd grabbed him around the neck when they'd walked out of the strip club. He could still feel the meaty fingers digging into his throat.

"I don't listen good, apparently." Kitty fluffed her hair so the marks were no longer visible.

"Okay, I've heard enough. I'm going to pay for breakfast. I'm assuming you can get... wherever... the same way you got here."

"Sure, cowboy."

Mark stiffened at the slang name. Dirty, suggestive, all wrapped up in her tone.

~

Ellie looked at Kitty as Mark walked away. Shaking her head, Ellie said, "That wasn't necessary."

Kitty grinned at her. "Jealous, much?"

"What? No." Ellie shifted in her seat. "You don't know Mark. He's ... we're... worried about Billy."

"Look, I like you. And if Billy really is in trouble, I'm glad you're looking for him."

"I like you, too. I get all of this tough talk. I don't even mind you asking for more money." Ellie rifled in her purse and pulled out her reserve cash. "Here's another twenty. I actually understand."

Kitty smirked. "You don't mind? Yeah, right." She scooped up the twenty-dollar bill and put it with the other cash inside her shirt.

One minute she was Billy's mom, the next, she was conniving and ugly. Exhausted by the constant changing of gears, Ellie locked eyes with her. "I really do. I get it."

"Girl, there's no way. And I don't like liars."

"Kitty, I was just like you. I'm not lying." Ellie shook her head. "And then I met a man."

Kitty snickered and hooked a thumb at Mark. "Him?"

"No, not Mark. We just recently met." Ellie blushed. "No, this was someone else. He introduced me to Jesus, and I was able to walk out of that situation, similar to yours, and leave it all behind."

"I don't need Jesus. I need a flesh and blood man with plenty of cash."

"You know how far that will get you. And when you're older and not as pretty, you'll be discarded for the next one. Trust me, I know."

"Lady, you're sweet and all, but full of it." Kitty looked out the window. "I trust me."

The sheen of unshed tears she saw in Kitty's reflection rocked Ellie to the core. "You know I'm right, and if you ever want to get out of this life, here's my card." Ellie handed her a business card, stood and made her way to Mark. Her own eyes filled up. Her heart was hollow, and her fingers trembled. She did know what Kitty was mixed up in and the guilt, shame, and self-preservation Kitty felt every time she crossed the strip club threshold.

"What's wrong? What did she say to you?" Mark put a protective arm around her and guided her through the diner doors and out to the truck.

"Nothing. I'm okay." Ellie glanced at the window where they had been sitting and met Kitty's sad eyes. She could never share the depth of feeling for Kitty with Mark. His tone showed just how much he didn't understand about self-loathing and desperation. If he found out Ellie's history, he would think the same about her. Plus, he had already aired his opinIon of women who sell themselves, how vulgar and disgusting. He could not find out Ellie's past.

The pain of doing what she had to do to survive. Not being able to change any of it. She'd learned how to take advantage of people from watching her mom, how to read the circumstance and capitalize on the misfortune of others. Her mother had been in and out of strip clubs and having no one to watch young Ellie, she was forced to go with her. Just like Billy, except Ellie's mom wasn't protecting her from an abusive dad. She didn't know what else to do.

Her mother was beautiful with long blonde hair, a heart-shaped face and soulful gray eyes that drew men in by the truckloads. She was popular wherever she went, at least among the male gender. Women could spot the spell Ellie's mom wove from a distance, keeping their partners close for fear they'd be drawn away into the magic.

On the rare occasions that Ellie and her mom were alone in their one-bedroom dump of an apartment, her mom was a typical mom. Doing laundry, questionable lingerie included, singing 80's cover tunes while cleaning the house, reading books at night that Ellie brought home from school. The nights in the apartment were a Godsend and precious few; usually it was a cot in the back of the dressing room with the sound of the bass to lull her to sleep. Despite no other children there at night, Ellie assumed it was normal to go to work with your mother, if you weren't rich enough to have an overnight babysitter.

"Are you sure you're okay?" Mark's voice brought her out of her swirling thoughts.

"Yeah, Kitty makes me sad."

"I'll be honest, she made me uncomfortable. I don't trust her, she didn't seem all that interested in Billy, and she wanted money."

Ellie sat quietly. Kitty was protecting herself with the strong body language and off-putting conversation. She suspected Mark felt like every other red-blooded male in the presence of a dancer. Drawn to, embarrassed by, struggling to keep their thoughts pure.

"What do you think about the cops following us?" Mark changed the focus of the conversation.

"Maybe they weren't actually following us, but rather ended up at the same location by accident? Is that possible?" Ellie responded. Mark glanced at her as she spun imaginary rings on her finger. She really needed a fidget toy.

"Pretty coincidental. Maybe." Mark started the truck. "What should we do now? I feel like we've hit a dead end."

"Me, too. Can we drive down the road a bit? Kitty is staring at us."

"Oh, yeah, sure. Sorry."

"No problem." Ellie took one more glance at Kitty and gave her the sign to call if she needed to.

Mark pulled out of the parking lot and headed back to Ellie's truck.

"I should go back to work." Ellie smiled pensively at Mark.

"I should probably, too. Or what looks like work. If you think of anything or hear any leads, you'll call, right?" Mark stopped the truck in the parking lot and turned to her.

"Absolutely." Ellie turned to him. "Same for you?"

"Yes." Mark hesitated. "Ellie? Can we go to dinner sometime? I've really enjoyed this time, despite looking for Billy. Doing something normal like a meal out with a pretty lady instead of a strip club or a diner with a prostitute would be much more enjoyable."

Ellie hesitated. She hadn't been out on a true date, but it was just dinner, not a date, right? What would Jason think? Ellie stared into his hopeful face. What would Jason *think*? What would he think of Mark? Or going out to dinner with a nice man? Would he be mad at her? Crazy talk, girl. Jason is gone. And what's the point? If he should ever find out her past, he would run as fast as he could away from her. So, why start something?

"This is all new to me. I don't know what widows do. Sure, I'd like that. But is it the right thing to do? I can't promise I won't have my mind on finding Billy, though. He's out there somewhere and there's people after him. At least the cops."

"Of course. I won't be able to sleep until I know he's safe." Mark rubbed his face with his hands. "And Ellie? I don't want to scare you or stress you out. I enjoy being with you, and we can figure this out together."

Not really. She had to define who she was without Jason. This was between her and God.

"Okay." Ellie opened the truck door and slid out. She stuck her head back in before closing it. "Goodbye for now, Mark."

"I will call you." Mark gave her a half smile.

She didn't want to leave him and if she was reading the room right, he didn't want to leave, either. Walk away now, girl, before you climb back in his truck and… and what? She'd see him again, his offer for dinner reverberating in her head. Mixed emotions played across her face, warring with each other. Stay or go. Be responsible. Be reckless, let your guard down, see what happens. Not safe. Go Now.

She caught Mark's wistful glance as she turned and made her way into her office.

Her boss growled at her as she walked past his door. "Mrs. Jenkins. I need to see you right now."

Ellie stopped in his doorway and crossed her arms. This was not good.

"Where have you been?"

"I was here this morning. I stepped out for a minute. Why? What's up?" Her boss didn't typically speak so gruffly to her. Her gut tightened.

"Want to tell me about this missing kid situation?"

Oh boy. Time was up. She filled him on as little

as she could, just the facts, glossing over the strip club conversation.

"Anything else you forgot?"

No, nope. Ellie shook her head.

"The police seemed to think you're hindering their investigation."

"What?"

"What I've been told."

"What you've been told?" Ellie sputtered. She sounded like a parrot. Were they at the strip club, like Kitty suggested? "How am I hindering their investigation?"

"Not important, but they are annoyed. And because you've failed to notify me of this particularly dire situation, I'm pulling you off the case. This is now Earl's case."

"Wait, sir, I've taken it this far. Please let me continue to work on it." Ellie pleaded.

"No. You failed to report a runaway juvenile to your superiors. You're lucky to still have a job."

"Sir, please." At the shake of his head, Ellie walked slowly to her office.

Slumping into her office chair, she straightened the items on her desk. Moved the calendar a half inch to the right, put pens in their holder, placed notes in the correct folder.

She was effectively cut off from anything related to Billy's case. He was no longer her client.

Chapter 14

"**Mark? Oh, here** you are." Aunt Eunice entered his office, turning on lamps in her path.

"Aunt Eunice, please. I was enjoying the fire." Only embers glowed in the big stone fireplace, so not quite a lie, but any other reason sounded so depressing.

"You can't sit in the dark all night."

"I'm thinking, and I do that best in the dark."

"You should be down on your knees."

"What?" Mark half rose from his chair. Aunt Eunice had never scolded him before.

"For Billy and that girl." Aunt Eunice switched off one of the lamps she'd just turned on. Her concession.

"What girl?"

"Billy's case worker."

"Why do I need to pray for her?" Heat rose up his neck. His aunt missed very little. If he were honest, he'd been thinking less of Billy and more about Ellie. How she handled herself, how she'd confided in him about being a widow, how she smelled like a breezy bouquet of flowers. How she twisted the ends of her blonde hair. Boy, good thing it's dark, you're in full blush mode.

"A feeling I get. Not all is right in her world, but she puts on a brave face."

Interesting.

"She told me she's a widow." Mark looked at Aunt Eunice.

She sat down on the ottoman next to his chair, her face full of compassion. She nodded. "I sensed the sadness. He must have been the love of her life."

Mark swallowed. He hadn't thought much of Ellie's husband. The man must have been amazing for Ellie to marry him, or at the very least, lucky. The wedding photo in her office told the story; they were in love. "I don't know what to do with that information."

Aunt Eunice cocked her head at him. "Why do you feel the need to do anything?"

Mark closed his eyes. Leave it to his aunt to cut to the point. He bit the inside of his cheek.

"I don't know. I just…she's…I don't know." Sheesh, he couldn't even put words to what he was feeling.

"You like her."

"Maybe." What was he doing? Crushing like a twelve-year-old boy? "I don't know yet. I'm definitely developing feelings for her. In such a short time. I've been holding back because I thought she was married. Now that I know she's not?" Worry creased his forehead as he squinted into the fire. "And love of her life?" He threw quotes up in the air. "How do I compete with that?"

"Compete? This isn't a race, son." Aunt Eunice

patted his knee. "You can love more than one person in your lifetime."

Mark caught a wistful smile on her face. "I'm sorry, how thoughtless of me. I forgot about Uncle Clarence."

"And my Charlie. God granted me two wonderful men to love."

Mark nodded. He had, indeed. Uncle Clarence had been gone since Mark was a baby and while his aunt and Charlie had never gotten married, he was the one Mark remembered the most before cancer overtook him.

"How will I know if she's ready to date someone new?" Mark asked, dreading the answer. He didn't share that he'd already asked her to dinner.

Aunt Eunice was silent for a moment. "You might never know. She has to be the one to decide. You can't force it."

Mark sighed.

"Do you know how long her husband has been gone?" Aunt Eunice cleared her throat. "Not that it matters. It's different for everyone."

"She just took off her rings. She had them on when Billy first ran away, and it's only been a couple of days and she's not wearing them now." He lifted hopeful eyes to his aunt's.

"Could mean a lot of different things, many of which have nothing to do with you." Aunt Eunice stood. "Pray and let God direct you." She pointed a finger at the painting of a narrow road leading to somewhere. Written in scrolling letters was "Lead me on level ground."

Mark put his face in his hands and closed his

eyes as his aunt softly left the room. She was right, all he could do was pray.

~

"What now, Lord? What do I do now?" Ellie lay on her bed, wrapped in her favorite crocheted afghan. Its colors of muted blue, dark purple, neon green, and ruby red complemented her light wood bedroom set.

Jason's murder was on her hands. Sort of. The ministry of helping girls out of prostitution and human trafficking was his passion. She'd encouraged Jason to continue with his ministry and get out as many girls as he could. But, on that night, she'd pushed all of his buttons, they'd argued, and he walked out angry. Wrong place, wrong time, the police said. She knew, though, he wouldn't have been out there at that time if it weren't for her selfishness. Essentially, she was the cause. If you connected the dots. Why couldn't she have encouraged him to get a real job like normal men, one where he worked in an office 8-5? Not out on the streets of Dallas, putting his life in danger for women who weren't stable enough to get out themselves. Stop it. She knew better. He would have gotten her mother out if she hadn't died before his ministry hit the streets. Oh, how her life could have been different. Instead, she modeled her mother's choices, followed in her footsteps. If only someone would have come alongside her mom, like Jason, and shown her a different lifestyle.

"Well, this is a lovely little rabbit trail you've found yourself on." Ellie unwound from the covers and padded into the kitchen. Maybe a cup of tea would help her sleep. She put the hot water on to boil and reached for her favorite mug, Jason's, the one that read "You know you love me". Ellie sucked in a breath. Yep, sure had. Jason introduced her to a love that she had never encountered. Unconditional, pure, he was always concerned about her needs. A Hallmark movie written just for her. She'd been blissfully happy. Happy wasn't even a strong enough word for how she'd felt with Jason. He hadn't been perfect; he was passionate about everything which equaled exhaustive in her book. And his love for Jesus? Infectious. She'd wanted what he had. The peace, the confidence, the belief in someone knowing her and still loving her. But now, Jason was gone and her whole world had tilted. Like sending a boat to drift in the middle of a large pond with no one at the helm. Was she still in God's graces? Or was she only connected to God through Jason?

Ellie texted her counselor friend. *Hi, Kari. I know it's late. Can you talk?*

Sure, came the quick reply.

Ellie took her tea and settled in the corner of the couch. Punching in Kari's number, she put it on speaker. "I'm really struggling tonight."

"Aww…girl. What's going on?" Jason had introduced Kari to her as a counselor, but they became fast friends outside of sessions, too. Kari knew people, loved Jesus like Jason did, and subsequently loved Ellie, too.

"I just don't know. I got pulled off a case about a runaway today. So, I'm totally ineffective to help this kid. I'm missing Jason. There's a guy…"

"Wait, there's a guy?" Kari asked.

She shouldn't have mentioned Mark, not yet, at

least. Not when she was missing Jason.

"Jason. I'm missing Jason."

"Tell me why. And what specifically you're missing about Jason." Her friend softly questioned.

Counselor mode.

"I took off my rings." Ellie looked at her bare fingers.

"Because of this guy?"

"No, of course not. They just didn't feel right anymore. Well, maybe. This guy kept calling me Mrs. Jenkins, and it felt like such a lie." She wound the fringe on the afghan around her hand, the heavy yarn soft and supple under her touch. Mark's face swept through her head; he was so gentle with her. His kind eyes catching hers, the sparkle when he tried to make her laugh, how safe she felt around him. How scared she was of Mark discovering who she really was. Such a seesaw of emotions.

"I can understand that, although no one can tell you when the right time is to take them off. You could wear them indefinitely if you wanted." Kari hesitated. "Unless you wanted him to know you weren't married."

Ellie frowned. Had she subconsciously wanted that? No, she just didn't want to lie.

"Has he noticed your rings? Did he ask about them?"

"No, he'd never do that. He just calls me Mrs. Jenkins all the time."

"Sounds respectful. Did you tell him you were a widow?"

"Yes, after the hundredth time of addressing me as Mrs." Ellie closed her eyes. "Mark makes me feel… I don't know… like he wants to protect me. Like my feelings are important to him. My opinions matter to him. I matter to him. That's not why I called you tonight."

"Why did you call?"

"I said I was missing Jason." Her tone was sharp and unnecessary. "Sorry. Okay, okay, this guy asked if he could take me to dinner, and I said yes and now I'm regretting that."

"Why?"

"Because I don't want to move on. I want Jason. I don't know this guy; he doesn't know me. And I'm sure if he did, he'd bolt."

"How did you meet?"

"The boy that ran off? He was sentenced to Mark's ranch. I was his case worker, until I got booted off."

"Sounds perfect. No conflict of interest."

"No reason to see him either. When we were on the case together, we had purpose. To be together." How did we get back to Mark?

"So, you're feeling guilty."

"Yeah, a little. I keep thinking what Jason would think about this?"

"Understandable. What would he think?"

"I don't know. Be happy?" Tears dripped off Ellie's cheeks. How could she ever be happy like she was with Jason? A dream that would never repeat itself.

"I think he'd want you to keep your eyes on Jesus. Let God work on the details of what's next."

"Probably." She swiped her hand across her face. She missed Jason terribly, his strength, his ability to challenge her, and yet provide the safety to grow. "I shouldn't have said yes."

"Now that you have, let's see where this goes. You're not cheating on Jason by being attracted to someone else. Jason loved you. He would want you to go on living. I'm not sure you've been doing that."

True.

"I think *attracted* is taking it a bit far." Ellie took a deep breath.

The sound Kari made on the other end of the phone line was just shy of a snicker. "Girl… right. He may be physically attractive, but you're obviously attracted to his heart, by what you've said. I know you, remember?"

Also true. No one had caught her eye all year and now she'd bonded with Mark in a span of a couple of days. Maybe she was taking this too far too quickly. Maybe a friendship was what she needed right now. It didn't have to turn romantic. A friendship wouldn't be dishonoring to Jason. Live a little. Yeah, right. You're not thinking friendship. You're thinking what it would be like to huddle in Mark's embrace and feel wanted again. He was kind and gentle, and although there was an edge to some of his philosophies, maybe there was also a passionate side, too. Ellie warmed to the thought of being passionately loved again. Ok, whoa girl. Dinner and see where this goes.

"I'll go. I may need to call you afterwards."

"Or not. This guy may surprise you. But remember, you're not locked into anything. If you don't want to go out again, don't. You don't owe anyone anything."

"Thanks, Kari. I appreciate you."

"Goodnight, my love."

Ellie smiled at the sentiment. Kari always made her feel ten times better, even as she asked the hard questions.

Chapter 15

Mark changed into his fifth outfit of the evening. The long-sleeved button-down shirt, tucked into dark olive green pants and his comfortable favorite dress jacket spoke casual and yet, tasteful. He blew out a breath and shrugged out of the jacket. Maybe untuck the shirt? Then he'd have to iron it again, pull the wrinkles out of the tucked-in look. Ugh. The last time he was with Ellie, he'd worn a hooded sweatshirt and old jeans. Why did this feel different? Because you like her. Because you want her to like what she sees. Good grief. He'd never been concerned about clothes before.

Plus, it *was* different. When he'd called earlier in the week to see how she was and re-ask about dinner, she'd confided her boss had pulled her off of Billy's case. The idea to not tell her boss hadn't turned out like they'd wanted, and he was sorry she was in hot water for it. Now he knew she was no longer responsible for Billy, and if he wanted to see her again, he'd need to be intentional about staying in contact. He was still concerned about Billy, and he thought she was, too. After their week, finding

Billy's dad dead, talking to Billy's mom, and then Ellie revealing she was a widow, it was a lot. And they were no closer to knowing about Billy.

God, keep him safe.

Mark tucked his shirt back in and looped a brown belt through the pants. As much as he'd like to look hip, or whatever the young ones called it these days, he was what he was. A late-30s single guy. Mark considered the shadow on his chin. He should have shaved. He debated pulling off his shirt and grabbing the razor for a quick by-pass. No. Nope. Wasn't it common for the ladies to like a little bit of stubble, the rogue look? That what you're going for, big guy? Again, no. Ease it down a notch.

"Whatcha doing?" Colton grinned at him from the doorway.

"Shut up."

"Going on a date?" Colton pushed. "Oh yes, you are. With Billy's case manager? Isn't she married?"

"Shut up. And yes, Ellie, except she's no longer Billy's case manager. Nor is she married." Mark held a tie up in front of the mirror.

"No tie." Colton suggested. "She was married when she came out here a week ago."

"Not really. She's a widow."

Colton whistled.

"What?" Mark spun around. "What's wrong?"

"Nothing. I've never known a young widow before. Just older ones, like Aunt Eunice." Brynleigh, Colton's fiancée, poked her head in the door, and Colton looped an arm around her.

"What's happening? Wow, you look nice, Mark." Brynleigh smiled at him.

"Have I told you lately how much more I like B than you?" Mark threw the tie at Colton, who grabbed it one handed before it could flutter to the floor.

Colton wrapped the tie around his head and danced around the room with an imaginary partner. Brynleigh watched with amusement until Colton caught her up in a fancy two-step.

"You two were made for each other." Mark feigned disgust. He struggled a little with his younger brother having a fiancée, shouldn't he be first? But Brynleigh was perfect for Colton and a Godsend to the ranch. With her taking over some of the teaching, it freed Mark to do other things. Like traipsing all over the countryside with Ellie. Although he'd rather be seeing the sights with Ellie and not visiting strip clubs. He sighed. This was crazy.

"Don't let them tease you, Mark." Aunt Eunice chided from the living room.

Must everyone be in on this evening? He was nervous enough. His thoughts were all bunched up, skidding sideways, bouncing off each other like a pinball machine. Of course, it wasn't like he dated very much. Or at all.

Mark walked into the kitchen where Aunt Eunice retreated. He kissed her on the cheek. Even though she was smiling at him, he could sense her sadness as well. Aunt Eunice would always be reminded of her own widowhood where Ellie was concerned.

"What was that for?" Aunt Eunice turned to him.

"Just appreciate you. I probably don't say that

enough." Mark gave her a half smile, his insides churning. How would he ever keep food down tonight?

"Go, have a great time. And, if you find you want to prolong your evening, come back here. I'm making a chocolate pie." She winked at him.

Bonus. Dinner and homemade chocolate pie.

~

Ack. Why had she allowed Mark to pick her up at her house? She'd once again be subject to his decisions, which was proving not to be a terrible thing. She felt safe with his decisions, so far. He'd know where she lived, not a bad thing. She'd have the opportunity to sit in his truck and allow his masculine smell to wash over her, sneak glances at him. Marvelous things. Mark had been nothing but a gentleman, even in the CATS club. Every outing they'd taken so far, despite the awful places, showed more of his heart. Wasn't that what she wanted? The intimacy of him being at her house, if only to pick her up, was unnerving, however, the pros certainly outweighed the cons. It will be fine.

Ellie put on her favorite gold necklace. She loved the way the single diamond caught the light. Jason had given it to her…take it off, take it off. She couldn't wear the necklace on a date… dinner… with another guy. Don't be foolish. The necklace didn't have any sentimental value to it other than it was a gift from Jason. This was ridiculous. Still, she put the necklace back in its place in her jewelry box and chose another one. It matched perfectly with her light gray sweater and held no connection to Jason. Turning in the mirror to see all sides, she liked how her black jeans complemented the rest of her outfit. Casual, yet classy.

She pulled on her cowboy boots, the glittery ones- every girl needed some glitter in her life, didn't they? A couple of squirts of perfume, one on either side of her neck and one under her heavy hair at her nape and she was ready. Clothed, at least, maybe not ready.

And waiting. Twenty minutes until the time he said he'd pick her up. Would he be early? Late? Circle the block until the clock said straight up six o'clock? Early, but not too early, she decided. Butterflies skirted around in the pit of her stomach. She had no idea where they were going for dinner. She should have asked. And then she'd be prepared, come fancy seafood restaurant or honky-tonk bar and grill.

She let Magic out the back sliding glass door for a bathroom break. Stupid door. It never closed right. She'd have to get that looked at some time soon.

5:55pm.

Magic was raising cane in the backyard when Mark's truck pulled into her driveway. What in the world? Ellie smiled. The dog had probably caught some poor, frightened animal between the house and the line of trees bordering her back fence.

Ellie heard the doorbell and opened the door. Looking ever so handsome in a wide black felt cowboy hat, a button-down shirt and nicely pressed slacks, she suddenly felt under dressed in her jeans. Oh my. Her heart squeezed a touch as she accepted the bouquet of wildflowers he offered her. How sweet. She didn't know men still brought flowers to a date…dinner.

"These are beautiful, Mark. Thank you." Ellie backed up. "Come on in, I've got to let my roommate in and then I'll be ready."

"Roommate?" Mark stepped past her, wiping his boots on the multi-colored rug by the door.

"Yeah, my hundred-pound rottweiler." Ellie's heart hammered as Mark followed her to the kitchen. She took a deep breath and pulled out a vase from under the sink. Another rule broken. She didn't typically invite people into her house without knowing them well. But what was she supposed to do? Leave him standing on the step? Calm down, girl. It will be fine.

Mark watched as she scooted the back door on its rails, causing a loud screech. "Dang door." She whistled for Magic. She could see him at the back fence line, barking his fool head off, growling in between loud warning barks.

She sensed Mark come behind her, could smell his cologne. His nearness unnerved her. Made her already sweaty palms sweatier. Moving out onto the covered back deck, she whistled again for Magic. Mark stepped out with her, bent on one knee to look at the door from the outside.

"Been having trouble with this for a while?" He pushed some dirt and leaves off the base rails.

How kind. "Yeah, it doesn't shut right either. Watch out." Ellie tried to warn him, however, her usually lumbering dog shot past her and pinned Mark against the glass.

"Um, should I be concerned?" Mark asked around Magic's huge head.

Ellie laughed. "No. He's being friendly. You'd know it if he wasn't."

"Magic word, please? Off? Down? Please stop leaning on the man friend?"

Ellie laughed out loud. "Magic is his name." Man friend? Friend? She liked the sound of that. Apparently, Magic liked Mark. "Come, Magic. Let the man friend be."

Magic turned, looked at the tree line again and with a snarl, went in through the open door and flopped on the rug.

Ellie shrugged her shoulders. "He likes you."

Mark stood. She couldn't read the glint in his eyes, but knew she liked it when he looked at her that way. All warm and molten gold.

"Ok, then." Mark dusted off his knees where he'd knelt examining the door. "I can look at fixing that for you, if you want."

He was proving to be one big surprise after another.

"That would be nice." She smiled at him.

"Do I lock this somehow?"

"It doesn't lock. It will be fine. Shall we go?"

Mark hesitated.

"What's wrong?" Ellie turned to him.

"Nothing." He locked eyes with her. "Everything is right. This is nice."

Oh. And the night had only begun.

"Mark, can I ask? Wherever we're going, do I need to wear something different?"

He shook his head, his eyes sharing more than any words could. She nearly melted into a puddle in his gaze. Despite the jeans, he made her feel like a queen. She resisted the urge to reach out and touch him when he opened the truck door for her, opting instead for a smile that caused him to smile back.

He played an easy country station on the radio, and she relaxed into the seat.

"Okay, what gives on the Tootsie Pops?" She picked a grape one from the cup holder.

"I like them."

Oh my goodness, if he didn't stop smiling at her… he was quickly becoming the most attractive man she'd been around lately. Good looking, smelled amazing, kind inside and out.

Chapter 16

He couldn't stop staring at her, mesmerized. Her sweater was a background canvas for her hair and perfectly flawless face. Silver earrings flashed beneath the layers of golden blonde. And the way she smelled? Good heavens, she was stunning. And he was falling fast. His heart beat at an irregular tempo every time he was around her.

The weather turned dreary, and a slight drizzle followed them to the restaurant. His choice of a steakhouse for dinner fit their mood. Delicious steaks, old cowboy I, heavy dark furnishings, and quality food. No dancing waiters or waitresses, no loud music, no roll throwing.

Inside, the roaring wood fireplace in the center added to the ambience.

The soft flickering candles reflected in Ellie's eyes, and Mark thanked the good Lord for allowing him time and opportunity to get to know this beautiful woman.

"Mark?"

He watched as her lips formed the word. His name. Out of her mouth. Was there anything better?

She said his name again. Sheesh.

"Yes? Sorry." A shiver went up his spine as he realized he was solely fixated on her glossy lips.

"You looked so far away."

Oh no, he was right here. Wondering…

"Sorry, you're just so beautiful." Had that come out of his mouth?

She smiled at him. A smile that lit up her eyes, exposed her teeth, made him lose his mind.

"You're pretty handsome yourself."

The waitress handed out menus and left to fill their beverage orders.

"The steaks are good here." He coughed. What a dumb thing to say.

"Oh really? I think I'll have a salad." Ellie chuckled at his discomfort. "Just kidding. I like a good steak."

"Can we talk about Billy for a second? Will that ruin your meal?" Mark hesitated.

"No, yes, of course. I'm kinda at a loss since I don't have access to his case anymore."

"I'm wondering if there's another way to find him. It's been almost two weeks."

"Maybe he doesn't want to be found. Maybe he did take off with the money."

"And maybe he's hurt somewhere or can't get back to the ranch because someone won't let him."

Ellie reached across the table and put her hand on his forearm. "Those are some big what-ifs. I know you think this is your fault, but I'm not sure you could have done anything to stop it. He took off on his own accord. We have evidence of that."

Mark heard her truths. He fought his body not to

respond to her touch and to stay focused on her words, losing that battle. He could feel the warmth of her hand through his shirt sleeve. Reassuring, confident. He could get used to this in a hurry. "I know. It just feels like a disaster."

"It kinda is, but not your doing."

"Aren't you worried?"

She retracted her hand.

"I'm sorry, of course you are. It's all so frustrating."

"I can't think of one thing we can do right now."

"Me, neither."

"We could pray about it. After all, God knows where he's at."

Mark rolled his eyes at her. "Wow, pretty, funny, *and* smart. How'd I get so lucky?" Oh criminy… his mouth had a mind of its own.

She laughed, though, and he drank in the sound of it. Her laughter found its way into his soul, burning out cold spots and creating holes in his overly guarded heart.

"Until God gives us some wisdom on Billy and what to do, let's talk about something else." She waggled her fork at him and took a bite of her salad. "Tell me how you came to own a boys ranch."

"That's not the most joyous topic," he started. How much should he say? What woman in her right mind would date a man whose father beat his mother? Might as well yank the Band-Aid off. "I didn't have the best upbringing. My father, who is also Colton's father, went to prison for physically assaulting our mother." He let that sink in, just in case she wanted to run screaming from the table.

When she didn't, he continued. "My mom died of breast cancer later. I decided I had the background and the history to help other young men through trauma, so I pursued the education and training needed, completed the licensing for the ranch to be certified to take in juveniles and that's the end of the story. Not really the end. I care for the boys that are under my authority. They aren't just a responsibility. I want them to know what happened in my childhood with my dad wasn't normal even if they saw it in their own house. I want them to know they are a valuable part of this world despite screwing up and how God views them. That's the real reason I do this."

Ellie was quiet through his story, leaning towards him, sadness in her gaze. "That's pretty amazing. I'm sorry about your mom, Mark."

There was his name on her lips again. He could listen to that all day long. And her compassion showed how beautiful her soul was.

"God brought good out of your own trauma and allowed you to speak into others' lives. To make a difference."

He'd never spoken those words out loud, but yes, that's what he wanted. He felt like a dictator most days, making decisions, keeping the accounting and credentials straight and updated, providing direction, handing out consequences as needed for the boys. Had he lost sight of why he started the ranch in the first place? Being the administrator required administrative duties, but he missed the personal relationships he'd formed with some of the boys in the beginning. Somewhere he'd lost focus.

He did want to make a difference, like Ellie suggested. He should re-evaluate what that looked like. When Billy was found.

"Not everyone could, or should, provide for boys like you have. And that's the truth. You are the founding father of a valuable institution."

Mark locked eyes with her. No one had ever validated him the way she just did. Her words warmed a deep spot in him that he'd covered up, not wanting to acknowledge what every boy, or man, wanted. Worthiness, a sense of value. And, for him, it came from the very alluring woman sitting across from him.

"Tell me about you. How did you get in the social work business?"

"Not very interesting. I wanted to help people, so I got my degree, sent out resumes and landed here in Texas. I, like you, wanted teenagers to see life differently, to see their normal may not be what God had in store for them."

Surely there was more to her story, he could see it in her eyes, but he let it drop for now. "Where are you from?" Mark started as the waitress brought their steaks and steaming loaded potatoes. "Oh, thank you."

"Everything to your liking?" the waitress asked.

Absolutely. Mark caught himself before actually saying the word. The night, the dinner, and the lady with him.

"Yes, thank you." Mark tucked his napkin on his lap. His steak was buttery and cooked to perfection. "Yours?"

"This is the best steak." Ellie cut hers up into

bite-sized pieces.

"Better than fries drug through mustard?"

"You can never go wrong with that. Sometimes a girl needs a good steak, though, too."

~

Thank goodness the rest of the dinner conversation centered around benign things. She'd dodged a bullet on the social worker question. She was not about to divulge her real reason for her degree and career choice. No one needed to know that. It would color how they saw her, who she was today.

The next conversation she dreaded, but one that would come up eventually, was about Jason. How could she possibly help someone understand how deep their love was for each other and not uncover her past? And did she want to share memories of Jason with another man? No, she did not. It was inconceivable that she was out on a date… dinner… let alone talk about her late husband. She supposed it was inevitable, though, to talk about past relationships. *You don't owe anything to anyone*, Kari's words came back to her. That's right. If she did want to talk about Jason with someone, it would be on her own terms. For now, she would keep the tone light and focus on subjects that were easy.

Finishing her steak and scraping the remaining potato out of its skin, she toyed with her food. She didn't want the evening to end. Strange what Mark's presence did to her. She was seen by Mark, listened to, safe. Allowing the waitress to take her empty plate, Ellie put her face in one of her hands and her elbow on the table.

"Thanks for dinner, Mark." Every time she spoke his name, he twitched. Was that a good thing? Maybe he enjoyed hearing his name as much as she liked hearing him say her name? There's a concept. She wanted to run headfirst into whatever this was becoming, but the walls around her heart weren't easily coming down. Just enjoy this right here. Enjoy this moment. She liked his scruff of whiskers. She liked his whole face. She liked how he listened intently to her, how he encouraged her to talk, to engage with her on so many levels.

"You're welcome. I have a surprise for you if you're open to it."

She watched his gaze travel from her lips to her eyes. When they finally locked eyes, his ears turned red. She cocked her head, waiting.

"My aunt fixed a chocolate pie and offered to hold it for us until after dinner. Keeping Colton away from it will be no small feat, I can assure you."

Going back to the ranch? And seeing his family again? What had Mark told them about her?

"Um…" she stalled.

"It's a casual thing, no pressure. Aunt Eunice was making it regardless. She offered to reserve a piece or two if we wanted some." Mark looked disappointed.

"That was very kind of your aunt." Ellie looked down at her hands in her lap. Why not? It couldn't hurt anything, she was enjoying herself, more time with Mark. Why not? She didn't have one solid argument why she shouldn't continue enjoying herself. "Ok, yes, I'd like that."

"Perfect." Mark smiled.

Ellie watched his ears turn red again. She giggled. Good grief, girl, don't giggle.

He laid cash on the bill and offered her his arm. "Ready?"

She nodded. He felt strong and solid and hers for the evening. Hers? Really? She let out a soft sigh. Enjoy the moment.

At the door, they looked out the window. It was pouring down rain, now.

"I'll go get the truck and bring it around." He started for the door.

"No, wait. I won't melt. I'll walk with you." She tugged on his arm. "Please?"

"It's pouring down rain, Ellie." He countered.

"Come on, I'll race you." She bolted out the door, splashed around the puddles on the wet gravel lot, careful not to soak her boots.

"Ellie, wait."

She ran, laughing, a child-like joy overwhelming her. Mark followed, his strides almost catching up with her. One more giant step. Mistaking a puddle for solid ground, in slow motion, she sank into the hole. Mark crashed into her from behind, pushing her to her knees in the dirty water.

"Holy smokes!" Mark blurted out, toppling over her.

His landing in the mud was more spectacular than hers, and she couldn't resist a chuckle. Dirty droplets of water covered her sweater, her jeans were soaked, and water was leaking into one of her boots. Mark looked just as bad. His tumble over her had ruined his nicely ironed pants and the rain had wrecked his hair and slicked his shirt to his body.

Water dripped from the curls at his neck.

Heaven, help me. Whether cleaned up or sitting in a mud puddle with her, he made her heart race.

She grinned at him.

"Are you okay?" Mark sat up on his haunches, eyes at her level, concern flooding his face. "Did you twist your ankle?"

Ellie shook her head. "I just stepped in a hole. I don't think there's any damage." She touched her ankle inside her boot. It didn't hurt at all. "I'm fine. Really. Are you okay?"

Mark took her hand and hauled her up to a standing position. "I'm okay. I thought I hurt you."

Ellie locked eyes with him. She could get lost for hours, watching the emotions fill his warm gaze. She didn't want to look away. His eyes sparked with desire.

Mark's hands remained on her upper arms. They were so close, she could feel the heat developing between them. Standing in a barely lit parking lot, rain pouring down, water-logged, and unaware of anyone or anything, but each other.

"You didn't hurt me." She managed before his lips came crashing down on hers. A second, two…she wound her hands into the front of his wet shirt and responded. Her head spinning, *please don't stop*. She felt his arms wrap around her and their clothing melded into each other's. His kiss turned soft, and he pulled his hands up to cradle her face. The pressure of his lips on hers, moving across them, searching, wanting more, hesitant.

They broke apart when headlights lit up the parking lot, a car swinging into a spot.

"Um…" Mark stepped back.

"Shall we get out of the rain? Or do you think it will make any difference?" Ellie looked down at her mess of an outfit. There wasn't a dry spot on her clothing.

"I have a blanket in the back." He pulled open the back door and brought out a rough quilt that had seen better days.

Winding it around her shoulders, she thought he might kiss her again. She jumped into the front seat before he could act. *Whoa.* She'd just kissed someone who was not Jason… and it was okay. She was okay. In fact, she enjoyed it. Maybe a little. Be honest, girl, that was good. She felt a shiver as a rock came down from around her heart. Maybe if she laid the rock close, she could pick it up again and return it to a similar place. Or maybe she left It off. It had served its purpose. Especially if the protective feeling she had with Mark was real. She was silent while he adjusted the mirrors and fiddled with the radio, not looking at her.

"I don't do that on a regular basis."

"What? Fall in mud puddles?" She teased.

He sighed, a big, throaty sigh. "I thought you might be upset."

"It's a little to unpack, but I'm certainly not upset." Ellie looked over at him. Despite his wet clothes, he had a twinkle in his eye. When he did make eye contact, it was everything she could do not to climb over the console and start the whole kissing scene again.

He 153rined as he backed out of the parking spot.

She couldn't stop the smile on her own face.

"So, to the ranch for homemade chocolate pie?"

"Can we stop by my house first to change clothes? I don't think your aunt will appreciate the humor in our soaking wet clothes." Ellie pulled the blanket tighter around her.

"Sure. I'll change when we get home… when I get home…"

They were silent on the short drive to her house.

"I'll just be a second." Ellie pulled her house keys out of her pocket.

"Okay."

She ran to the covered stoop, leaving him in the driveway. The rain had let up, but the wind howled around the corner of the house. Unlocking the door, she stepped into the house. She could hear Magic barking wildly from the back of the house. Why was he doing that? She turned on the living room light and screamed.

Mark bounded up the steps and froze behind her. "What in the world?"

The entire room was torn apart. Cushions on the floor, plants overturned, cupboard doors opened. So much damage. Someone had been in her house.

Chapter 17

A hand snaked out and grabbed a fistful of Ellie's hair. The ski-masked man drug her across the living room, screaming. Ellie's arms flailed as her body bent at the waist and tried to keep up. Magic wildly hit a door towards the back of the house.

Mark dove onto the lunatic and rammed his arm into the guy's windpipe, all three of them plunging to the floor. A gun skittered across the wet floor, its metal casing bouncing off the coffee table, skidding to a stop under the sofa.

"Where's the money? Where is it?" The intruder yelled. He let go of Ellie and wrestled with Mark, legs vying for position, toppling over each other. Mark on top, then twisted to the floor. The man growled and punched him in the face. Crunch. A fountain of blood let loose from Mark's nose. Mark bucked hard, toppling the man. Mark stood and kicked at him, aiming for his face, but the contact glanced off the man's shoulder. Mark fell to the ground, grunting at the impact. He could see Ellie scrambling back to the front door, the rain and wind blowing leaves inside.

The man clawed his way on hands and knees to the sliding glass door. Mark grabbed for one of his legs. The man turned and swung again, connecting with Mark's face. Ellie screamed.

"I don't-" Mark couldn't get the words out, blood dripping into his mouth, his nose gushing blood. Laying on his stomach, he put his head down on the cool floor. He needed to check on Ellie. He needed- The room spun as he lifted his head and tried to roll to his side. A string of blood followed him.

"Ellie?" he whispered.

Her hands touched his back, light, feathery touches that made him want to cry. She put her face down close to his, stroked his cheek.

"Ellie?"

"I'm right here. I don't think you should move. I'm calling 911."

He reached out a bloody hand to her. She tucked it into hers.

"I'm okay."

"I'm calling anyway. Mark, you're hurt." She dialed 911, told the dispatcher what happened. "An ambulance is on its way. Along with the police."

"Are you okay?" Mark asked. "He's gone?"

"He went out back. Through the sliding door. And, yes, I'm fine, just a little shaken up."

Mark could hear the big dog yipping and growling, his nails clicking on the tile floor, circling the room. An occasional thump as the dog hit the door with his weight. "Magic?"

"I'll let him out in a bit. I think he's locked in the laundry room, but he sounds ok, just mad."

Ellie sat on the floor next to him until the police

and EMTs arrived. She moved away as the medical team went over his body with latex gloves, Mark groaning at the prodding.

"Mr. Bruens, can you tell me where it hurts the most? Was there a weapon involved? Did you get kicked?" The big EMT spoke slowly.

Mark spit the blood gathering in his mouth out on the floor and swung up to a seated position at the protest of the first responders around him. Blood ran down his chin onto the front of his shirt. "He punched me in the face. Twice."

A clean rag was pushed I157ot his hand, and he attempted to stop the flow of blood.

"Okay, good information. Are you light-headed?" At Mark's shake of his head, the EMT put a blood pressure cuff on his arm and a pulse meter on his finger. "So, it looks like you've been in quite a fight." The man looked around the disheveled room.

Mark could feel the cuff squeezing, doing its job.

"Your blood pressure is high, but everything else checks out. I think your nose is the only concern, so I'm going to pack it with gauze until you can be seen at the ER." An EMT pulled the rag away from Mark's nose and gently inserted two small wads of gauze. "If you start feeling light-headed, say so."

Someone handed him an ice pack and he held it against his face, the coolness easing the pain.

"You're probably going to be sporting some black eyes and if your nose is broken, they may be able to reset it at the hospital. I'm not going to try that here." The EMT in charge paused. "What'd you say happened?"

"There was an intruder in my … friend's house, and he was dragging her, and I jumped him, and then he got a couple of good swings in on me."

His friend. Mark looked up at Ellie, who was still talking to a police officer. Other officers were taking photographs of the scene, picking up possible pieces of evidence, congregating in the kitchen. Several plainclothes officers, detectives he assumed, were in the living room listening to Ellie's story.

The EMT stood and approached Ellie. "Ma'am? Do you need medical attention?"

"No, thank you. What about Mark?" Ellie answered, arms wrapped around her waist, eyes on Mark.

"Okay. His nose will need to be looked at." The man returned to Mark's side. "Do you want your friend here to drive you to the hospital? Or someone else we can call?"

Ellie nodded at him.

"My friend can take me."

"Perfect. She said she didn't need any attention from us, and you are free to go to the hospital on your own." The EMT shook his head. "Not everyday you walk into your house with your …uh, date… and find an intruder."

Mark pulled the ice pack away from his nose to correct the EMT, but decided it wasn't worth explaining. They *were* on a date, a nice date, until this happened. Couldn't just be normal, could it, Mark? It had to be ruined. That was normal.

~

"Okay, I'll say it again. We were on a date… really, just dinner… we fell into a mud puddle being silly. That's why our clothes are wet." Ellie colored. And we kissed. Not a detail she was going to share with the world, or these officers in her living room. The room itself, swarmed with men in jackets that read Dallas PD on their backs, men touching her things, asking tons of questions.

"And then what?" the older detective asked.

"We went home... to my house, so I could change clothes, and we walked in on a burglar. He pulled my hair and tried to force me out the back, but Mark jumped on him, and they fought. He kept yelling, 'Where's the money?'"

Several officers turned her way as her voice rose in frustration.

"Do you know what he was talking about?" the tall detective scribbled in his pocket notebook.

"Maybe. I was working a case recently, I'm a juvenile social worker, and one of my clients supposedly stole money from his dad. A lot. Like casino jackpot money." No way was she going to divulge the whole story.

"So, you think the burglar, which now becomes a robbery case since you came home and interrupted the burglary, thought you had the money?" the gray-haired detective asked.

Another plain-clothed officer stepped up to the conversation, behind Ellie. "Evidence bags, sir."

Ellie turned to the voice. Where had she heard that voice before?

The older detective took out a permanent marker and signed his initials below the officer's. Ellie couldn't see the evidence, had no idea what they were taking from her home.

"I don't know. I don't have the money, for sure. We can't even find the kid. And I'm not interested in the money." Ellie watched the officer with the evidence bags step around her. There was something about him… "Excuse me, were you one of the officers at the motel on this case with the missing boy and money? The one with the two dead bodies?"

The officer looked at her and then his supervisor. "Yes."

"So, you're familiar with the case."

"Yes."

Ellie watched as they sat Mark up. He had to be okay. She left the detectives standing looking at each other.

"Mark, what are they saying? Is your nose broken?" She got down on her knees next to him. She wanted to gather him up, hold him in her arms, but the pain on his face discouraged her from doing anything other than hold his hand. The now-stained cloth he'd held to staunch the bleeding lay by his side. She ran to the kitchen, soaked a tea towel in warm water and brought it back to him. Gently, she pulled the ice pack away, wiped the dried blood off his cheeks, around his nose, and across his lips. She had an insane desire to kiss all of those places once they were clean. Her shoulders slumped. "I'm sorry."

"Not… your… fault." He covered one of her hands with his.

"Good grief." Even his hands were bloody. Taking each one in hers, she rubbed the blood away. His fingers were long and handsome, if fingers could be handsome. She ran her fingers over each knuckle, traced the lines in his palm, avoided looking in his face.

"Ellie," he cleared his throat. "Stop."

She did look at him then, which was a mistake. He was smiling at her, although only through his eyes. Everything below that was not a pretty sight, but those eyes. They said unspoken words to her soul. Care, concern, desire. Oh my. She searched them. Tried to put a pin on what she felt when he looked at her like that. Warm, Dangerous. She could feel another rock drop off the wall around her heart.

"They want me to go to the hospital and confirm there's nothing wrong."

"Of course, let's go." Ellie helped him to stand and then held his arm as he closed his eyes and steadied himself against the wall. "Is this a good idea? Maybe you should ride in the ambulance."

"No, I'll be fine." He wound his arm around her neck, pulling her close.

Oh. She rested against his strong frame until he was ready to make the trek to her truck. One foot in front of the other and she settled him in the passenger seat.

"I'm going back to ask what they'll do with the house, and then we'll hurry on to the hospital, okay?" Ellie squeezed his shoulder. He looked brighter and more alert, less pasty. *Thank God.*

At his nod, she returned to the first detective.

"I'm taking him to the hospital, but what do I need to do when I get back?"

"Lady, I'd advise you not to come back here. Even when we're done, it'll still be a mess. You'll feel safer at a hotel for the night. We'll lock up as best we can and put tape over the rest."

"Okay. I'll grab some clothes and I'm going to take my dog with me." Ellie rushed through the house, mentally noting things she might need, toothbrush, pjs, her phone charger. Last stop, the laundry room door. Magic bounded out and then stopped and growled at the strangers in his house. Many of the men cast a wary eye at the unleashed Rottweiler. Ellie snapped a lead on his collar and pulled him close to her.

"Do you always keep him locked up when you're gone?" The detective asked.

"No, the burglar must have locked him in there."

"Based on what I'm seeing, why would the dog willingly be locked up?" The detective spoke from a safe distance as Magic continued to growl.

"He loves treats. Maybe the guy threw something in the laundry room?"

"Before he could tear his head off?"

"I don't know." Ellie shrugged and wrapped the lead around her right hand, preparing to walk through the throng of strangers.

"It'd have to be a steak for that guy." The detective made a huge berth around them and pushed the laundry room door open further. "I'll take a look around. You go ahead and take your guy to the hospital. We'll be in touch."

"Heel, Magic." Ellie made it down the hall and almost to the door when Magic stopped and side-licked an officer who was too close. "Sorry."

"No problem."

Same officer that had been at the hotel.

"He isn't usually friendly with strangers." Ellie paused.

"I'm a dog guy. They can sense that." The officer turned and went into her kitchen.

Chapter 18

Mark groaned. Ellie stepped outside to the waiting room, so Mark could change into a gown. Why the flimsy, barely-covered-anything gown was necessary since it was only his face that was caved in, he didn't know. Suck it up, buddy.

A thin, older doctor came in after the nurse checked his vitals and wrote notes on a tablet.

"Well, it looks like, Mr. Bruens, that you had quite a tousle tonight." She gently probed his face, over his cheekbones, under his eyes, and carefully across his nose. He closed his eyes briefly after she waved a pen light in them. "Eyes dilate appropriately, and I'm not concerned about a concussion unless you failed to answer the first responders' questions in the field correctly. I don't see evidence of any broken bones either. It could have been worse. The hits could have shattered your nose, your eye sockets, your cheekbones. You're going to look atrocious for a while until the bruising turns. I'm going to add a butterfly clip over this gash," the doctor pulled out a sterile bandage from a drawer and placed it across his nose, "to keep it together. You may have a slight scar. A manly one." She touched him on the shoulder. "You can go ahead and get dressed."

He watched her leave the room. Gingerly moving off the exam bed, he sat in the chair opposite the cabinets and put his face in his hands. He avoided the butterfly clip and disrupting what she had done. His whole body ached.

He stood up and waited for the room to stop spinning. He may not have a concussion, but everything in him wanted to lay down and sleep for a week. Mark put his arm through the sleeve of his still wet shirt, dismissed the idea of putting on the red stained undershirt, and turned at a knock on the door. What more could they do to him? Release instructions?

Ellie stood in the doorway.

What a relief that she was unharmed. He reached out to her. All he wanted to do was hold her. And sleep. And maybe kiss her again. He heard her soft gasp.

Ellie stared at his bare chest. "Oh sorry, I'll see... out in the ...out there." She hastily closed the door.

Well, that was interesting.

As he stuck his other arm into the sleeve, he caught his image in the mirror. The white bandage across half his face, his hair all awry. He checked his muddy pants. At least they were zipped. He'd look even worse in the morning when his eyes turned black.

"Is that really necessary?" Mark grimaced when the nurse brought in a wheelchair.

"Standard procedure. I've already told your lady friend to bring her car around." The nurse laid discharge papers in his lap.

Mark blinked hard. He did not need a wheelchair, but the nurse didn't seem concerned with his excuses or groanings.

Ellie was standing outside her truck, concern etched in her frown.

He stuck out his hitchhiking thumb and asked, "Going my way?" Locking eyes with her, he winked. Blush spread from her neck to her ears. He was going to be fine, she needed to know that, and a little levity was helpful. As he stood, Ellie wrapped her arms around him. "Easy. Please."

She stepped away with apologies on her lips, and he caught her, pulled her back in.

"Just be easy." He wrapped her in his arms and savored the moment.

The nurse coughed loudly. "Can't go back in until you're safely in the vehicle." She huffed.

Ellie laughed, her hair tousled, her jeans dripping little puddles on the sidewalk.

"We've got to get out of these wet clothes."

"I grabbed some from the house. The detective said I couldn't come back tonight and to check with him tomorrow about when I could return." Ellie shut the passenger side door, said thanks to the nurse, and got in the driver's seat.

Mark slowly blinked. He already missed the warmth of her in his embrace. Magic whined from the back seat and tried to lick him, his long tongue stretching between the frame and the seat.

Mental note number one, go get his truck

tomorrow.

Mental note number two, kiss this girl. Right here.

"Ellie?" He turned to her. The parking lot lights glowed on her face. "Are you really okay?"

Mark reached for her, cupping her face with his hand. Slid his fingers through her soft hair. Gently kissed her. Tasted the sweetness of her lips. Hungry for… more. More everything with this woman. Two weeks and he was fully smitten. She scooted closer to him, leaned into his body. Flames lit up his spine, firing off sparks all the way up his torso, winding around his heart, threatening to engulf them both in molten lava.

Mark broke free, his breath ragged.

Ellie leaned back with a slight smile. "Let's get you home and then I'll find a hotel for me and Magic."

Mark kept his eyes locked on an unseen image in front of him, willing the world to stop spinning. If he looked at her, he was going to repeat his actions of a couple of minutes ago.

Wait, she's going to a hotel for the night?

"I can't let you do that." He sputtered.

"What? Take you home? You want to stay here at the hospital?"

"No, no, of course not. You can't go to a hotel. That's what I meant."

"Mark, I can't go home. I told you what the detective said."

There was his name on her lips again. Music sounded in his ears, some corny love song. But it wasn't corny at all.

"Stay with me."

"Ha." Ellie chuckled. "No."

"Not with me exactly. Stay at the ranch. There's plenty of beds." He scrambled to convince her.

"Bunk with the boys?" She smiled.

"No, Aunt Eunice's living quarters have two bedrooms. You can stay in her spare room." That was the best idea he'd come up with yet. She'd be safe… and close.

"I can't do that, Mark. I wouldn't want to intrude."

"She saved chocolate pie for us. She already likes you."

"Mark, I'm going to a hotel. I have Magic to think about, too."

"At least consider it."

She patted his hand. He hadn't convinced her yet, but once Aunt Eunice was involved, she'd have no grounds to refuse.

~

She thought they were both dead when the guy at the house caught her hair and drug her across the floor. Ellie rubbed the top of her head. Getting out alive was the goal. And when Mark fought with him? Ellie could only stare at the men wrestling for the upper hand. She should have picked up something to help, but she'd just stood there. She hadn't done anything. The whole thing happened so fast, and she froze. The guy had to be talking about Billy. Why would he think the money was at her house? Did he think she was hiding Billy? None of this made sense.

Eunice and Colton were standing on the wraparound porch when they arrived at the ranch. She'd get Mark settled, and then look for a place to stay with Magic in tow. Hotels were much more open to pets, now-a-days, right? She shouldn't have any trouble. She was not staying in the same house as Mark. After seeing him half in, half out of his shirt with the slightest glint of light colored, curly chest hair, she'd nearly come undone. He was so attractive with all of his clothes on. Thankfully, he had pants on. Seeing his wide shoulders, bare chest, and a peek at his biceps… ok, stop. And then his kiss in the truck. He couldn't get enough of her, touching her hair, pulling her face close to his. So romantic, her hero. The guy had a mangled face because of her.

"So sorry to meet again like this." Ellie put an arm around Mark's waist and smiled at his grateful look. Telling Magic to stay, she helped Mark up the steps.

"Mark called us. You poor thing." Eunice reached out to Ellie as Colton took the weight of his brother.

"I'm fine, I'm fine." Mark tried to walk in the door, but bumped the corner instead.

"Uh-huh." Colton led them to the couch in the living room.

"My clothes are still damp." She didn't miss the exchange between Colton and Aunt Eunice. Oh dear. How did Mark explain their wet clothes? And did he mention the kiss? Ellie sighed inwardly. "I brought some clothes from my house. May I use your restroom to change?"

"Absolutely, and if you bring them to me, I'll wash them so they're wearable again."

"Oh, there's no need for that." Ellie stopped as

Aunt Eunice pooh-poohed her.

She quickly changed into a navy-blue hoodie with TEXAS emblazoned on the front and a pair of softly worn blue jeans. When she returned to the living room, Colton and his aunt were in the kitchen, and Mark had his head back, eyes closed, unmoving on the couch. His chest rose rhythmically. The image of him half undressed floated in front of her, and she gulped. Even in sleep, he exuded safety. She did not want to curl up next to him, run her hand over his whiskers, and well, kiss him. She did not. Yes, yes, she did. She wanted to do all those things.

As if sensing her, he opened one eye and patted the seat next to him on the couch. Ellie obliged.

Girl, you didn't even hesitate.

"I have coffee." Aunt Eunice handed her a warm mug.

"Come on. It'll help." Colton nudged Mark with his boot.

"Only if it's laced with whiskey." Mark accepted the coffee and spread his wide frame out so there was no longer space between them.

She could feel the coolness of his clothes through her jeans. She didn't care. The warmth of his gaze heated up her insides.

"Just kidding. I will probably need some type of pain reliever."

"I've got plenty at the house." Colton answered. "Aspirin, that is."

Mark grinned at his brother and sipped his coffee. "Magic?"

"He's out in the car." Babe was on the tip of her tongue, and she bit it hard. Way too intimate, girl.

"What's Magic?" Aunt Eunice and Colton looked at each other.

"He's my dog. The man who broke into my house locked him in the laundry room. My plan was to find a motel for us after I brought Mark home since I can't go back to my house yet."

"Can we bring him in?"

"Oh, I don't know. He's a Rottweiler and pretty big. He'll be fine."

"We love dogs. I'll go get him." Colton was halfway to the door.

"Bandit?" Mark asked.

Ellie raised her eyebrows. "Burglar?"

Mark chuckled. "Bandit is Colton's dog."

Good grief, she thought Mark was being delusional.

"He's down at my house. It's fine."

"Ellie, I'm so sorry about your house." Eunice rocked in an old wooden chair. "I turned down the bed in my guest bedroom for you tonight. It's quite cozy."

Ellie looked at Mark who leaned back with his eyes shut again. He smiled without opening them. Oh, this was a set up. They'd already decided for her.

Magic bounded into the room like a bull and pushed his big head onto her lap. He stepped on Mark's boots, gained his attention, and then ran to Aunt Eunice and bumped his head on her leg until she gave in and scratched behind his ears. He didn't look traumatized and for that, she was grateful. Whoever broke into her house had not touched her dog, other than to lock him in the laundry room.

"I think he'd get on my lap if I invited him to."

Aunt Eunice kissed him on the snout.

"I'm certain about that." Ellie clapped for Magic to come sit by her. "About staying the night, I really can't-"

"Good luck," Mark whispered.

"Yes, yes, you will. There's nobody in that room, and I'll enjoy the company." Aunt Eunice chided.

The battle was over. Ellie would never be able to turn down such kind hospitality and not offend Mark's aunt.

"I'm not sure what to do about Magic, though."

"Does he normally sleep with you?" Aunt Eunice gave him another pat.

"He does. He's gotten used to the bed ever since-" She couldn't bring herself to mention Jason. Not in the presence of Mark and his family.

Aunt Eunice saved her by interrupting, "Well, that bed is big enough for the two of you."

"Oh goodness. You're too kind."

"Come, let's get you settled." Eunice led the way through the kitchen and around a half wall covered in old farmhouse wallpaper. A side door opened into a short hallway and then a small family room, complete with an oversized couch with tons of multi-colored pillows, a smaller loveseat, and a TV. "This is your room to the right and this bathroom is yours."

The bedroom was small, but housed a full-sized bed, matching end tables and a good-sized closet. The bathroom was just as colorful with upgraded furnishings and a shower. How many guests stayed in this delightful spot?

"The boys built this side of the house for me when I came to the ranch. My girlfriend from Austin comes to stay occasionally, and we have the best time. The boys think we're too old to be devilish, but we manage to get in just enough trouble to remind them that we were young once." Aunt Eunice's eyes twinkled.

Ellie bet they did.

"This is my bedroom and ensuite." Aunt Eunice led her into the other room. The large four poster bed had an intricate lace canopy and a royal feel. It was plush with white fuzzy pillows stacked upon more pillows. Totally different from every other room in the house.

"Oh my." The room was stunning.

Aunt Eunice trailed a hand along the heavy, dark dresser. "The furniture, including the bed, were my late husband's. I added the pretty. He wouldn't be caught dead under that lace." She chuckled.

Late husband? Aunt Eunice was a widow, too? Ellie looked at her, wistfully. She wasn't ready to share with this nice lady, but it was comforting to know someone else knew what she was experiencing if she did decide to talk about Jason. However, she was Mark's aunt. How would that feel?

Ellie followed Aunt Eunice into the most glorious bathroom she'd ever been in. "The boys did right by you." She exclaimed.

"They call it my bougie bathroom. The floors are heated, the towel rack is heated, and the tub…girl, I could soak in there forever." It did look fantastic. No jets, just warm water, filled to the top, coaxing out the stress.

"This is really beautiful." Ellie took the older woman's hand. "I really appreciate this, Eunice. I wasn't sure what I was going to do."

"Ellie, the Lord always provides."

Ellie grew teary-eyed. "Yes and amen." She backed out, called for Magic who had made his home at Mark's feet, and settled into her room. *What a gift, Lord.* If nothing happens with Mark, Eunice could be a forever friend.

Chapter 19

Mark wrestled in his bed, sheets twisted, no comfortable position. His nose hurt, his body ached. He turned over for the millionth time and willed sleep to come. Impossible with Ellie under the same roof. His old alarm clock read 1 a.m. He blew out his breath, the motion hurting his chest.

The visions just kept coming. Ellie, her hair in disarray, sitting in the puddle, rain falling on them both. Him, skidding into her, their kiss in the moonlight. For crying out loud. Her face contorted in fear. The mad man dragging her by the hair, his blood on her hands. Shocked, terrified, rage filled his body and then relieved that it was over, in pain. His insane desire to lock Ellie away from any more harm. His body was barely able to keep pace with his emotions.

He threw off the covers in exasperation, drew on a pair of sweats. Tiptoeing across the old kitchen floor, he knocked softly and then opened the door to his aunt's living quarters.

"Hi." Aunt Eunice met him in the short hallway. "I thought I might run into you."

Mark grimaced. He felt like a teenager sneaking

out of the house to meet a girl.

"Where you headed?" She asked, head cocked to the side, arms crossed. Ellie's self-appointed guardian.

She obviously knew. He was standing in her house… or her part of the house.

"I just want to check on her." Just a peek. He couldn't sleep knowing she was so close and yet, isn't that what he wanted? For her to be close? But not untouchable. Which is what she was with Aunt Eunice blocking the way. No way was he pushing past his aunt, though. Too much respect under that bridge.

"She's fine, son. We talked a little and then I sent her to bed."

"What did you talk about?" Me? Hopefully. Aunt Eunice was on his side.

"We actually have a lot in common." She uncrossed her arms.

Obviously not sharing with him. Or if their talk was about him. He'd never felt like this about anyone. Like he needed to keep her safe, happy. And kiss her. A lot.

"You're not going to let me see her, are you?"

"No, I'm not." Aunt Eunice put a hand on his chest. "Son, she's okay. She's already in bed. Go get some sleep."

"Impossible." He growled but obeyed.

He managed to fall asleep quickly after taking some aspirin and assuring himself that Ellie was okay. On Aunt Eunice's side of the house.

When he awoke, the sun was shining in his window, and the air had turned chilly, the early fall making its debut. He pulled on the sweatpants from last night and added a zippered jacket over a Texans' t-shirt. He stopped at the bathroom on his side of the house and raked fingers through his hair. He leaned close to the mirror, the bandage still in place through the night, although slight traces of blood leaked out around the bottom. Black and blue marks dotted one eyelid and both eyes had dark half-moon bruises under them. He was a sight. But alive. He'd thought he'd seen a gun at one point in the struggle, but then he never saw it again, so maybe he imagined it in the ferociousness of the fight. *Thank God.*

A quick brush of his teeth, no need to astound Ellie with bad morning breath, and he was ready to face the day. And see Ellie.

When he entered the kitchen, Aunt Eunice was at the stove, and Ellie was seated at one end of the long dining table. Colton was next to her, regaling her with stories of Mark's youth. Before it had all taken a nosedive.

Oh boy.

Some of the boys filtered in, and they stopped and stared at Mark's battered face. He closed his eyes. What was he going to tell the boys?

"This is what happens when you disagree with Aunt Eunice." Colton saved him.

"Oh psh, you know I love each and every one of you." Aunt Eunice ladled piping hot gravy over biscuits and handed each boy a plate.

"Actually, Bandit did it. Mark was telling one of his bad jokes and Bandit had enough." Colton continued.

The younger boys began to giggle. The older

ones skidded to a stop when they noticed Ellie at the table, Magic at her feet, swishing his tail. Would the boys recognize Ellie as Billy's case manager? He didn't think any of them were around when she came out to the ranch initially, but she'd be pretty hard to forget, with her golden hair and wide smile and…

"Boys, this is my friend, Ellie. And her dog, Magic." Aunt Eunice rescued him this time.

Mark swiped a heaping plate of breakfast, touched Ellie on the shoulder as he passed, and sat on the other side of her.

"Good morning." He smiled. She was stunning, no surprise, with her hair caught up in a loose bun and her face glowing.

She dipped her head, so her bangs fell covering a portion of her face. "I forgot to grab makeup."

"I did not notice." He covered her hand with his. "I think you're beautiful."

Colton snorted.

Mark glared at him and retracted his hand.

Ellie blushed and put another forkful of biscuit and sausage gravy in her mouth.

"What's the plan for today?" Mark pushed food around on his plate, his stomach in knots.

"Well, I'm going to clean up the kitchen." Aunt Eunice chimed in.

"And I'm going to see to it that this ranch continues operating until the boss gets back in the game." Colton grinned.

Very funny.

"I meant, Ellie and I." He was grateful Colton was keeping the ranch running smoothly with the boys, he really was. Mark hadn't thought much about what was happening beyond Billy. And Ellie.

Ellie caught his gaze and held it for the briefest of seconds. Bolts of electricity sped through his veins from his toes to his heart.

"I need to call the detective and ask if I'm free to go back to the house." Ellie picked up her plate, rinsed it in the sink, and piled it with the others.

"When you're ready, I'll go help put things back together and fix that back door." Mark offered. "Plus, I need to get my truck."

"Oh, I'd forgotten about your truck. Are you up to fixing the door?"

"I'm sore, but, yes, I can fix it for you."

She touched his arm on the way to call the detective. He stood, rooted to the spot, all synapses firing in his arm.

"Dude, you've got it bad." Colton piled his own plate next to the sink, and kissed Aunt Eunice's cheek.

"Shut up." Mark's ears burned.

"You can't deny it." Aunt Eunice turned from the sink. "Can you?"

"Can we talk about something else? Like why her house was ransacked?" He knew his emotions were out and visible. Part of him didn't care, the rest of him wasn't used to having any feelings worth sharing. He had never in his life felt like he did towards Ellie. Ever. It was crazy. He felt alive and hopeful and weird. Mushy.

~

Ellie smiled to herself as she climbed onto the comfortable bed. She'd slept okay but awoke several times to re-orientate herself on where she was. The different location hadn't bothered Magic at all, and his snoring had been reassuring. Mark's words to her this morning about being beautiful without makeup rested in a spot in her soul that didn't accept compliments very well. She wasn't a spring chicken, by any means, and she used more concealer than she used to. But what if the things he'd said were true? Maybe only to him. Which warmed her heart a little. He was the kindest man she'd met in a long time. thoughtful, considerate, and obviously crushing on her. Ellie curled around one of the fluffy pillows. She might be crushing, too. It had been different with Jason. Their start had been one-sided with Jason pulling her along, out of the mire created by her own decisions. She'd come to need his assuring words, and then they'd fallen in love. Everything with Jason was passionate and fast-paced and overwhelming to her, but he always made her the center of his world, a place that she was always thought of, cared for. No one had ever treated her like something special. And his love for Jesus? Surpassed his love for her, and she was okay with that as she began to know his Jesus, too. Mark was comfortable, slow to speak, quick to protect her. She felt an inkling of that specialness again. Happy to be with him, sad to be apart, desire for more of him left her breathless sometimes. Especially when he kissed her. She didn't deserve a second chance at happiness, but her feelings for Mark were quickly overshadowing the doubt.

"Hello, Detective? This is Ellie Jenkins. Yes, from yesterday." She cradled the cell phone in the crook of her shoulder. "Can I go back to my house today? Really? Did you catch him? Oh, okay. Thank you."

She sat up on the edge of the bed as someone knocked on the door.

"Ellie, can I come in?" Mark said from the other side.

"Yes."

He left the door open and sat next to her. "Did you reach the detective?"

She nodded. Heat flooded her face. They should move. Off the bed. Control yourself. There's bigger things at play than you sitting with Mark. On the bed.

"What did he say?"

"That I can't go back to the house today. Maybe tomorrow."

Mark tried to hide his enthusiasm, but Ellie caught the slight smile.

"That doesn't mean I stay here, though." Ellie looped her arm through his. She could feel his warmth, his strong forearm.

Watch it, girl.

"Why not?" Mark turned to her, keeping her arm still locked in his. "Is it because of my stupid brother?"

"No, Mark. It's because of this..." Ellie unengaged her arm and put both hands on his face. His whiskers brushed her fingertips. She'd intended to mention the bruising, the swollen nose, but all she could manage was to stare at his lips and the pleading in his eyes. The green flecks showed up more with the black marks surrounding his eyes. And then she kissed him. Softly. Unassuming. Kissed him. She couldn't help herself. They were so close, and she loved him kissing her. Why not kiss him? She felt his arms go around her shoulders and they were falling…

"Ahem." Aunt Eunice said from the doorway.

Mark stood and silently watched his aunt.

Would she chide them for being inappropriate? Ellie couldn't describe whatever this was between her and Mark. Inappropriate, sure. How many times did 'Get Off the Bed' clang in her head? Would Eunice see her as some people had in her past? Careless? Lustful? She'd defend that all day long. Not that anyone asked her. And besides, this, whatever this was turning into, was not sinful. She knew what sin felt like. This was not that. Eunice couldn't know that, though. Would she judge Ellie?

"Mark, would you help me for a moment in the kitchen?" Aunt Eunice wouldn't make eye contact with her.

What did that mean? Would Eunice tell him to stay away from her? Ellie couldn't read her face. Ellie rubbed her hands on her jeans. She probably screwed up. Again. Let her emotions transmit into action.

"Yes, absolutely." Mark moved to the door and gave her an apologetic smile.

"I'll be out in a second."

Oh boy. Had she ruined her relationship with Eunice? Why had she kissed him? In her… his house. She knew better. Just because it felt right didn't mean it was right.

She picked up her overnight bag and took it into the living room. She'd get her clothes, claim Magic from the boys in the backyard, and find another place to stay for the night.

Ellie watched Mark and his aunt have a hushed conversation. She startled both of them when she said, "If you'll show me where my clothes are, I'll be going."

"What? No. Mark said you couldn't go back to your house yet." Aunt Eunice shot Mark a hard look. "I washed your clothes, but you can stay here as long as you need to."

Ellie locked eyes with her. Was she mad? Ellie didn't know her well enough to tell. "Look, I'm sorry. I've overstepped, obviously…"

"Ellie, come sit down." Aunt Eunice pulled out a chair next to her at the dining room table. "Come."

Reluctantly.

"Mark, you come, too." Aunt Eunice patted the chair on the other side of her.

Ellie sat, her legs like Jello, eyes on everything other than Mark or his aunt. Here it comes…

"Listen kids, I know you like each other and all…" Aunt Eunice started.

Oh boy. *Like*?

"Aunt Eunice…" Mark looked as dismayed as Ellie felt.

"Hush, let me finish," Aunt Eunice grabbed Mark's left hand and Ellie's hand in her small, hard-working ones. Turning to Ellie, she said, "I mentioned my late husband to you for a reason, Ellie. And yes, Mark might have mentioned your late husband."

Mark put his head down on the table, but Aunt Eunice held tight to his hand.

Ellie's stomach turned over.

What in the world…

What next? Mark's aunt wanted to talk about Jason? Huh, uh. No way. Despite Aunt Eunice's warm hand, Ellie felt her own grow cold. She pinched her lips together. Kari said she didn't owe anyone anything. She could get up from the table right now if she wanted. Respect kept her seated. Aunt Eunice had been nothing but kind.

"What I want you to do for me, Mark, look at me." Having gained his attention, she continued. "As a widow speaking to you, my oldest nephew and one of the sons I love, be careful and gentle with this young widow's heart."

Ellie raised her eyebrows. What?

Mark leaned around his aunt and gave her a solemn look. "I swear, Aunt Eunice."

"Mark, being a widow is tough and we're not always easy to love, especially when you realize that a widow never gets over her first love. The second love just looks different."

Oh.

Mark smiled at her. Not the cheery one she'd seen in the past, but a smile that spoke of promises given and kept. She smiled back.

What was she thinking?

She was thinking this might work, that's what. Aunt Eunice nailed it. She would always love Jason, but maybe this was a different sort. Not love, of course, they'd only been seeing each other for two weeks, but something was growing.

"Ok, back to work." Aunt Eunice stood, put Ellie's hand in Mark's, and said, "He'll be good by you."

Chapter 20

By her? Like beside her? Or *to* her? Mark looked at their hands intertwined and moved over into Aunt Eunice's warm, vacant chair. "Ellie, I promise to always be kind and intentional and aware of you and your heart."

Ellie rubbed her thumb over the top of his hand. There was the molten lava again. Every touch from her left a blaze unlike anything he'd ever experienced.

"Thanks, Mark. I can be a lot." No excuses, no questions. "Aunt Eunice is right. I do want to talk to you about Jason sometime, just not in your house, not here."

Mark glanced away. He knew Aunt Eunice was right. Didn't make hearing another man's name on her lips any easier. "Ok." Maybe he should kiss her thoughts of another man away. No, that wasn't fair. He and Ellie would forge their own way through a relationship, however, knowing her history… Jason…he nearly bit his tongue off saying the man's name. If Ellie wanted to share with him, he'd sit and listen. He didn't have to like it, but if the two of them were going anywhere, he'd need to know this former husband, wouldn't he? Maybe, maybe not.

"You're staring at me. What are you thinking?" Ellie chewed on her lip.

He had an insane desire to kiss her at the dining room table. What was insane about that?

He leaned over and she met him halfway. Yep, perfect. She tasted like gravy and blueberries. Lava, indeed.

"Do you want to take the horses out? See the property? You can borrow a jacket." Mark wrapped his arm around the back of her chair. Stole another kiss. He could do this all day long.

"That sounds wonderful. We definitely can't sit here doing this." Ellie pushed away from the table.

Mark chuckled.

"Let me clean up my boots and change into jeans and I'll be ready." She commented over her shoulder.

"Your boots are already clean."

Ellie turned back to him.

"I- I couldn't sleep, so I cleaned them." Mark pushed his chair back and brought her boots from a spot near the front door.

"Oh."

"It'll cost you, though."

"I didn't ask you to do that."

"True. For a service well done, you have to expect some type of payment." Mark grinned at her. This was fun. He held up the mud-free boots. "Spotless."

She stepped closer to him, a glint in her eyes. "How much?"

He considered what he could get away with. And hesitated too long. Ellie snatched the boots out of his hands and scurried sock-footed to Aunt Eunice's side of the house.

"Well played." He called after her. She was a huge distraction, and he was loving every minute of it.

Mark joined Aunt Eunice in the kitchen. He kissed her wrinkled, soft cheek.

"You're giving a lot of those out lately." She turned back to the pie she was working on.

"Blueberry?"

"And peach."

"We're going out riding for a bit. Anything in the fridge I can wrap up and take for lunch?"

Mark grabbed what she suggested and placed a couple of water bottles and napkins in a small backpack. On a whim, he pulled down a bag of Tootsie Pops from the cabinet and added a few to the bag. "Can you tell Ellie that I'm out in the barn?"

"Sure. Have fun. Don't forget what I told you, though."

"I won't, I promise."

Out at the barn, Mark pulled his big sorrel horse out of its stall and picked the smaller, gentle mare named Belle for Ellie. He had no idea what her experience was with horses, but Belle was the best they came. Easy-going and well-behaved, she'd follow Mark's horse all the way to Missouri if she was told to.

"Mark!"

He dropped the saddle in the middle of the floor and ran outside of the barn. "Ellie, what's wrong?"

He opened his arms, and she flew into them in tears. He pulled hair out of her face.

"Tell me."

"Magic killed all your goats." She cried into his shirt front. Magic pranced around them, hearing his name.

He looked across the paddock as little and big legs shook in the air. Slowly, the goats recovered and stood. Oh my goodness.

"No, he didn't. Look." He turned her, keeping his arms around her waist, so she could see the goats coming back to life. He chuckled, then laughed into her shoulder. Tears ran down his face and he let go of her, bending at the waist in full belly laughs.

"What? Why are they alive? What are you laughing at?" Ellie crossed her arms and glared at him.

"Sorry." He tried to compose himself, but the laughter kept coming. If he didn't stop and explain soon, she'd think he had lost it. The laughter felt so good, a release from all of the emotional issues. "They're fainting goats. They're bred to fall like that when they're startled. It's ok, Magic. You're okay." He patted the big dog's head.

"I've never heard of that." Ellie watched as the goats popped back up as if nothing had happened. "And it doesn't hurt them?"

"Nope." Mark wiped his eyes. "They're bred to do that."

"Wow, I thought he'd killed them all." Ellie swatted him when he began to chortle again.

"Come on, I've got our horses almost ready." Mark took her hand and led her into the barn. His horse, Bart, whinnied loudly. "Looks like he's itching to go. This is Belle, your horse. You'll love her."

"Does Magic come with us?"

"No, he'd better stay. The burrs and tall grass will stick in his fur, and he'll be a nightmare to clean up." Mark whistled at one of the boys nearby who coaxed Magic into the fenced backyard.

He finished up saddling, showed her how to mount, and gave her a leg up onto the horse. He led them out to the south, away from the east where Billy had climbed over the fence. He also didn't want to take her in the direction of the casino that was built in a neighboring lot. Colton had nearly been shot to death over the casino. He, himself, wanted the ride to go perfectly without the hint of anyone intruding. They deserved a break to be Ellie and Mark, together. She learned quickly, and he picked up the pace past a trot, so she could experience the full effect of riding like the wind.

They came to a small creek at the far end of a pasture and both horses crossed with no hesitation. They rode for several miles, seeing cattle, a few deer, and a coyote. Ellie was silent most of the way, and Mark looked back often, checking on her. He was thankful she didn't talk non-stop and could enjoy the stillness around them. The open spaces made him contemplate life and how big God was and good and the creator of many beautiful things. Including the woman with him.

"Mark, can we talk about-" Ellie called to him from behind and the wind snatched away what she wanted to talk about. Please don't let it be her late husband. Please. And there was the intrusion, an invasion on the perfectly peaceful day. He'd expected it, hoped it wouldn't come, and now it had.

~

"...Billy?" Ellie nudged her horse up next to his. He had a concerned look on his face. She knitted her eyebrows together and repeated the question.

"Oh, Billy. Yes." came his reply. He swung down in a gully, and she was forced to fall behind again. "There's some trees and an old barn over this hill we're going to stop at. We can talk then. I brought lunch."

He turned in his saddle to talk to her, and she drank in the sight of him. His cowboy hat hid his curls and shadowed his amazing eyes, but his smile was contagious, and she found herself smiling back. He was so pleased with himself for packing a lunch. She let her eyes wander across his wide shoulders, trim waist, and easy way of riding.

They rode their horses into a small patch of tall pines, their boots scuffing across brush that had grown up around the base of the trees. Magic would not have liked this hike. The barn was more like a storage place for several large bales of hay and enough cover for cattle to get into if they wanted to get out of the sun or rain. Ellie shivered. A passing cloud gained speed across the sky, followed by several other darker clouds.

"We may get rain." Mark swung his boot over the saddle and landed on the ground. Ellie followed his method and pulled her horse next to his inside the three-sided wooden barn. A fallen log served up seating well, and Mark placed it just inside the barn, so they'd be protected if it did decide to rain. "Are you cold?"

"A little." She smiled as he undid the satchel on his horse's saddle and handed her a warm, flannel-lined jacket with a hood. The slick outer coat made the inner lining even warmer. He pulled a second one out and a backpack filled with lunch.

As he spread out his treasures, he presented them to her one-by-one.

"Cheese. Crackers. Ham slices. Iced tea. Brownies. And Tootsie Pops."

Oh my. He'd seen to it all. How sweet. She was falling fast for this man who'd only been in her life for a short while.

With their backs up against the log and the delicious spread in front of them, Ellie moved closer to him. He put an arm around her.

"Now this, this is really going to cost you." Mark teased and then landed a kiss on her cheek.

"Wow, that's it?" Why had she said that? She blinked hard. He was too hard to resist.

And then he kissed her soundly on the lips. She put her other hand on his chest and kissed him back. Oh, she could do this forever. Forever? Really? Wait until he finds out who you really are. A voice from the past screamed in her head. Everything good always changed when they found that out. She pulled away.

"Can we talk about Billy for a minute?" She tried to cover the sound of her racing heart.

"Sure." Mark cleared his throat.

He was upset with her. Not upset, that was the wrong word. Confused? She'd said she was a lot, and she'd meant it.

"I think we're at a dead end with finding Billy." He bit into a sandwich. "The guy in your house seemed to think you might know where he is or at least where the money is. We should wait and see what the police come up with."

Ellie nodded. She thought the same. While they were on sobering thoughts, she might bring up another one.

She closed her eyes and took a deep breath. "Do you want to talk about Jason?"

He looked at her from the side, his mouth full of crackers. "Do you?"

She wrung her hands, tried to spin her rings. Dang it.

"We're away from the house. We need to, sometime."

Mark was silent. Maybe this was a mistake. Maybe they didn't need to.

"Ok." he finally said, quietly. "I'm going to be honest. I don't really want to, but I know he was important to you. I'm struggling with wanting to be the only man right now that is important to you."

"You are." Was he? Yep, he was. The only one right here and now. She knew Aunt Eunice's words of advice were running through his head. Trying to be gentle and understanding about another man she'd loved. That was a tall order.

He locked eyes with her.

She saw the insecurities flit across his face. "This is going to sound crazy, and we don't have to, but can I hold your hand while I tell you about Jason? It's weird, I know." Ellie licked her lips. It was different, for sure. "It's a technique I learned. If you're touching someone during an argument or hard conversation, it creates a safe space, kinda like we're in this together. Physical touch-kind of psychology. We don't have to, though."

"No, it's fine." He interlocked his fingers in hers.

Rain started to drip onto the metal roof, making the barn even more appealing, secluded, cozy.

"We were married for almost four years, no kids. He pulled me out of-"

Mark interrupted. "Ellie, can I say one thing? I don't care about your history, everyone has a past, you've been wiped clean from all of that. Tell me what kind of person Ellie Jenkins liked enough to marry?"

Oh.

One day, he was going to want all the sordid details. They always did. However, today, he'd given her grace, and she didn't have to relive the past or shoulder the embarrassment and shame of who she was before Jason.

"Okay." She turned and gave him a quick peck on the lips.

He folded her into his chest as they watched the rain pick up speed, dripping off the roof, making puddles in the entryway. He was warm and close and smelled like ham sandwiches.

She told him Jason's best qualities first, carefully choosing her words. "Well, Jason never judged, he always put others first. He was attentive to everyone but managed to make me feel special. He chose me. He introduced me to Jesus and helped me see myself through God's eyes."

Mark's arms tightened around her. This had to be hard, hearing about another man. If Mark had questions, he stayed silent.

"His downfalls? He was exhausting, always hyped up, like the energizer bunny. He only required a little sleep before he was off again, thinking of some way to help people. I couldn't keep up most of the time. But he was okay with that, and we made a pretty good partnership."

When she looked up at him, still in his arms, he was smiling. She wrinkled her nose. She'd gone on for twenty minutes about another man, and he was smiling? She pulled back so she could look him full in the face.

"You're smiling."

"Sorry. I hear all of these great things about Jason, and I'm thinking to myself, Mark? You've got all of those qualities, too. There's hope for you, yet."

Oh.

He wasn't upset. Wonder of all wonders. *So grateful, Lord.*

"I guess I have to look at it like this and I know it's not the same thing, but it's what I can relate to. Mom had two sons that she loved deeply, not one of us more than the other, but equally. Do you think that's possible?" He ran a hand across his eyes.

Ellie looked outside at the buckets that were now falling from the sky, none of which were landing on the inside. Was he asking if she could love him like she loved Jason?

She moved away from him as he sat up and started repacking the lunch. "Do you want the last brownie?"

She'd waited too long to respond. "Mark? Stop." She put a hand on his arm. "I don't know how to do all of this right, and I'm going to make mistakes, but yes, I think that's possible. Assuming you're referring to-"

He kissed her hard. The longing, the questions, the hope all wrapped up in his kiss.

"Good gravy, dude. I've never been kissed by someone so many times in one day." She pushed away. Be still, my heart. Enjoy the moment. Don't cloud it with 'what ifs'. "What are we going to do until the rain stops?" Wrong question as she saw options flick across his face. Desire. She saw desire land in his eyes.

She laughed when the rain abruptly stopped.

"Guess God thinks we should move on." He laughed with her as they put the picnic items back in his saddlebag and prepared to go out into the sloshy world.

Probably very wise as she couldn't seem to keep her lips off his. Or vice versa.

Loaded up, they went back the way they'd come, across the creek that now flowed much faster, through the pasture where they'd seen the deer, and back to the barn. Couple of hours with an amazing man out in the most delightful places. Their talk, now light-hearted and easy.

Inside the house, someone had built a fire and the embers crackled and threw off a warmth that can only come from a wood fireplace.

"Can I help with anything, Eunice?" Ellie loved being around the older woman. Her peaceful demeanor, the way she spoke to both Mark and Colton, the way she wrinkled her nose when she tried to be funny. She'd made it clear at breakfast her expectations of Mark and Ellie, and they were doable and kind. Just no more 'talking' in the bedroom.

"Well, I'd love that. I'm making biscuits for dinner tonight. Stuffed chicken, fresh vegetables, and homemade biscuits. The pie is already done."

Ellie put on the apron Eunice handed her. The apron said on the front "A Whole Lot of Nothing." She laughed. "What does this mean?"

Eunice looked over her shoulder at her. "It's from Romans 8. In the Bible."

"And what does that say?" She loved to watch Jason read the Bible, and he'd share things with her occasionally, something he read that made an impact on him. But her reading the Bible herself? Reading was not her forte.

"Paul, the writer of Romans, listed out sixteen things that could never separate us from the love of God." Eunice stuck floury fingers in the air as she ticked them off. "Not trouble, not calamity, not persecution, not hunger or being destitute, or danger, or the threat of death."

Ellie took the rolling pin from her and finished rolling out the dough.

"Let's see, that's the first seven. Then there's the last nine. Not death, nor life, nor angels or demons, or our fears for today or our worries for tomorrow. Not even the powers of hell can separate us. No power in the sky or in the earth below. Nothing, nada, zero. Nothing in creation."

"I don't even know what half of those things

mean. I've heard of angels, and I've met a couple of demons-" Ellie stopped at the look on Eunice's face. She'd said too much.

"I suspect you've met more than a few." Eunice commented.

Ellie felt the eyes of her soul connect with Eunice's. She had. How did Eunice know that?

"The important thing to note is that Paul listed those things, because there is absolutely nothing that can separate us from God's love. Nothing. And he left no loopholes or opportunities for 'what ifs'."

Ellie's eyes welled up. She bet she could think of something. Jason basically said the same thing, especially that her sins had been washed away, like she was brand-new, similar to what Mark had said in the barn. Hard to fathom. Even Jason hadn't known everything she'd endured. Only God knew. And He never stepped in to help. She'd done what she had to do. She finished rolling out the dough and started cutting out biscuits with the round, metal biscuit cutter.

Eunice left the kitchen and came back with a large, weathered Bible. Turning the pages with a freshly scrubbed finger, free of flour, she pulled out a piece of paper. "I heard a pastor say this about that verse. I think he was quoting a commentator. Let's see, Cranford was the man's name. Cranford said it's not by any courage, endurance, or determination that keeps us connected to God, but rather His hand around us. Or something close to that."

Ellie methodically pushed the round biscuits onto a baking sheet. Jason always said we could do nothing to earn God's love, but what about the opposite? Could we undo God's love by our own actions? Not according to that scripture. But the things she'd done? Unforgivable. Plus, Jason was gone. Did God still want her in His hand without Jason, the good one?

Her cell phone startled her.

"Hello? Yes, this is she. I can? That's great. Thank you." Ellie handed the baking sheet to Eunice. "The detective said I can go back to the house tomorrow. They've finished processing it, and they'll let me know what they've found soon. Good news. I have to tell Mark."

Chapter 21

Mark pulled into Ellie's driveway and shut off the engine. She'd let him drive her truck, which felt a little boyfriend-ish and made him smile. She trusted him with her truck, a good sign.

"I know this is going to be tough." He reached across the console and took her hand. She half-smiled in return.

"Seeing all of my stuff broken and tossed around…" Ellie took a deep breath.

"We'll all be here to help." Mark looked in his rearview mirror as Colton and Brynleigh pulled in behind them, Brandon and Selena parked on the curb.

"I appreciate you."

She looked so sad this morning. Or rather, right now. Their evening had gone silky smooth although she appeared distracted. The trepidation of returning home to a mess must be wearing on her.

Dinner was amazing with all of them around the table. After Ellie shared the news about being able to return to her house, they all agreed to come help after church. He was thankful for their help, regardless if it cut down on their alone time. She'd not be under the same roof as he, 200iplocr. Savor every moment, dude.

They'd left Magic with Aunt Eunice, so he wouldn't slice his paw on something broken. That's all they needed was to have to take the dog to the vet. One thing at a time. *Please, God.*

Ellie unlocked the front door. Crime scene tape stuck to the bottom of the door and flew off into the yard when she pushed it open.

Images of Ellie in the hands of the lunatic assaulted him, and Mark tripped over the lip of the entryway. He caught himself and schooled his face. This truly was a disaster. Ellie didn't need the memory of being accosted on top of this mess, although it had to be somewhere lurking. A person didn't just wish that type of trauma away.

Brynleigh brushed past them and took charge. She tore black trash bags off a roll and gave one to everyone.

"We can start in the kitchen, and you guys, the living room. That okay, Ellie?"

Ellie shrugged.

"We can work our way to the back." Mark suggested. He gave her a brief hug and then joined Brandon and Colton in the front area.

Ellie shuffled to the small kitchen. Even the fridge had been rifled through. Flour and sugar dumped out on the counter, leaving empty canisters scattered. Drawers and cabinet doors open, cereal boxes dumped, even the drawer with the Tupperware lids was disturbed.

Mark stepped into the kitchen, frowning. "Colton and I decided to fix the back door first, so, well, so it's fixed." Really good words there, buddy.

Ellie didn't acknowledge him and continued to slam drawers and doors shut.

Mark started toward her when Selena stopped him with an upright hand.

Not right now, she said with her eyes. He'd leave the consoling to the women. For now.

Mark and Colton pulled the glass door out of its tracks and scrubbed the railing down. Fresh air into the house smelled glorious as the sun peeked around a cloud. Leaves were turning more golden and red, beautifully ignoring the chaos inside the house. They finished the task, tested the lock on the door, a small victory.

Mark looked over at Ellie, furiously scrubbing the counter, wiping away any sign of the burglar. This was terrifying. He wanted to comfort her, tell her she was safe, and that this would never happen again. Empty promises. He'd never be able to guarantee that. The person who broke in was definitely looking for something. The money. Despite what the man yelled, Mark doubted Billy was really his concern. Billy was just the vehicle for the stolen money. Maybe. Maybe, Billy hadn't taken the money and time with his father had gone horribly wrong.

So, why did the crazy man break into Ellie's house? Why did he think Ellie had the money, or Billy, or both? Unless Kitty said something at the club to the cops she thought were following them. Kitty was definitely money hungry. What if the cops had promised some type of finder's fee to her? Would she be foolish enough to believe them?

Greedy enough?

"Mark, can you come in here, please?" Brandon called from the living room.

The ladies made significant progress in the kitchen and were working their way to the dining area where the living room connected. Brynleigh scrubbed up the drops of blood from where Mark had laid on the floor.

Colton and Brandon had moved her oversized couch away from the wall. Sitting half way in the living room, they pushed the coffee table and rug off to the side. A huge mirror that originally hung behind the couch had dropped to the ground and splintered into a million pieces. If he'd just tarried with the door for a little longer, he would have missed the chore of picking up a gazillion mirror fragments. He brought the trashcan closer to the mess.

"Your girlfriend got a gun?" Brandon bent at the waist behind the couch, sweeping shards into a dustpan.

What? Girlfriend?

Colton punched him in the arm. "Dude?"

"Well, first, she's not my girlfriend, and second, we haven't talked about home security-" Mark stopped. "What? She's not my girlfriend." Could be. Should be. There was something there that made his heart pound out of his chest. Something? Ellie. Ellie made his heart pound. Call it like it was.

"Oh my gosh, dude." Colton rolled his eyes.

"One more time. Does. Your. Girlfriend… ok, Ellie… have a gun?" Colton stood. Tipped the dustpan towards him. Amongst the dust bunnies, gum wrapper, and pieces of the mirror sat a gun. A real one. Like shoot to kill gun. Mark hesitated. He *knew* he heard a gun clank to the floor in the scuffle.

"Ellie?" Mark yelled. Brandon and Colton looked at the gun like it was a lab specimen.

"What?" Ellie, Brynleigh, and Selena came around the corner. "What is that?"

"So help me, if that's a mouse, I will never forgive you." Brynleigh backed away from the huddle.

Brandon tilted the dustpan again, careful not to dump it out on the floor.

"Ellie, do you have a gun?" Mark asked. He cast worried eyes her way. There *had* been a gun. They both could have been killed. Even more terrifying.

"I do, but that's not it. Whose is that?" Ellie reached out to pick it up. The guys scrambled to stop her.

"Don't touch it." Brandon pulled the dustpan and gun out of her reach.

"How do you know it's not yours?" Mark asked.

Ellie looked at him like he'd grown two heads. It was a legit question, wasn't it?

"Because mine has a pink grip on it."

That one was definitely not pink. Only shiny metal gray.

"What caliber?" Brandon looked closer at the gun.

Ellie shrugged.

"Do you know where yours is?" Colton asked. "Bryn, can you find a 203iploc bag for us to drop this in?"

"Why didn't the police find this?"

"I don't know. Maybe the mirror hid it. Is your

gun still in the house?" Mark stared at her. She had a gun for protection. That was good. And even better that the gun they found wasn't hers. That meant the gun could very well belong to the one who he'd wrestled with and who trashed her house. And the guy hadn't used it on them.

~

Ellie turned without a word and walked back to her bedroom. The mattress was skewed, the cases off her pillows and flung around the room, every drawer open, her closet destroyed.

Apparently, the burglar thought she'd stashed the money somewhere in the house. Did she lock Billy in the basement, too? How dare they? She blew out a breath, counted to ten. Her head was about to explode. She was a social worker, for Pete's sake. Not a co-conspirator in a money heist with two dead bodies and a missing boy. And why couldn't he shut the drawers after he ransacked them? She wanted to Scream.

And the gun? She had no idea what to think about that. It wasn't hers. He must have dropped it fighting with Mark. She shivered. It could have gone off.

The only thing in the bedroom untouched appeared to be the safe, bolted to the floor by the bedside. Jason often carried a gun through the slums and sketchy places he worked, and he had taught her gun safety. She'd given his away to a friend that worked alongside him, knowing she'd never be able to carry the heavy gun.

Sitting down on the floor beside the safe, Ellie noticed her stand-up jewelry box was open, its lid cracked. There wasn't anything of value in it, except…

She'd moved her rings to the safe, hadn't she? She'd told Kari she was going to, but…

She spun the dial on the safe, breathing hard, hands shaking. Stupid combination. She hated these things, could never remember the numbers, couldn't get it open. She should have insisted on a fingerprint locking safe. She spun the lock again. Whispered the numbers. No go. She slammed her palm down hard on the top. She'd tear it apart with her bare hands if she had to. If they weren't in there…

Slammed her hand again on the unmoving steel box. Screamed.

"Ellie, what's wrong?" Mark crouched next to her, barely enough space between the wall and the bed. He crowded around her and grabbed her hand before she could punch the safe. Blood dripped from a torn fingernail. The rest of the crew stood by the doorway, watching her lose her ever-loving mind.

Reaching around him, Ellie said the numbers out loud as she turned the dial. Click.

She heaved a sigh of relief. *Thank God. Please God, please let them be in there.*

Mark knelt behind her in the tiny space.

No, no, no! Her gun lay in the cavernous hole on top of legal papers and a fireproof envelope that contained her passport. Those were the only things. The. Only. Things.

She sagged against Mark. She was stupid, stupid. This was her final, stupid mistake. If the darkness would only consume her and she could truly be done. No light, no more mistakes, no more life.

Done. She could feel Mark's arms around her and hear the others questioning him.

"What happened?"

"Is the gun in there?"

"Did she pass out?"

And Mark's voice, concerned and high-pitched. "Ellie? Ellie?"

If she stayed here, in the dark, maybe this nightmare would end. A flutter of her eyelids and she knew, knew she was still here on earth. Not with Jason. Where she wanted to be. Maybe she'd never be with him. She was so stupid. She'd never be allowed in Heaven.

Nothing can separate you. He has His hand on you.

Yeah, right.

Ellie kept her eyes closed but shifted against Mark's chest. His hand stroked her hair, pulled her closer to him. She could hear his heartbeat. Unlike Jason's, whose would never beat again.

"Ellie?" She could hear the fear in Mark's voice.

It bore asking, yet she already knew the answer. Because she was stupid. She pointed over his shoulder without opening her eyes, "Are my wedding rings in my jewelry box?"

Someone in the room walked over to where she pointed.

Silence.

"Um, no." Brynleigh then. "I'm sorry."

She knew it. The burglar had gone through her jewelry box, found hers and Jason's wedding rings, and took them. He. Took. Them. She hadn't moved them to the safe like she said she was going to. She'd gotten all caught up with another man and forgotten the two most tangible things she had left of Jason.

Ellie pinched her eyes closed tighter. And then the hot, angry tears came. She banged closed fists on Mark's chest. "Please let go of me!"

"Ellie, I'm sorry." Mark wrapped her up tighter.

"Let go of me." She screamed. "Just let go."

Her sobbing filled the room.

Mark loosened his grip on her, and she scrambled out of his embrace. Knocked her knee on the corner of the bed. Screamed.

"Everybody get out! Get out! Get out!"

Brandon, Brynleigh, and Selena backed into the hallway. Mark stood and joined his brother on the other side of the room. "Ellie-" Mark stepped toward her.

"No. Get out." She looked officially crazy now by their faces. No more. She couldn't do any more. "Please."

"We'll be in the other room." Mark pulled his brother into the hallway.

"No. Out. I want you out of my house." She slammed the door behind them and crawled into the bed. Wrapping the comforter around her, she willed the darkness to come again.

Chapter 22

Mark backed away from the door she'd just slammed. He turned and looked at Colton, who shook his head.

"I don't know what to do," he said, quietly.

"Me, neither." Colton raked fingers through his hair. "I'm guessing her rings were stolen? So maybe this wasn't about Billy?"

"No, the man actually asked about the money and Billy. I think the rings were stolen to make it look like a burglary." Mark blew out a hard breath. He could still hear her sobbing, guttural, deep, painful.

A nightmare. How could he comfort the woman he had deep feelings for, if she'd just ordered him out of her house? She was distraught, for sure. The whole ordeal from Billy missing to now was like an avalanche rushing downhill, swallowing people and homes, wrecking lives. God? What now?

Trust Me.

Be still and trust Me.

Fat chance he was going to be any good at that. The weeping had stopped, he couldn't hear anything on the other side of the door now.

He walked into the living area, the couch still pulled away from the wall, the women sitting on the love seat, concern etched on their faces. Colton and Brandon continued to sweep debris and set things right to the best of their knowledge.

"Any guesses on what's happening?" Mark slumped into a gray rocking recliner.

The ladies looked at each other. Brynleigh leaned her head onto Selena's shoulder.

"Best guess? I'd say grief just caught up with her. She said her wedding rings, so…" Selena looked to Brandon for confirmation.

"She's a widow. The wedding rings were hers and her…husband's." Crap.

"That's even worse. I wouldn't care so much about wedding rings from someone I divorced, unless they were super expensive, but if they were the only thing I had left of Brandon…" She wiped her eyes.

Mark caught the glance between Colton and Brynleigh. They felt the same. The love, and loss, and the fear that someday the person they loved would be gone, every emotion he read on their faces made his gut churn. Him, with no clue how to respond, and the lady he was falling for, behind a closed door. She might as well be in Timbuktu.

"You'all can go. I'm going to sit here for a while. Maybe she'll get some rest and come out later. I want to be here when she does." He watched the couples silently agree and leave the house, hand in hand. "Oh, and Colton, would you tell Aunt Eunice what's going on? And that Magic will stay with her for a bit until we figure this out?"

"Sure." Colton responded.

Brandon bounded back to the open door. "I'll drop off the gun at the police station. I took pictures of its location that I'll give them, too. And tell them about the rings." He grabbed the plastic bag they'd put the gun in to preserve evidence.

"Ok, thanks." Mark had totally forgotten about the gun.

The house was quiet when he closed the front door. He straightened a painting on the wall and picked up a magazine that had fallen from the end table. He did what he could to restore things to their original spot as he made his way into the kitchen. She might be hungry when she came out and although he was no cook, he could heat up soup or tea or whatever she wanted. How did you feed grief, though? He'd promised to protect her heart. To be understanding about her being a widow. He hadn't thought the understanding would have to spread to Jason as well. Wedding rings, of course, were important, but she'd taken them off. He needed to get a better understanding of how he was supposed to respond to her. Unless she never let him back in. A possibility he didn't want to consider. If that happened, it meant she'd chosen her memories of Jason over him, the here and now. He couldn't take that. How did you compete with someone who's passed on? *God, what are you doing here?*

Long after the tea grew cold and a shadowy dusk settled over the living room, Mark rose for the umpteenth time and went to stand by her bedroom door. Nothing, no sound.

He needed a plan, something to do, something

to make the situation better. He'd go get Magic and bring the dog back to the house. Maybe having her companion with her would help. He certainly wasn't being any.

Grabbing keys from where Ellie first dropped them and what felt like a lifetime ago, Mark left the house. Driving away from her was the hardest thing he'd done to date. The sadness in his heart matched the tears freely falling down his cheeks.

~

"I said go away." Ellie shouted from under the covers.

A large nose sniffed at her. Magic pushed his face under the comforter.

Ellie started to cry again, wetting the caseless pillow. She took the big dog's head in her hands and ruffled his ears. Magic, satisfied that she was safe, curled up next to her with his heavy body and promptly started snoring. She heard the bedroom door softly click shut. She didn't want to see anyone and had no plans to come out. She couldn't get the open jewelry box out of her mind. She remembered setting the rings in the box, could recount the conversation with Kari about putting them in a safe spot, and then she just didn't do it. She hadn't planned on having her home broken into, either.

She had very few pictures of her and Jason, but tons of memories. The rings, however, were things she could hold in her hand, things that brought on a slew of memories. How Jason had proposed in a poem, the rings tied with white ribbon and attached to the bottom of the paper. How he'd held her shaking hands in his while he slipped on the wedding ring. How she'd trembled everytime she ran her thumb across the top of his hand and the cold metal. Her rings, and his, had a grounding effect on her, a reminder that Jason had chosen her. She'd taken them off, started to feel her own strength, her own ability to walk through life, alone, but still doing it. Now, the rings were gone. Her lifeline to Jason was gone. Neglect on her part, but some of this was Mark's fault, too. And Billy's.

If Billy hadn't run away. If Mark hadn't dragged her into this mess, her personal space would never have been vandalized. A lot of 'ifs'. *And where are you, God? You took Jason from me. What do you expect from me, now?*

Ellie unwound from the bed and padded to her bathroom. Magic lifted his big head, noted the direction she was heading, and let it drop again on the cozy comforter. She did her business and then stood in front of the mirror washing her hands. She opened the medicine cabinet. Nothing was touched. The burglar missed taking the meds she kept. Of course. Not the oxycodone left over from a past surgery, not the headache medicine that was prescription strength, not the sleeping pills.

She'd forgotten about the sleeping pills prescribed to her after Jason's death. If she took a couple now, she could sleep through tomorrow and maybe the day after.

"You know those won't change anything. He'll still be gone." Kari had said to her when Ellie told her about the prescription. Truth in love. The doctor had only written a half prescription, with more available if needed, for fear that Ellie might abuse them. To be honest, she'd thought about taking all of them together numerous times. Not something she was proud of, but then again, what was one more thing to be ashamed of?

Ellie popped two in her mouth, swallowed, and made her way back to Magic. So be it if something happened in her sleep.

She awoke ten hours later to her cell phone ringing. Mark. Nope, not happening, buddy. Two other missed calls from him. She ignored Magic's half-attempt to get out of bed and slid back under the covers.

The next time she awoke, she had cotton mouth from the pills and her stomach grumbled. Magic danced around her feet, needing time out in the backyard.

"Okay, okay."

Everything was cleaned up in the rest of the house, something Mark must have done before he left to get Magic. She squinted at the clock. 2:37pm. Twenty-four hours after she discovered her rings stolen. Thankfully, she had slept. No dreams. The pills had done their job. She might be able to squeak another couple of nights out of the bottle. Then, she'd have to switch to something else. Or deal with this. Nope, not until she had to. And she didn't plan on that anytime soon. She'd call her boss, tell him she had the flu and wouldn't be in the rest of the week. He wouldn't be very happy, but she didn't care. She could call Kari, but she'd tell her to stop taking the pills. Which she also wasn't ready to do.

Jason always said things looked better in the morning. Well, she'd missed the morning and things didn't look any different later in the day.

I lost our wedding rings, Jason. How do you like them apples? So sorry. Oh, and I took them off due to another man. How do you like me now? Still proud of me?

Ellie leaned over the sink and threw up. This is what grief looked like in the flesh, a churned up emotional mess. She knew, deep down, that she was spiraling and couldn't stop it. Maybe if she sunk low enough, she'd cease to exist.

Someone rang the doorbell. She tip-toed and peeked out the eyehole. Eunice stood on her steps, holding a casserole dish. Ellie closed her eyes. Mark must have sent her. She had no desire to see the woman who'd become a friend in such a short time. She couldn't ignore her, though. That was incredibly rude.

Ellie blew a breath out her nose and opened the door. Be smiley, assure her you're fine, and send her on her way. Ellie looked down at her sweatpants and hoodie. Her looks alone told a different story.

"Hi." Ellie attempted a smile.

"Hi, sweetie. I brought you something to eat."

Ellie tried to snatch the dish, but Eunice skirted around her and went head-long to the kitchen. She shut the door, resigned to have to make chit-chat.

"You didn't have to."

"It's how I know how to help. You're devastated about your rings. Mark told me."

Oh yeah? Did he also tell you I'm certifiably crazy? That I have no interest in him or you or Billy? Her thoughts whirled, her mouth silent.

"I suspect you're grieving." Eunice stretched out

her arms.

And Ellie walked right into the embrace. With no hesitation. So much for her resolve to never speak to any of them again. Ellie was taller than Eunice, but she laid her head down on the older woman's shoulder and sobbed. Seems she had no control over anything.

"It's like I opened that crack, and all this grief came pouring out. After Jason died, I buried it, knowing someday it would come spilling out, and then I managed to forget it was there. Waiting. Waiting for an opportunity to burst out." Ellie cried, her voice muffled.

"That's exactly how sneaky grief is. When you least expect it." was Eunice's soft reply.

"It's just been lurking."

"Now's the time, then. Let's deal with it." Eunice handed her a tissue. "I'm not a counselor or anything, but I do know this subject, and I'd be happy to listen. Do you have a counselor you see regularly?"

"Yes." Ellie blew her nose. The effects of having not eaten were catching up to her. "But you're Mark's aunt."

"And a widow." Eunice searched her cabinets, pulled a plate down, and served a bite of the casserole to Ellie. "Sounds like you need some food in your belly. It's still warm."

Ellie ate every piece of it. "I don't know what to do now."

"What's changed? God still loves you like my boy does."

Ellie rolled her eyes.

"What? It's true." Eunice patted her hand. "Your beautiful rings were stolen. Mark had nothing to do with that. Remember that scripture we talked about? Nothing above or below can separate you from God. This isn't penance for you being or not being a good person, although I can't see you being anything but caring and kind."

What she didn't know couldn't hurt her.

"My rings are still gone." Ellie pushed her plate away and laid her head down on the table.

"Yes, that's true. You still have your husband in your heart. That can never change. No one can take that away." Eunice gathered up the plate and silverware and cleaned them in the sink. "Did you tell me that your husband introduced you to Jesus?"

A lot of good that did.

"Yes. Well, maybe *I* didn't tell you, but that's how it happened." Ellie said, head still down.

"This is what I tell people when things seem very dark, like right now for you," Eunice dried the dishes and put them away, along with the casserole into the fridge. "God is never not working on your behalf because you love Him."

"Do I, though? Really?" She lifted her head. Anger, hurt, sadness pushed through her tone.

"Let me take out the double negatives and turn it around. God is always working, even when you can't see Him at work, on your behalf because He loves you."

Ellie stood. "Eunice, thank you for the meal. It was really good."

Eunice took the hint. "If you don't finish off the casserole soon, it does great in the freezer."

"Thank you." Ellie opened the front door. "And please tell Mark that I appreciate him bringing over Magic."

"Can I also tell him that you'll call him? He's so worried about you, Ellie."

Nope.

"I don't know if I'm ready for that. Bye, Eunice."

Chapter 23

"Holy crap, man. Would you stop moping around? It's been three days. She's not going to call." Colton slapped Mark on the shoulder.

"Leave it." Mark stomped out of the house. He didn't need his brother telling him how long it had been. He was well aware.

Out in the barn, he picked up a shovel and started cleaning the stalls. The manure piles were huge, and the straw packed down. Whose job was it to keep up on the cleaning? The boys were all assigned jobs. Rules were rules. Someone was slacking. It felt good to get his hands dirty in the fresh air, despite the smell that arose from the manure.

He finished the three stalls on the west, broke a healthy sweat, and stopped for a drink of water.

Miserable. Nice descriptive word. How about inadequate? Or heart-sick? Good grief.

Nothing could sufficiently describe how he was feeling.

Trust Me.

I do. Really. Ok, not so much. I had a plan. And then Ellie came along, and the plans changed. And this isn't the plan.

I have a plan for her, too.

Ok, but us together?

Silence. He sucked in air and waited. Listening. He could hear the goats jumping from platform to platform in the pen nearby and one of the boys calling Bandit. Nothing from God.

So, that's the way this goes? *I'm not walking away from you, God, but I'm confused and don't feel like you're listening to me.*

Trust me.

For Pete's sake.

He heard his brother come in from the south gate and turn on the barn radio. Mark leaned back on the hay bale, felt the old wooden planks scratch his neck.

"What are you doing? You switched places? Instead of pouting in the house, you're pouting in the barn?" Colton came around the corner with a pitchfork.

"Shut up. You don't know what you're talking about."

"You are correct. I've never felt the way you do."

Wow, he agreed? Colton rarely agreed with Mark. Choosing to be the devil's advocate most of the time.

"You've never seen me pout, either."

Mark rolled his eyes. "Who's supposed to be mucking these stalls?"

Colton kicked Mark's boot. "Billy."

Oh. Lovely.

Colton pulled another haybale up next to Mark's. After a few minutes of silence, Colton said,

"I know this is hard-"

"I don't even know who to be mad at. Billy? Ellie? Me? You? God? Who gets credit for this mess?"

"Not me, for certain. If there's one thing I do understand, it's anger. It's my go-to response. When I'm angry and don't know why, it's usually because I'm not angry, but some other emotion."

"Wow, did your therapist teach you all that?"

"Shut up." Colton shoved Mark with one hand. "Well, maybe."

"So, counselor boy, what's my underlying, not angry, emotion?" Mark gave him a hard side look.

"Hurt. Jealousy."

Yep. No doubt.

"Heart sick."

Mark launched off the bale and tackled Colton. The two fell on the barn floor, laughing.

"I'm not wrong, though." Colton stood and swiped straw off his jeans.

"Yeah, I miss her." Mark stood, too.

Colton frowned. "Let's finish Billy's job and then you should consider what to do now."

"Like I haven't been doing that already. I keep hearing these words 'Trust Me' reverberating in my head."

"Reverberating? Big words." Colton tossed stagnant hay into the wheelbarrow. "You asked advice from me? Your little brother? Who's just as messed up as you are? Even though God's been speaking to you already?"

Mark stopped and looked at him. "I guess."

"Are you going to trust Him?"

"I guess."

"There's your plan, man." Colton wheeled the stall contents out of the barn.

There's my plan. *I trust you. I trust that you have a plan for Ellie. I trust that even if it's not us together, you have a plan for each of us.*

His heart still hurt, but his mind was clearer. There was a plan.

~

Ellie had picked up the phone to call him numerous times but hadn't the guts to do it. He must think she was a lunatic, screaming at them, telling her new friends to get out and leave her alone. "Mark?"

"Ellie?" Mark sounded breathless.

"Where are you?"

"I am currently shoveling out the chicken coop. I started with the manure in the horses' stalls, and I've moved on to more of the same in the poop department. Just smaller."

Ellie chuckled. "Sounds fun." She heard the smile in his voice. "Listen, I- I've been a real jerk."

"No, Ellie, please don't say that."

"I should never have led you to believe that I was ready for-" She paused. For what?

Silence.

He was not going to fill in the silence.

She started again. "I wasn't expecting to have as much fun with you as we did. And I thought I was ready to live outside Jason's world... on my own. You kinda changed that." Were her words even making sense?

"In a good way?" Mark whispered.

"Yeah." Ellie heard a commotion on the other

end. "What's happening?"

"Oh, um, I startled the chickens."

"How did you startle them?" Curiosity killed the cat, Ellie.

"I might have, um, done a little dance?"

Truth was as dangerous as curiosity sometimes.

"I'm not saying we pick up where we left off," she stammered, "but if you want… hang on, I have another call coming in. It says it's from the police department."

"Answer it. I'll hold."

Ellie could hear the chickens squawking again. She smiled as she switched to the in-coming call. "Hello?"

"Mrs. Jenkins?"

"Yes?" She ignored the title, although her heart pinged a little. She'd have to get used to that.

"This is the Dallas Police Department, Sergeant Bolivar speaking."

"Yes?"

"We caught a case north of town, a woman was found in the yard of an apartment complex up here. Your business card was on her. We have some questions…"

"Wait. What was her name?"

She'd given her card out to many people over the years, but only one in the northern part of Dallas recently. Kitty.

"Her neighbor called it in. The old lady appeared a little frazzled and we're not sure she was completely lucid when we talked to her. Pretty typical around here. Pretty boozed up, I believe. She said Catherine, Cat, something like that."

"Kitty?"

"Yeah, that was it. Any idea if that was her real name or not? Or a last name? The old lady mentioned a kid was waiting outside her apartment for her to get home, but he was gone when we arrived."

A kid? Billy?

"Okay if I come to you? I'll bring any information I think is relevant with me." She took down the address of the police department and disconnected. "Mark, are you still there?"

"I'm still here. What did they want? Do they know who broke into your place? Who the gun belonged to?"

"No to all of those questions. This was north patrol, on the other side of Dallas. They found Kitty dead! And Billy was spotted in the vicinity." Ellie changed out of her sweats and pulled on a hooded sweatshirt. "I'll come get you."

"Are you sure you want me to go?" Mark sounded hesitant.

Ellie paused. "Don't you want to?"

"Yes, but- never mind, I'll be ready." Mark rushed.

"Ok, see you in twenty."

By the time she pulled up in front of the ranch, Mark was standing on the porch, waiting.

He looked good, a smattering of whiskers across his face, his blue eyes watching her with tenderness. Maybe this wasn't a great idea. She faltered. They had to find Billy, and she hated the news about Kitty, but maybe this was what they needed. What she needed. In all of her memories of Jason and the all-consuming grief that was stirred up, she continually saw Mark in the little things. How he'd smoothed her hair in the barn. He'd been willing to share head space with Jason, although she struggled with it. What had he said? She could love two people. She'd loved Jason, for certain. Her feelings for Mark? Well on their way to that conclusion. She'd let her stolen rings trip her up, plunge her into a darkness that grief was so good at.

She missed Mark. She missed Jason, too, but he wasn't coming back and there was nothing she could do about it. This, this she could do something about. Be brave, girl.

"Ellie, are you sure?" Mark got in the passenger side.

Her blue eyes met his. She had so much she wanted to say, although now was not the time. They could talk later. She searched his eyes and finding hope, slid her hand over to his.

His eyebrows raised as he clasped her fingers and squeezed.

"Tell me how this is going to go."

"We'll stop by the police station and then play it by ear. I'm sorry about Kitty and all that, but if Billy is hanging around, I want to find him."

Chapter 24

Mark couldn't keep his eyes off her. She had purplish half moons under her eyes, but they held a little of the sparkle he'd missed since their time at the ranch. She had raw spots on her cuticles, a sure sign she was picking at them in worry. He couldn't believe it when she'd called. He figured they were done, over, stopped before their journey could fully begin. He wasn't sure why she'd called originally, she certainly wasn't being a jerk. The call from the police department couldn't have been timed more perfectly. She'd been back in close proximity within the twenty minutes she proposed, even though he knew driving the speed limit should have taken her longer. Who cares? Always the rule-follower. Well, he'd change his whole way of thinking if it meant she'd give him a second opportunity. Second? He'd barely started with the first.

Mark glanced over at her. She was so beautiful with her hair pulled back and layers framing her face. Little makeup, jeans and boots, he didn't think she could be prettier.

"What?" Ellie asked, catching his glance.

Mark shook his head and turned to the window. Ellie drove the long way around to the north part of Dallas like they had driven the first time, skirting the crazy downtown traffic. The day was cooler than most Texas days and the greens were starting to be overtaken by the browns. The ground needed another good soaking to push the season fully into fall.

Trust Me.

Yes, God. He understood now. God was always working just like Aunt Eunice constantly said. He was openly grinning now, his very soul bursting with joy at the nearness of her. No, not everything was settled between them, they had a ways to go, but she'd wanted him to come with her. That said something, didn't it? He stole another glance at her as she released his hand and made the turn into the police station.

"I'm going to call the detective and let him know we're here." Ellie pulled out her cell phone. "Detective Bolivar? Yes, we're at the police station. Oh. Sure."

Mark watched her mouth move. Some stupid song went through his head, 'Say my name, say my name'.

"He said to meet him at the apartment complex. Maybe we'll spot Billy." Ellie backed out and handed her phone with the address on the screen. "Can you punch that into GPS for me?"

"Sure." The screen locked before he could add the address. A fuzzy picture of Ellie and a guy, presumably Jason, dressed to the nines, flashed in his face. She was in a lightning blue, off shoulder formal, and he was in a tux. He hesitated, blinked. Not an image he wanted to see again. "It locked."

She snatched the phone back, opened it with the combination and her thumb, and handed it back to him.

Had she seen his reaction to the photo? Hopefully not. Her look was guarded, so maybe. Regardless, his heart hurt. Though not very clear, she was stunning all dressed up and the camera caught her looking at the guy with unabashed love.

He supposed he would run into things like that photo for quite a while. Like Aunt Eunice said, it would be up to Ellie to make those changes when she was ready.

If this thing between Ellie continues, there will be a different photo on her lock screen. Calm down, buddy. This would be much harder than he'd ever anticipated, especially if reminders of her first love popped up often.

Mark flipped to the maps app and put in the address of the apartment complex. Not far from the diner where they'd met Kitty for breakfast and close enough to the strip that she could have walked to work.

Ellie pulled in behind a police car on the street. "I don't know what to expect. I certainly hope they've already taken Kitty away."

"Me, too." Mark resisted the urge to take her hand. They'd seen enough dead bodies to last a lifetime.

They followed a concrete sidewalk into a U-shaped courtyard. Three sides of the pitifully grassed area were surrounded by triple layer apartments, glass broken on several windows, all desperately needing a coat of paint. Mark could see people standing in the apartments, curtains pulled back, watching the policemen congregate in the center. Empty beer bottles littered the area, cigarette butts piled high in cans next to stone benches. Could have been a pretty park area for residents at one time before the strip had moved in next door.

A heavy-set man with Dallas PD on his vest broke free from a group of uniformed officers and approached them.

"Mrs. Jenkins?"

Mark shuddered. That, he would never get used to.

Ellie glanced at him, and he looked away. "Yes, that's me. Detective Bolivar?"

The man stuck out his hand and Ellie shook it.

"This is my… associate, Mark Bruens," she introduced him.

Associate? Mark shook his hand as well.

"We've already sent the body with the coroner." Detective Bolivar said with a sweep of his hand. "Can you give me some idea of your involvement with this Kitty character? Why she had your card on her person?"

"Sure. I'm a case manager for juvenile offenders and a boy ran away from the group home. We tracked down his mother, Kitty, who hadn't seen him, so it was a dead end for us. I did give her my card in case he showed up."

Mark noticed she failed to mention that it was his ranch Billy walked away from. When had Ellie given Kitty her business card? He'd given Billy's mother his in the strip club, but he didn't know when

Ellie had given out hers. Not that it mattered.

"Ah, I see. Well, the old lady mentioned a boy, but she's pretty nutty."

"Can we talk to her?" Ellie looked around at the apartments. Curtains dropped into place, curious, but not enough to get involved.

With the outside looking so rough, Mark could imagine the insides housing people with warrants, kitchen tables loaded with dope, and guns hidden in couches.

"I don't care. If you get anything outta her that fits with this Kitty case, let me know." The detective pointed to Apartment 26 on the first floor, tucked in a corner, and walked away.

"I don't know, Ellie, this seems a little dangerous." Mark uttered as Ellie made her way to the apartment.

"There's tons of cops out here. We won't go in."

"Wait, Ellie. Let me knock." Mark stepped in front of her to the torn screen door. The flimsy panel door behind it sported a large crack down the middle. If a shotgun blast came through the unopened door, it would hit him first. Who was he kidding? It'd go through both of them, leaving them as dead as Kitty.

Hesitantly, he knocked on the metal part of the screen door, the sound reverberating down the walkway.

An old lady, food stains on her apron, and a look in her eye that would cause a bear to back down, opened the door. She looked at Mark, surveyed his clothes, and spit tobacco juice into a paper cup.

Ellie stepped out from behind him. "Hi, ma'am. We're hoping you could help us."

"No cops." The woman started to close the door.

"Wait, we aren't the police. We're looking for a boy you might have seen. He may have been waiting for his mother, Kitty, to get home? But, as you already know," Ellie pointed to the knot of officers still in the courtyard, "Kitty is dead."

"Nope, no cats. I don't have any cats."

Ellie and Mark looked at each other. Maybe she was as looney as the detective had said.

"We're not here about your cats. Was Kitty your neighbor?" Mark asked.

"I only have one cat. Catherine liked her. She was nice to Tabitha."

Mark struggled to keep up with the woman's thoughts.

"Catherine, said to call her Kitty, but I've already got a kitty cat. Don't need no more." The woman spit in her cup.

Oh, she called Kitty Catherine to keep Billy's mom separate from her cat.

"A boy. Did you see a boy hanging around?"

The old woman squinted an eye at them. "A boy?"

"Yes, a boy." Mark could hear the excitement in Ellie's voice. They were finally getting somewhere.

"He was waiting for his mom. I asked if he wanted to see my cats, but he said no. Is he still here? I can show him my Tabitha." She stepped out of the doorway and looked around.

"I'm not sure. Was he taller than you? Brown hair? Maybe a baseball hat on?" Ellie pushed.

"Do I know you? You the cops?" The old woman scrunched back behind the screen door, sliding out of reality.

"Ellie, I think we're done here." Mark turned Ellie back to the courtyard with a hand on her arm as the woman slammed the interior door.

"So close. We were so close." Ellie blew out a breath. "Definitely some mental illness there."

Definitely.

Mark and Ellie watched as Detective Bolivar walked toward them.

"Anything?" he asked.

"Not really." Mark dropped his hand on Ellie's arm.

"I may have a few questions for you all," The detective pulled out a small notebook.

Mark and Ellie exchanged glances.

"This boy you mentioned… we've identified the body and when we ran her info through our records, she was flagged as a potential co-conspirator in a double homicide slash robbery south of Dallas. Along with her son. Is this the same kid you're looking for?" He turned his phone around so they could see a picture.

Billy.

~

Ellie sucked in a breath. "Yes."

They reluctantly nodded when the detective asked them to meet him down at the station.

"Mark, they're still actively pursuing Billy as a murderer." Ellie walked beside Mark.

"We knew that."

"I'm not sure what they do with deaths like Kitty's if in fact it was an OD. But, for Billy's sake, I want to find out. Like is there a service? If Billy is her only kin, where do they bury her?" Turning back to look at the scene, Ellie bumped into a man walking briskly toward the courtyard. "Oh sorry."

The man tilted his head and looked at her.

Ellie stopped.

Samson?

His shaven head made him look more intimidating now than when she'd known him before. Before Jason. She swallowed. This couldn't be happening. They were so close to finding Billy, and she runs into the bouncer at the club she used to work at a million years ago? *Please, God.*

Mark looped his arm in hers and steered her to her truck. "Do you know that guy?"

Ellie looked over her shoulder. "No." Pleaded with her eyes for Samson not to acknowledge her.

She reached the truck, keys in hand, and stood watching Samson disappear around the corner.

"Do you want me to drive?"

"Yes, please."

Gently, Mark took the keys from her.

She went around the truck, straining her neck to catch a glimpse of Samson, and got in the passenger side. Why would Samson be here? Had he recognized her? Of course he had. Her hair had changed color, and she was totally clothed from the last time he'd seen her. Oh my. Ellie stared out the window. Did she really think she could just waltz out of that life and live happily ever after? With Jason, she had. She'd changed, met Jesus, believed, no, hoped, the past would never catch up to her. A dream. A nightmare, actually. Because now, it had.

"Are you okay?" Mark asked, offering his hand.

She patted it and then jammed both hands into the pocket of her hoodie. He withdrew it. She shook her head. Her world was crashing, and she was powerless to stop it. Again. If Mark figured out who she really was, he wouldn't want to hold her hand or have anything to do with her.

"I'm going to stop for something to eat before we go to the police station. It might be a long day." Mark turned onto a busy street.

"I'm not really hungry, Mark."

"I can hear your stomach." He glanced at her, worry etched in his gaze.

"Ok, maybe a drink. Something to settle it." Like hard alcohol.

Mark pulled into a fast-food restaurant, ordered fries with mustard packets, please, and two Diet Cokes.

"Thanks." She sipped her drink. Not touching the fries.

When they arrived at the police station, Mark ran around to open her door and let her lead the way in. They stepped into a congested foyer with a wide range of people settled in plastic chairs, visitors waiting to see inmates in the basement jail of the justice center, and people standing in line in front of a long plexiglass window. A harried receptionist with a police uniform sat behind the glass, arguing with a man in a suit.

"Good grief. This is a mess. Why is it so busy?" Mark whispered, behind her. With the number of people crammed into the small room, he was nearly pressed up against her. She blew out a breath and tried not to hyperventilate. The atmosphere was stifling.

From across the room, Ellie felt someone's eyes on her. She shifted her vision, scanned the faces in front of her. Locked eyes with Samson. Why was he here? How did he get here before they did? She looked down at the ground and then back at Mark. He was busy with something on his phone. Back to Samson. Please, she mouthed. He put a finger over his lips, assuring her he'd be quiet. She briefly closed her eyes. Samson would keep her secret. Maybe she was safe.

"Hey, isn't that the guy we ran into over at the apartments?" Mark pointed at Samson.

"What?"

"The guy. The one who you ran into." Mark pulled her out of line and over to Samson.

"The detective-" Ellie stammered.

"We're here, he'll wait for us." Mark answered. "Didn't we see you over at the apartments? Why are you here?"

Samson pulled off the wall and stood up to his 6'7' frame. Mark's eyes narrowed.

"Who's askin'?" Samson looked at Ellie, then at Mark, and then lowered his gaze back to Ellie.

Mark looked at her then, too. "I am."

"I ain't nobody, mister, and I don't know you or her." Samson pointed at Ellie.

Ellie glanced to the left and the right.

Detective Bolivar walked out a side door and stopped between Mark and Samson. "You know each other?"

"No." Mark said.

Ellie didn't meet anyone's eyes, especially

Samson's. Or Mark's.

"Well, this fine upstanding man was the bouncer at the club your Miss Kitty worked at." Detective Bolivar placed a hand on the big man's shoulder.

Samson crossed his hands in front of him and looked directly at Ellie. "She was one of my girls. I always protect my own."

"How noble." Mark said, under his breath.

Ellie held Samson's gaze.

Please, God. I'm begging you. She didn't know Samson worked the same strip club as Kitty. He wasn't around when they first located her, thank goodness. This chance reunion would have happened sooner.

"I'll talk to you guys first and then you, big guy." The detective punched numbers into the door lock and ushered them through.

Ellie looked over her shoulder. Thank you.

Samson gave her the tiniest nod and then put his hand over his heart, a sign he'd always given her indicating she was safe with him. She was always safe with him, even now, when she wasn't his any longer.

Chapter 25

"**Really, that's all** we know." Ellie said after thirty minutes of questions and sharing information about what they'd done to find Billy.

Mark watched her talk, willed his brain to stop.

He'd seen her mouth words to the guy in the waiting room, the one they'd run into at the apartment complex. It looked like 'Thank You', but he couldn't be sure. Why would she be thanking him? When Mark looked over his shoulder at who she was sending the message to, the man had met his gaze and then looked away. He was the bouncer at the club where Kitty worked. He wasn't the one who choked him and threatened more harm if they didn't leave. So, who was this guy?

Mark stood when Ellie and the detective did, assuring them that he didn't have any additional facts than what Ellie had given him. He hadn't heard much of the exchange, of course, his head was elsewhere.

He walked silently behind her to the truck, through the throng of people still waiting to be seen. The guy was no longer in the foyer.

"Do you want me to drive?" He asked, digging

her keys out of his pocket.

"No, I can." She accepted the keys and unlocked the truck.

They sat in silence for a moment.

Ellie turned to him in the seat. "I don't think we're any closer to finding Billy."

"No." Mark stared out the windshield. He pursed his lips and avoided looking at her.

"Mark-"

"Ellie-" He stopped. He didn't know what to say. A piece was missing. Who was this Samson character? And what didn't Ellie want him to know? "Sorry, go ahead."

She reached across the console and offered her hand.

Oh. Uh-huh. A gesture of reassurance or was she indicating this was going to be a hard conversation? Nope. And yet, how could he deny her? He couldn't resist touching her. He didn't want a hard conversation, but he did want to hold her hand. Hadn't they been through enough? Begrudgingly, he put his hand in hers, hypocrite screaming inside his head. She squeezed his fingers. His stomach turned over.

She backed out of the parking lot, one hand on the wheel and the other in his.

"Wanna tell me what's wrong?"

Mark blew out a breath. "I keep thinking about Kitty and how all-consuming it was for Billy to get back to his mom. I mean, she didn't even want him." He'd get to the guy at the police station, eventually.

"How do you know that?" She kept her eyes on the driving, but he could feel the tension in her hand.

"He told the foster family that over and over. He even mentioned it to Colton."

"No, I mean about Kitty not wanting him."

"Well, she was a prostitute. How is that being a good mom?"

"Or a dancer. Maybe you don't know the full story."

"I know the full story on my mom. She was beaten by my dad, and she still protected us boys from him. Loved us, brought us up right, all while dealing with an abusive husband. She didn't toss us away. I will never understand prostitution. How can someone be so selfish and greedy that she'll do anything, including sacrificing her son, to get money?"

Ellie removed her hand from his. He instantly felt the warmth leave, and something else as well. Like he was teetering on an abyss and her hand in his was the only thing keeping them up on the ledge.

Ellie drove faster than her norm.

Had he upset her?

Trust Me.

Wasn't that what he was doing?

After a silent hour, she pulled into his drive and kept the engine running.

"Do you want to come in, say hi to Aunt Eunice?"

She shook her head. He studied her face, worry lines creasing her forehead. She swiped at tears. Was her sadness about Billy?

"Ellie, what's wrong? Did I say something wrong? Help me understand."

She turned to him, then. Tears fast-pacing down

her cheeks. "How do you have all this knowledge, this Christian walk of yours, and yet you have no grace? Zero."

What? Grace for what? Mark's brow knitted in concern. "A stripper, who sold her body to strangers, and didn't give one filthy fig for her son?" Bars started slamming down around his heart. Protect, protect, his brain screamed. "I'm not sure what you're talking about. Kitty didn't seem too concerned about Billy when we laid down money for information or bought her lunch... wait, does this have something to do with that guy... Samson... the bouncer? The one you mouthed thank you to at the station? Didn't think I saw that? Well, I did." Mark slammed the truck door. "Not sure why you didn't want me to see that. Maybe you knew him in some former life... " Mark trailed off as understanding dawned and he saw the blood leave Ellie's face. "Interesting." Mark climbed the steps to the porch.

Ellie jumped out of the truck and stomped to the bottom step. "That's right. You get it now? I was just like Kitty. I was Kitty. Just like my mom. Except I didn't have the privilege of having a son like Billy. Kitty was such a bad person in your eyes. So, what does that make me? Huh? What, Mark?"

Mark stared down at her.

Their yelling drew Aunt Eunice to the door. "What is all the fuss... oh, Ellie, it's so good..."

"Stop, Aunt Eunice. Go back inside. I'm coming in, she... is not." Mark said, harshly.

"Sorry, Eunice. Your perfect nephew thinks he's better than me, or anyone, because I've had a rough go of it and made some bad decisions along the way."

"What in the world?"

"Yeah, sorry. You know, that scripture you pointed out to me? The one about nothing separating you from God's love? Well, it's horse crap. This, this right here is what separates. You want the truth, Mark? Think you can handle it, Mark?"

Mark blanched, uncertain of what was going to come next, but her tone indicated he wasn't going to like it.

"I did know Samson. He protected me from all of the perverts that came around. He saw me as a person who deserved better and believed I just hadn't gotten my chance to get out, yet. And he's the one who introduced me to Jason, my husband, and gave me money to start a new life. With Jason. Jason, who is not you!" Ellie whirled around, jumped in the truck, rolled the window down. "And another thing, when you said you didn't care about my history, didn't want to hear it, and how I was wiped clean from all that? You're a liar."

"I've never lied in my life. You, however, have been lying this entire time. Being someone you're not. Sweet Ellie. You fooled me for a bit, but it never crossed your mind that I might find out? I wasn't lying when I said those things, but that was before I realized I never knew *you*. I only knew the *fake* you."

Her truck spun rocks as she flew down the lane. Mark watched her leave, his hands in tight fists. Trust you? Nope.

~

Ellie pulled into her driveway and shut off the engine, her hands over her face.

Why had she ever thought she could escape her

past? She hadn't been a strip club dancer for almost eight years and now here it was, back up in her face. Jason had constantly told her she was washed clean from that lifestyle when he talked about Jesus. Apparently, only Jason thought that. Mark condemned her for her past. Blindly, she'd believed Jason, had desperately wanted it to be true. Mark stole her confidence, chopped her heart up in pieces, shouted she wasn't worthy of a new life. And now that Jason was gone, she suspected God had withdrawn any favor she'd gained by listening to Jason. The truth was she would forever and always be something less than those people who claimed they were Christians. Judgy, hypocritical people who felt she could never be anything other than a dancer for men. A person like her didn't deserve good things.

Aunt Eunice told her nothing could separate her from God's love. What a crock. As if He'd ever been on her side to begin with. Maybe Jason's, but clearly not hers. Separated from God. How could you separate something if you'd never been together to begin with?

Ellie unlocked her house and patted an over-enthusiastic Magic. Sliding the newly fixed back door open so Magic could do his business, she curled up in a rocking lawn chair and stared out into the yard.

Nothing had changed in the world. The birds still sang. The squirrels chattered. Magic still chased the leaves blowing across the backyard. But, inside her heart, everything had changed. It was like winter had come early and frozen over all the good in her life. Maybe, the good was just a I. A way to control the way people looked at her, the upstanding citizen… .neighbor… friend. Maybe the ice was always there, covering, protecting. In her soul, she imagined the rocks that had fallen away, gathering themselves back to the wall that protected her heart. Maybe she was a terrible person, and Jason had been lying to her. And God? It'd always been hard to believe He accepted her as she was and not concerned about her sins. She'd gotten past the idea that the other shoe might drop after Jason's death, now it had.

Could she even go back to her job as a social worker, knowing that she was unworthy to help others, kids, out of hard places when she herself hadn't made it out of the muck? She thought she had, but Mark was proof that she hadn't. She sat down at her writing desk and wrote out a resignation letter, signed her name at the bottom, and stuck it in an envelope. She'd drop it by work on her way out.

Samson, he was the only good that had happened recently. With Mark, it had been good, but fake, she realized now. He hadn't known the real her and when he did find out, he hadn't wanted anything to do with her. She needed to see Samson, thank him in person, not just a passing word mouthed over her shoulder.

Ellie loaded Magic in the truck, dropped her resignation letter by work, gathered some of the things in the office, and drove back to northern Dallas. Hopefully, Samson would be done at the police station and back at the 24/7 club.

She pulled into the back parking lot where the

employees parked and sat staring at the back of the building. Different club, same Samson. How many times had Samson escorted her to her car in the early morning hours, threatening anyone who watched her walk out? How many times had Jason met her back there, begging her to trust him, and to step away from the club's lifestyle? As she began to see the light in his eyes when she came out on Samson's arm and the care he took of her, she started to believe she wasn't just a ministry or project for him to save. He really liked her, current work status and all.

Ellie startled when a hand banged on her window.

"Ellie?" A thin black man asked, a hood covering his head, jean jacket frayed, but clean.

"Anthony?" Ellie rolled her window down part way.

"It's me. In the flesh. What are you doing here?" Anthony gestured toward the parking lot. "Rebecca will be so happy that I saw you."

"It's a long story." She saw the concern in his eyes. "Oh no, I'm not back. I ran into Samson earlier today and he helped me out, so I wanted to thank him. What are you doing here? Is this your area now?"

"I see. We kinda follow Samson around. When the club starts I' suspicious about losing girls, he jumps to another club, and we follow. His shift doesn't normally start for a couple more hours." Anthony explained.

"You the lookout now?" Ellie asked. That had been Jason's job, watching over the parking lot, who came and went, offering help to girls that Samson deemed ready to get out or who needed a break.

"Ever since… well, you know, Jason…"

Ellie got out of the truck and hugged him. "I know."

"Hey, since you have a few hours, why don't you come see Rebecca, have dinner with us?" Anthony's wife was a fabulous cook as Ellie could attest to on several nights.

"I don't want to impose."

"Girl, you're family. You aren't imposing. You can fill us in on everything you're doing. Big things, I'm sure."

Yeah, right. Big things. Big mistakes.

Anthony gestured to a beat-up vehicle sitting in the alley. "Do you remember how to get there?"

"I'm not sure. Can I follow you?" It had been awhile. Ellie backed out of the dismal parking lot just as two young girls wrapped in furry jackets, long bare legs exposed, exited the building, their cigarette smoke trailing behind them. Ellie shivered. She saw herself in them. Tired. Hating herself. Coping the only way she knew how.

Chapter 26

Mark lay in bed, way past dawn, way past the boys coming in for breakfast.

A knock on the door. Aunt Eunice brought in a tray laden with breakfast items. "I'll come back for it later." She tip-toed out.

He needed a lock on the door. He wasn't interested in talking to anyone or eating anything. He stared at the ceiling, sheets twisted around his torso, his bare chest, sweaty.

How could he be that deceived? He was smart, observant… clearly not. He'd let a pretty blonde lady invade his carefully protected heart and wreck his head.

Betrayal, that's what this was. Ellie hid things from him, deliberately. She'd camouflaged herself, not allowing him to see the real Ellie. He'd seen a future with the woman, for Pete's sake. Fat chance. A prostitute. Not a prostitute, a stripper for certain. She trickled the truth out, but he would have figured it out eventually. Would it have been too late? How long could a relationship survive built on lies? He'd forced the confession out of her about who she really was. She hadn't been up front and honest. More like manipulative even. Keeping a secret like that from him was plain manipulative.

Mark drug himself from the bed, showered and put on work clothes. Not that he planned to do anything constructive today. He picked up the untouched tray and returned it to the kitchen.

With a snort, Aunt Eunice wrapped up the breakfast items and put them in the fridge.

Mark leaned on a counter. "Something wrong?" His surly mood was ready for this.

"I asked you to protect her heart." Aunt Eunice exclaimed.

"Which Ellie? The widow or the stripper?"

"She's one and the same, Mark." Aunt Eunice slammed a dirty dish into the sink, "if you'd see that through Jesus' eyes."

"She lied to me." he yelled.

"No, she didn't. She protected herself. Out of fear. Fear that you'd act just like you are now." Aunt Eunice pulled chicken breasts out of the fridge, wrapped them in cellophane, and began pounding them into thin pieces. "She isn't perfect. And, quite frankly, neither are you."

"What about my heart? She lied to me."

"Don't be selfish, it's unbecoming. Tell me, Mark, were you ever to a point where she could trust you with her past? No, you were not. And for good reason, apparently. The good Lord knew what He was doing when He allowed this whole relationship to blow up in your face."

Mark took a step back, shocked. Aunt Eunice had never spoken to him in that tone.

"You vowed to me that you would protect her heart."

"I clearly never had her heart if she was keeping things like this from me."

Silently, Aunt Eunice placed the chicken in a casserole dish and moved it to the fridge. Stalking over to her side of the house, she turned for one last glare, and then slammed the dividing door.

Now Aunt Eunice was mad at him, too.

"I'm going to the barn if anyone cares." He yelled.

Silence.

He flung the door shut behind him.

This was shaping up to be a perfect day. He never should have gotten out of bed.

He mucked out the stalls that were again gross, cussed Billy for leaving and starting this whole thing, and managed to break a shovel. The metal part broke away from the wooden handle causing Mark to fall off balance into the pile of manure he'd just picked up. He threw the metal scoop just as Colton entered.

Colton ducked, narrowly missing the splinters as they ricocheted off the barn wall and gave him an icy look. "Whoa, man."

Mark let loose a string of expletives.

Colton crossed his arms. "You done?"

"Maybe, maybe not. What's it to you?"

Colton pointed to the broken shovel. "I meant with that. Clearly, I don't care about the words that come out of your mouth."

Mark stopped his tirade and looked at him.

"I mean, your hissy fit doesn't bother me, and your words? They don't carry much weight with me either, right now."

"You heard me yelling at Aunt Eunice." Mark's

shoulders slumped.

"And your words to Ellie." Colton added. "They were pretty harsh."

"Any grand words of wisdom?"

"Shut your mouth, comes to mind. Or act your age. Or here's one for you, love your family and friends like you do *yourself*."

Mark glared at him. "It's neighbor, love your neighbor."

Colton squinted at him.

"Finish that verse. Go ahead, finish it." Colton stepped toward him.

This was exactly what Mark needed, a good argument, an opportunity to blow off the tension building in his body. Come'on Colton, let's go.

"It's 'love your neighbor like you do yourself'." Mark met him halfway.

"You are so pig headed. You love yourself and your perfect little world so much, it's disgusting. Grow up. You're not perfect, and you don't deserve someone like Ellie. Maybe I should sit down and have dinner with her, show her she picked the wrong brother."

Mark roared and closed the remaining space between them. Toe to toe, eye to eye. He rounded his fist, took a step back, and swung on Colton, connecting with his jaw.

Colton leaned in, punched him in the gut, knocking the wind out of him.

Mark doubled over.

Colton tackled him to the floor.

"Stop it!" Brandon rushed into the barn. Much stockier and heavier than Mark, Colton sat on his brother, fist cocked, ready to smash his nose in, split it wide open again. Brandon hauled Colton off, both of them falling into a hay bale in the middle of the alleyway. Brandon pointed at Mark. "Stay down."

Mark wiped his nose, a trickle of blood on his hand.

"What is going on?" Brandon used Colton's shoulder to push to a standing position. "I came around the corner and you two are brawling like a couple of idiots."

"My brother *is* an idiot." Colton stood and reached over to help Mark up.

Mark refused. "You said you were interested in Ellie-"

Colton blew a raspberry at him. "I did not. Basically, I said I was much more in tune with what she has gone through than you in your perfect little world."

"You *did*. You know my life hasn't been perfect. And you can't possibly know what she's gone through, because *I* just found out."

"Oh, that she has a past? I have a past, Mark. What of it?"

"I know yours. She lied about hers."

"Did she really? Or was she keeping it from you because she knew you'd respond this way? You are so shallow."

That's funny. The second time he'd heard that in less than an hour.

"She was disrespectful."

"Like Dad?"

No. Maybe. Their father was far more than disrespectful. He was mean.

"I think *you* disrespected her." Colton crossed his arms again.

Brandon frowned.

"Who, Mom? I would never-"

"No, Ellie, you idiot."

"How? She was a stripper and didn't tell me." Mark spat the words out like poison on his tongue. Mark snorted.

"She's one now?" At Mark's head shaking, Colton added. "Oh, at some point in her life, she made bad decisions and did bad things, and you're punishing her now?"

Punishing her? Was he?

"Who died and made you God, O self-righteous one?"

\Self-righteous? Mark stared at the floor.

"She should pay for the past forever, and you're the person to dole out the punishment? She was clearly someone different *then*."

"I could never- Knowing she had-"

"Isn't she a Christian? So, God has forgiven you, but you can't forgive her? Hypocrite."

Hypocrite.

Brandon pulled up a hay bale and sat down next to Mark, their back up against the base of a stall. "I think it goes a little deeper than that even."

Both Colton and Mark looked at him.

"Could be wrong, but I think Billy running away has really thrown you for a loop."

"You think?" Mark drug his fingers through the straw and the dirt.

"Like it was your fault." Colton contributed.

"Wasn't my fault, but he was my responsibility.

Don't you get it? I failed. And if I failed at that, what else am I failing at? Huh? Clearly relationships should be added to the list. Maybe I should just quit this business, turn the ranch into a goat farm. I've fooled everyone into believing I'm capable of running a ministry for troubled boys, of which I'm not. No one will ever believe I can do this."

Colton whistled. "So, one mistake will forever ruin you to be anything other than a failure?"

Mark looked at his brother. He *was* a hypocrite.

~

"Rebecca, this is so good. I have missed your soup." Ellie dipped crusty bread into the cheesy potato soup. Their four-person table had seen better days, but it fit perfectly with the cozy kitchen. Warm sunflowers in hues of reds and golds were on potholders, curtains, glassware, making the room sing with sunshine. Being with these friends of old, in their safe place, lightened her mood. She could, would, put the ugliness of her conversation with Mark on a back burner. Ellie rolled her shoulders, praying the knot would release soon.

"Tell me, what did you want to thank Samson for?" Anthony smiled gently at her, his thin, arthritic-knotted fingers laced in front of him, his chocolate brown eyes seeing far too much. Rebecca patted him on the shoulder and cleared the table.

It had been a long time since Ellie had seen either of them, and yet, she let down her guard and swallowed, tears threatening. Ellie looked into Anthony's wise face, glanced at Rebecca. The woman was a saint, feeding everyone who crossed their door stoop, calming rough waters, listening to all.

Ellie took a deep breath and started at the beginning. She bared it all, laid every sordid fact and emotion on the table. Never once did she read anything, but compassion on Anthony's face. Rebecca, however, clucked her tongue at some of the details, like Mark's attempt at a picnic in the barn, cozy despite the pouring rain. Ellie chipped at her fingernails, refusing to gloss over anything. Anger at Mark, God, herself. Shame of her past. Vulnerability in believing Jason, for thinking Mark would actually like her.

"Girlie, that is some story." Anthony winked at Rebecca as she handed him a mug of hot coffee. Rebecca gave Ellie one as well and then added sugar and creamer to the table.

"I know, right? And now I'm here."

"What are you going to do?" Rebecca sat down next to Ellie.

"I don't know. I quit my job, so I'll have to find something to do that I qualify for." Ellie ticked off skills. "Babysitter, answering the phone, writing reports, collecting money, prostitution."

Anthony rolled his eyes. "Whoa girl, you were never a prostitute. Let's call it what it was. You danced for money to make ends meet because your momma danced. That doesn't spell prostitute."

"What about all the good you did with Jason?" Rebecca added.

"That was Jason. I was along for the ride." Ellie chewed her lip.

"Nonsense. Some of those girls didn't trust Jason's offer to help, and they were plain scared of my old, black butt. But they trusted you. Because you proved they could get out of that lifestyle if they wanted. That was you."

"What about God, honey? What's he speaking to you lately?" Rebecca asked.

Ellie looked at her, thoughts tumbling. Speaking to me? Silence. Nothing. "Since Jason died…"

"Ah, honey, you thought God left, too?" Rebecca pulled her into a side hug. Rebecca's ample bosom perfect for the next onslaught of tears. "There now, child."

Anthony waited until her sobbing slowed. "You know I don't mince words."

"Always the truth. I know."

"When Samson first said to Jason, 'I got one for you, she needs to be out, she needs Jesus,' Jason said 'point her out, let's go.'" Anthony coughed into his hand and looked apologetically at Rebecca.

Ellie lifted concerned eyes to him. Oh no. Was Anthony sick?

"A cough, that's all it was." Anthony patted Ellie's hand.

Still, there was something much more serious that passed in the look between him and his wife.

"Anyways, Jason waited for you and was instantly smitten. He thought you were the most beautiful thing that had walked into his life. He mentioned more than once how he was going to marry you someday."

"He even spoke those words to me when he was living here at this house." Rebecca included.

Ellie had forgotten that Jason stayed with them to be closer to his ministry work.

"You know what I told him? Don't you go marrying that girl," He paused as Ellie raised her eyebrows.

"Because I was hopeless?" She couldn't believe her ears. Mark was right, she didn't deserve happiness. Ellie felt her heart break. Jason *had* married her as a project.

"Yes." Anthony raised a hand as if he could stop her thoughts from spiraling.

Too late.

"You needed Jesus more than you needed Jason." Anthony said, quietly.

"I knew Jesus because of Jason."

"You've got it backwards. You were first written on the heart of God. He's the one that put Jason in your path. You could have been at any club, other than that one, and never met Jason. God wanted you to be at the club where Samson was and therefore, where we were. Our ministry hadn't targeted any other club yet, because we didn't have an inside man like Samson."

"Let me get this straight. I was in that place because God wanted me there? That's reassuring."

"We all got free will. You were doing what you thought you needed to."

"So, why did Jason marry me then, if you said he shouldn't?"

"If I remember correctly, you became as sold out for Jesus as Jason was which simply made you ten times more attractive."

"I wasn't a project?"

Rebecca chortled. "Heaven's no, girl. Jason was so in love with you. It took every ounce of strength I had to hold him back until *you* knew how much Jesus loved you more."

Oh.

Ellie had felt closer to Jesus in those early years after meeting Jason. Because of that feeling, she'd immersed herself in the ministry of saving other girls like herself with Jason and Anthony and Rebecca. She certainly didn't feel that closeness now.

"I need some time." Ellie stood, abruptly.

"Time for what?" Anthony and Rebecca stood, too.

"To figure out my next steps. I'd better go if I'm going to catch Samson before the evening crowd comes in."

"I have a thought. Why don't you stay with us for a couple of days? Get your feet back under you." Rebecca asked.

"Oh, I couldn't do that. I've got Magic… and…" Ellie stuttered.

A time out sounded amazing, though. Just set the world aside for a bit.

"We have a spare bedroom. A couple days. Get some rest and Lord knows, it's quiet here. And your dog is welcome, too. It'd be nice having a pet in the house again, wouldn't it?"

"Let me go talk to Samson. I promise I'll think about it." Ellie hugged both of them and kissed Rebecca's leathery cheek. "Thank you. I'll call you when I decide."

Anthony put his hand over his heart and patted his chest. Like Samson had. She knew she had their heart.

Chapter 27

Two weeks later

A loud buzzer sounded through the house.

"Mark, there's someone at the gate." Aunt Eunice hollered from the kitchen.

"I see them. Thanks, Aunt Eunice." Mark put down the book he was reading in his office. He was absorbed by the book, finding the author to be direct and unrelenting when it came to Godly men's responsibility regarding life, relationships, and work. He could only read one chapter at a time, needing space to let the writer's words soak in. More than once, he'd been moved to tears by how inadequate he felt and the complexity of mistakes he'd made. Thankfully, the author also taught grace. After the initial feeling of failure, there was the encouragement to be better. A better friend, a better person, a better man. With Colton and Ellie's words ringing in his ears about how hypocritical he was, Mark vowed to be better, to do things differently. Not for Ellie's sake, he hadn't heard from her for weeks, but rather his own. *He* needed to be a better version of himself.

"Hello? What can I do for you?" Mark said into the microphone attached to the speaker at the gate.

"Good morning." A nicely dressed older man stepped out of his vehicle and stooped over the gate speaker, clearly unfamiliar with the gadget. "I'm looking for Mark Bruens. Does he live here?"

Mark hesitated. "What can I do for you?"

"I'm here regarding Billy Kramer."

"I'm sorry, who are you?"

"Terribly sorry, I should have stated that first. I'm Billy's case manager, and I wanted to talk to you a bit about his disappearance."

"Do you have any ID?" He knew Ellie had been tossed off Billy's case, and it stood to reason that someone else had been assigned. But why didn't Ellie tell him? Because he ticked her off by being such an idiot that she was no longer talking to him, that's why. Still would have been nice to hear it from her.

"Certainly." The man pulled an ID out of his wallet and held it up facing the house.

Mark snorted. "Can you hold it facing the camera, please?"

"Technology…going to get the best of me…" He placed the card almost directly on the camera.

Mark was able to make out the state ensign, the man's name, and the authoritative title. "Come on up the lane to the ranch house."

"Thank you." The man stepped back into his vehicle and drove as directed.

Mark watched him unfold from his car and offered his hand. The man shook it with confidence.

"We'll sit inside. Aunt Eunice, can you put on

some coffee?" He led the man to the dining room table.

"What's this about?" Mark's gut tightened. They were no closer to finding Billy than before, he wouldn't have much to offer.

"Again, I'm his case manager, Earl Rogers," the man started.

"Have you talked to Ellie?" Mark interrupted, as Aunt Eunice placed steaming cups of coffee in front of them along with a plate full of homemade granola bars. Her sidelong glance asked the same thing.

"Mrs. Jenkins? No, I have not. She is no longer with the organization." Earl smiled his thanks at Aunt Eunice. "Now, I do want to talk to you about Billy, but I also have some questions for the other boys who are staying here. Can you make those arrangements for me?"

Mark felt the knot in his chest tighten. Ellie was no longer with the organization? Why? Where was she? He met Aunt Eunice's eyes. Ellie was so good at her job, helping the kids whose paths she crossed. Surely, she hadn't left because of him. His heart clenched. What if she had? Solely based on his words and lack of grace and understanding. *Lord, please. In spite of me, please take care of her. She's not the one for me, but she's still a human being that You love. Don't let me be the cause of her turning away from You. Please.*

If…if she's not the one for me. Because she could be, if he could get past his own jacked-up mindset.

"Yes, of course." Mark agreed, half-heartedly.

Earl asked random questions, confirmed the

reports, all the way back to the initial drop-in by Billy's father. Mark answered what he could. Vague about what happened after finding Billy's dad dead in the motel and unsure how much trouble Ellie could get in since she'd been ordered off the case. Which if she didn't work there any longer, maybe she wouldn't get into any trouble? He'd done enough, he wouldn't take the chance of doing her any more harm.

"Okay, let's have a go at the boys."

"It might be easier to go out to the bunkhouse, so you can talk to them in their living space." Mark stood.

"Of course."

Mark led the way out the back door, through the fenced yard, and into the bunkhouse.

"Are the boys locked in at night?" Earl asked.

"No, this isn't jail. The step before jail."

"But you have security cameras."

"Yes, I need to know that everyone's safe and no one from the outside has come onto the grounds without my knowledge. The boys all know that if they leave here unescorted and without permission that when, or if, they're found, they'll go straight to juvenile detention. They all understand those consequences."

Mark rounded up the boys by ringing a large bell outside the bunkhouse. "We usually use this for meals, but occasionally for other things."

They watched the boys come from various parts of the property, most from a side room on the bunkhouse used for academics. Brynleigh, Colton's finance and the boys' teacher for various subjects, popped her head out of the room.

Mark forced a smile at her and informed the boys who Earl was and what to expect. All of the boys were solemn and cautious. Mark ducked into the room with Brynleigh to give Earl some privacy without being too far away.

"He's here to see if any of the other boys want to leave like Billy did." Mark explained to Brynleigh. "You know, to see if I'm going to fail them, too." He put his head down on one of the plastic tables that was full of books and wooden pieces of a project one of the boys was working on.

"Hey, Mark? That's pretty cynical. This probably has nothing to do with you and is standard procedure. Don't jump to conclusions. In fact, come here," She motioned him to the open door. "Listen…"

She was right. Numerous times, he assumed everything reverted back to himself, when nine times out of ten, it had nothing to do with him. He could now add narcissism on top of lacking grace. Mark shook his head. He would forever be trying to undo the negative thoughts that floated through his head four million, two hundred and seventy-five times a day.

Mark stepped to the other side of the door frame from Brynleigh. The youngest of the boys was in tears talking with the case manager. Mark released a shuttered breath. He would do anything for these kids. His biggest desire was always to see them grow into their own potential and to navigate away from behaviors, learned or situational, that landed them where they were.

"And Mr. Mark helps me when I get angry. He doesn't judge…"

Mark's heart lurched. Yes, he did. Just not with the boys. Why couldn't he do that with adults? Specifically Ellie? He knew why. He wanted to appear perfect, despite knowing he wasn't, and wanted respect from his peers. How could he respect Ellie knowing what he did about her? Ugh. She deserved respect, just like everyone else. *He* was the louse.

"Sounds like the kids view you a little differently than you do yourself." Brynleigh tip-toed away from the door and left him to listen to the other boys talk to Earl.

Mark groaned and wiped his nose. Every single one of the boys mentioned God and how Mr. Mark was teaching them how to follow Jesus. He didn't deserve any one of these kids. Maybe that was the part of grace he didn't understand. He believed God was sovereign so it wasn't a stretch to believe that each of the boys were sent to his ranch purposefully, even Billy. He was constantly humbled by how much they taught him.

He wished he could share this newly-discovered knowledge with Ellie. He was so wrong in how he'd treated her, how little grace he'd shown, how arrogant he was to believe he was better than her. Here in the space of weeks, she had done the same thing. Opened up thoughts on how selfish he was, how misguided his intentions were, how lost he really was. Mark leaned his head up against the door frame and closed his eyes. Ellie…

After Earl left, satisfied that all was fine at the

ranch, Mark hurriedly donned a jacket and left, too. He'd drive by her house, see if she'd talk to him, beg her to. He was so stupid. Had been all along. Wanted her to know, he was changing, growing. Wanted her to know he saw her like Jesus did, and nothing else mattered.

Clouds raced in again, threatening to drop rain at any second. The wind whipped his truck around. Mark pulled onto her street. His heart pounded. What if she didn't believe him? She had to. He needed her. Not the other way around. Her confidence in him and the gentle way she approached him, her own strength took his breath away. He needed her.

And, if he were being honest, he wanted to be those things and more for her. Her safe spot with no judgment. Shoot, he'd already ruined that. But maybe, with God's help, he could turn that around. He wanted to be her rock. He needed her to know she could tell him anything, no matter how ugly or embarrassing, and he wouldn't leave. They needed each other.

The clouds unleashed a downpour as Mark pulled into her driveway and hit the brakes. Was that a sign in her yard? He could hardly see through the windshield. As the defogger cleared the glass, he made out bold black and white letters that made him feel sick to his stomach. SOLD.

~

Ellie struggled to get up and start the day. Just ten more minutes. She thought back over the last couple of weeks. Watching Anthony and Rebecca continue the SAFE ministry, ministering to strip club dancers and the prostitutes on the corners, Ellie remembered how grateful she'd been to leave that lifestyle and to be surrounded by people who cared about her. Despite the voices battling in her head, telling her she wasn't worthy to help someone else, she tagged along with Anthony, hoping for opportunities that would prove differently. They had stayed out much later than normal last night, falling into bed way past 4am.

Around 2 a.m., Samson had signaled to them out the back door. A dancer was being seriously harassed by some drunk college kids, and while he gave them the boot out the front, Samson was concerned for the girl. With whispered encouragement from Anthony, Ellie waited for Samson to open the locked security door and rushed into the back room. The dancer, probably a teenager, sat crying in front of her makeup mirror. The rest of the dancers skirted around her, sympathetic. The show must go on or there would be consequences. The others turned a blind eye to Ellie, allowing her to console the girl. She spoke quietly, assured her she wanted to help.

An older woman, with makeup caked on her face, had crouched next to Ellie at the girl's feet. "Clara, this business isn't for you. You need to take her offer."

The woman left as quickly as she'd come and redirected a hard-looking man away from the dressing room.

"I have to finish this shift. I'll meet you tomorrow." Clara promised.

Ellie took a sigh of relief and used the same door Samson let her in through. Her heart skipped erratically as she met with Anthony and told him what had happened. Clara was just one girl, but if she could help others, then everything was worth it. She had a purpose again.

Ellie swung her legs over the bed and for the umpteenth time looked at Jason's Bible sitting on the bed stand. After selling her house, she'd agreed to stay with Anthony and Rebecca until she figured out her living arrangements. She'd slept on the couch the first couple of nights, unwilling to sleep in the bedroom Jason had occupied before they were married.

Oh Jason.

She picked up the Bible. Jason's neat handwriting greeted her on small slips of paper that fluttered to the large rectangle rug as she paged through it. He hadn't shirked writing in the margins, either. Blue, black ink, and yellow highlighting graced the pages. Ellie let the tears fall. Jason had loved his Bible, loved his God, loved her.

She was captivated by the verses he had underlined.

The Lord is my strength and my shield, in Him, my heart trusts.

May the God of hope, fill you with all understanding…

Ellie used her shirt to wipe her face. This was where Jason gained his strength, strength to do what he felt was right, how to treat the people God loved. All of them. Jason was steadfast, unwavering, in his determination to turn people to Jesus.

Someone softly knocked at her bedroom door.

"Come in." Ellie wrapped the comforter around her shoulders.

"I wasn't sure you'd be up, yet." Rebecca came into the room. "I made pancakes, but I can warm them up later for you, if you'd like." She glanced at the Bible in Ellie's hands. "He always had that big old Bible with him."

Ellie leaned down and picked up some of the scraps of paper. "Funny, Mark's aunt tried to get me to believe this one. Really hard, though."

Rebecca sat down on the edge of the bed. "Which one?"

"The one about how nothing can separate you from God's love. I'm pretty sure I've already done that. Separated myself." At the look on Rebecca's face, she continued. "I know God loves me, I think. Oh, I don't really. Sometimes, I think He tolerated me because of Jason."

"Child..." Rebecca put her bony hand on Ellie's. "God loves you for you. Not Jason. Jason was just the instrument to get you to Him."

"How do you know that?"

"Because I know God. I know who He is. I know what He promises in the good book." Rebecca took the Bible in her own hands, rubbing the worn cover. "Ellie, He wants you to know Him, too."

"I don't know how to do that. I only know what Jason told me." Ellie shook her head. She thought she did at one time, but the feeling faded, and the whispers choked out the feelings.

"It's time, then. Read that verse again, about God's love and how there's nothing you can do to stop Him from loving you."

"I appreciate you, I really do, but you don't know what I've done. I'm sure you can suspect, or

Jason may have told you some of it…" Ellie drifted off. All she wanted to do was hide under the covers, not lay bare her past before this kind old lady.

"Let me ask you something," Rebecca put a warm arm around Ellie, "do you love these girls you're helping?"

"Sure. I want to help them in any way possible."

"But do you know them? Really know them?"

"Of course not. Sometimes I hear their stories, but do I really know them? No." Ellie looked at Rebecca. "Oh, I get it. God does know me and still loves me."

Rebecca nodded. "God loves you with or without Jason." Rebecca flipped open the Bible to Romans. "Let's read it again, in a different way. Start here." She put a gnarled finger under Chapter 8, verse 35.

Ellie began to read. "Can anything ever separate us…"

"Me, can anything ever separate me," Rebecca interrupted.

Ellie started over, "Can anything ever separate me from Christ's love? Does it mean He no longer loves us…me…if I have trouble or calamity, or are persecuted, or hungry, or destitute, or in danger, or threatened with death?" Tears slid down her face.

"Keep going, child."

"No, despite all these things, overwhelming victory is ours…mine… through Christ, who loved us."

"Do you see Jason's name in there?" Rebecca waited for a response.

"Yes, and mine." Ellie whispered.

"And Mark's." Rebecca held Ellie's hand.

Ellie continued to read. "Neither death nor life, neither angels nor demons, neither my fears for today nor my worries about tomorrow – not even the powers of hell can separate me from God's love. No power in the sky above or in the earth below – indeed, nothing in all creation will ever be able to separate me from the love of God that is revealed in Christ Jesus our Lord."

Huh. She'd let her thoughts get all twisted up. She was still the same Ellie and had the same strength Jason relied on within her grasp, despite what Mark said. She believed the Bible was true, she'd just never inserted her name as the recipient of His complete and perfect love. It was always Jason and his love for her that connected her to God. Like a dot-to-dot coloring page, she was always one, or two or three, steps away from the starting dot. And yet, the verse spoke to her specifically. How amazing that she could experience that love firsthand, not just through Jason. Her thoughts about herself were no match for the love revealed in those verses.

Ellie hugged her and wept.

"Now about Mark…" Rebecca stood. "I know he said some harsh things, but he's going to make mistakes, and you have to forgive him. I didn't say marry him, I just said forgive. Don't let your grief over Jason ruin what might have been good with Mark. Give it a little time."

"I don't know. I've pretty much cut all ties with him."

"Well, the good Lord knows. What are your plans for the rest of the day?"

"Clara, one of the girls Anthony and I talked with last night, wants to meet today."

"Be careful." Rebecca said over her shoulder. "And come get pancakes."

After a shower and a couple of bites of breakfast, Ellie left the house to meet Clara. The clouds were still out, and a cool breeze skittered leaves across her path. The coffee shop they'd agreed to meet at was around the corner from the club, in an out of the way, off the strip low building. Ellie had never been there; however, Anthony knew the owners and agreed it was a safe place to meet.

The quaint decor and friendly owners ushered her in. While she chose a drink, she noticed Clara slide in, at least she thought it was her. The large sunglasses and huge scarf covered most of her face and head.

"Clara?" Ellie turned to her.

Clara removed the scarf. "Yes, it's me."

"Oh good. What can I get you?" Ellie motioned to the wide range of beverages, both hot and cold.

"Something hot and sweet, but you don't have to get it. I can pay."

"Oh, it's my treat."

Ellie felt, rather than heard, the rush of air flow out of the shop when the door opened. She made eye contact with the barista, who was backing up into a smaller room behind the counter. Fear raced up Ellie's spine. She could hear Clara's sharp intake of breath. Other patrons in the store hit the floor and hid under tables.

"Don't turn around." An evil-laced voice behind her shouted. A gun was jammed into Ellie's back, the cold metal sitting right at her kidneys.

"You're coming with me."

Clara screamed.

Ellie twisted away from the gun and tried to reach out to her.

"Run!" Ellie shrieked.

Clara made it to the door.

Boom.

Boom.

Ellie felt the white-hot sear through her shirt and watched as Clara crumbled before her, a blood stain spreading quickly from Clara's chest. Ellie dropped to her knees.

Chapter 28

Restless, unable to get the sold sign from flashing in his mind, Mark lit into physical labor when he returned home. He tried Ellie's number again for the billionth time. Just the automated message saying the number was no longer in service. The rain clouds backed off, leaving puddles in places. Work on the ranch was never done, and he needed to work. Shut down the thought that Ellie was gone for good. She'd packed up and left without... without what? What had he expected? After their last conversation? His plan was to work until exhaustion took over, so he could sleep without thoughts of Ellie swirling.

His cell phone rang as he pitched fresh hay into the goat pen. The same unknown number had come through a couple of times, and he refrained from picking it up. He didn't need new windows, to enter into a scam sweepstakes, or give to any charities. He might as well get rid of the caller before they called a dozen more times. "Hello?"

"Mr. Mark?" the timid voice said over the phone.

"Billy?" Mark dropped his phone, scrambled to pick it up before one of the goats ate it. They were already crowding around him, curious, feet making sucking sounds in the marshy ground. He listened to the hiccups on the line.

Billy calling never occurred to him. Foolishness. He'd been praying every day for some breakthrough with Billy, a sign he was alright, but he hadn't been expecting Billy to call. The kid didn't have a cell phone while he was at the ranch.

"Mr. Mark? I want to come home."

Oh my.

Mark ran into the barn, nearly knocking Colton down.

Mark mouthed "Billy" and pointed to his phone.

"Billy, where are you? I'll come get you, tell me where you are." Mark shouted into the phone.

"Stop shouting." Colton thumped him on the shoulder.

"Is that- is that Colton?"

"It is. Tell him where you are." Mark passed the phone to his brother, putting it on speaker so they both could hear.

"Hey. Are you okay? Safe?" Colton asked.

Mark pinched the bridge of his nose. *Please God, please let him be safe.*

"I want to come home."

Mark heard the tears in Billy's voice. They matched his own.

"We'll come get you, just tell us where you are." Colton eased.

"I don't know where."

Mark grabbed the phone back. "Do you see any

landmarks? Any gas stations? Who's phone are you calling on?"

"The lady I was staying with. It's her phone. She said I could use it to get back to the ranch, and I tried to hitchhike part of the way, because I didn't know if you'd come get me. The driver left me."

Mark and Colton exchanged worried glances. Hitchhiked?

"Are you at a gas station now? Or a truck stop?"

"There's a lake close by. I'm in a pancake place."

"Are you still in the Dallas area?"

"I think so."

Colton pulled up a map of Dallas and pointed to a large truck stop, one that catered to semis, near a corner of a lake.

"Billy, can you ask a waitress or somebody nearby?"

They could hear Billy's muffled question to a person on his end.

"I asked a mom eating with her kids. She looked safe."

Mark closed his eyes. How much had Billy gone through since he left? He knew down in his soul that Billy hadn't killed his father or the other man in the hotel room. Might have seen him killed, though. *Lord?*

"What did she say?" Mark urged.

"She said I'm in an IHOP. There's a lake nearby and an arbo- arborat- I don't know how to say it."

"Arboretum?"

"Yes, that."

Colton widened the map with his fingers and

searched for an arboretum, restaurants nearby. "There's an IHOP right there. That's got to be where he's at."

"Billy, we're coming for you. Don't move, okay? If you need to eat something, go ahead and order. I'll pay for it when we get there." Mark ran after Colton to his truck.

"I have money." Billy said, quietly.

Mark hesitated. Billy had money? The casino payout from the hotel?

"Am I going to jail, Mr. Mark?"

"We'll talk about that later. Not if I can help it." Mark wouldn't make promises. "We'll be there in about thirty minutes, just stay put. Please."

"Okay. Just you and Colton, right?"

"Yes, and we're in Colton's big truck. Do you remember what it looks like?"

"Yes. Okay."

Mark hung up the call. "Colton-"

"I know. We'll deal with whatever after we make sure he's safe." Colton spun out of the driveway. "Call Aunt Eunice and ask her to pray. And tell her why we left."

Ellie should be a part of this. Mark pulled out his phone and dialed her number again. He wanted to throw the phone out the window when he received the same "this number is no longer in service" message as before. How he wished he knew where she was.

Twenty minutes later, they pulled into the IHOP and could see Billy inside, watching out the window.

"Thank God. Billy, we were so worried." Mark pulled him into an embrace that had both of them crying. Colton hugged him next.

"I'm sorry."

Mark sat in the booth next to him and handed him a napkin. Billy was crying in earnest now, and other patrons started to look their way.

"I thought my dad had news about my mom, and I knew you turned him away, so I went to him," Billy paused as the waitress came over to the booth.

"Everything okay, here? You boys want anything? Coffee?" An older woman looked at the three of them with concern in her eyes.

Both Colton and Mark shook their heads at the food offer.

"The bill, then?"

"Yes, please."

A good Samaritan, for certain, concerned for Billy.

"Billy, do you still have your hearing aids?" Mark had so many questions for him, his physical well-being down the line, but the easiest to assess.

"No." The boy solemnly met Mark's gaze. "I threw them away. I'm sorry."

"It's not a problem." Mark could see the darkness in his eyes. The emotional toll the weeks away had taken. His heart hurt for the boy.

"Billy, what happened at the motel?" Colton asked, gently.

Billy raised sad eyes at him. "My dad was drunk and couldn't remember why he'd come out to the ranch in the first place. When I asked about Mom, he started calling her names and then passed out. I woke him up when two guys broke into the room. I think my dad may have hurt one of them. I grabbed my backpack and my dad's and ran out the door. I knew the police were coming, and I'd be in trouble for leaving the ranch."

Mark looked at Colton, a warning in his eyes. "So, that's all you know about the motel?"

"Yes, why? Did my dad hurt that guy? They were trying to rob us, he can't get in trouble for self-defense, can he?" Billy started to cry again.

No, especially when his dad was dead.

"I didn't know about the money in my dad's backpack until later. I thought he might have food stashed in there."

Great. Billy did have the money but wasn't aware of the bloody scene he'd escaped from. What were they going to do now?

"I think I found my mom, though." Hopefulness showed on his face. "She lives next door to the lady who said I could stay with her until my mom got home. The crazy cat lady, although she's really not crazy. Mom never did, though, and I waited long enough."

What? He and Ellie had talked to a crazy cat lady next door to where Billy's mom died. Did Billy know his mom was dead? Both parents? The detective mentioned the crazy lady said there was a boy waiting outside the apartment. Could that have been Billy, like Ellie thought? Ellie, where are you? We should be doing this together.

"I think I know where that is." Mark shrugged his shoulders at his brother's questioning look.

"Of all the crazy cat ladies there probably are in all of Dallas, you think you might know where *this* one lives?" Colton blurted.

"I do." Please, I'll tell you later, he said with his eyes.

"Can we take her phone back to her?" Billy sat up in the booth.

"We can."

"Am I going to jail?"

"Let's get the phone back to her first." Mark put his arm around Billy. "On second thought, Billy, I think we should let your case manager know about all of this."

"Ms. Jenkins? Why? You said I wouldn't be going to jail?" Billy cried.

Mark glanced at Colton.

"I didn't say that. I said we'd figure it out together." Mark put an arm around him. "You have a new case manager now. Ms. Jenkins is somewhere else, but I've met your new one and he was worried about you, too. We'll call him and find out what the next steps are."

"But what if he wants you to turn me in?"

"I'll still be with you every step of the way. Right now, all he's aware of is that you left the ranch without permission." Mark refused to look at Colton. There was more… like three dead bodies, but the facts only pointed to leaving without permission. Everything else would need to be proven in court.

~

Ellie heard the jingling of the bell above the coffee shop door. Someone had left, then multiple people scurried around her, rushing free of the shop.

Quiet. No sound except for her own labored breathing.

"Clara? Anybody?" Ellie tried to sit up, hand on

her side, watching blood drip through her fingers.

The barista crept out of the back room and knelt down beside her. "Shhh…stay down. I've called the cops, not sure if they'll come or not." She pushed a dish rag into Ellie's hands. "Use this."

"Thought this place was safe." Ellie turned her body, so she could see the front door. "Clara?"

The barista moved in front of her, blocking her view. Ellie could see the soles of Clara's shoes, unmoving. Was Clara dead? Unconscious? Why wasn't she moving?

"Clara!" Ellie covered her face, leaving bloody hand marks on her chin and cheeks. An avalanche of tears unleashed, and she gasped for breath.

"Lady, you gotta calm down. You're making it bleed more."

Ellie lay back on the floor and stared at the sneakers by the door. She could just shut her eyes and drift off… wouldn't that be glorious? To leave this world behind, to see Jason again. *Oh Lord.* Mark's face floated in front of her eyes. She'd never see Mark again, though. Fight to live or fight to die? One would be much easier. She could feel the stickiness on her fingers, her life leaking out onto the dirty floor.

She opened her eyes when an EMT put an oxygen mask on her, pulling her hair in the elastic. *Lord, please help me.* Another uniformed man slid a stretcher under her side, lifted her gently, and then rocked her onto the sterile cot. 1… 2… 3 one of the men counted, and she was lifted and taken outside to an ambulance. She didn't miss the brief zig zag in the EMT's pathway to the door, avoiding Clara on the floor. Ellie couldn't see her, but the fact that she'd received medical attention first… there wasn't any reason to help Clara. Clara was dead.

Lord Jesus. Why? Had someone heard that she and Clara were meeting today, afraid she'd pull her away from dancing? That they'd lose money without Clara working? But why kill her? What good did that do? God? She was so close to getting her out, to helping her be free of that lifestyle. Clara had wanted that, too, right?

"Ellie, can you hear me? Is there anyone I can call? Anyone at all? Family?"

Ellie's eyes fluttered open and she stared at the kind man. How did he know her name? He had been gently talking to her, telling her every step he was taking to keep her alive. This is going to pinch, you're going to feel a rush of warmth through your body, you're doing great.

Emergency contact. No one. She had no one to call. Wait, Anthony and Rebecca should be called. They'd worry if she didn't return. Ellie moved the oxygen mask askew. "My purse." She squeaked out and then gritted her teeth as a wave of pain rolled over her.

The EMT heard her and rifled through her purse. She never kept much cash or any credit cards on her for fear of being robbed. The EMT held up the one business card she stashed in her wallet. She nodded at him. God bless Anthony for making up cards for her to pass out that had the ministry's name on it, his name, the church's address, and a burner phone number that couldn't be traced back to his and Rebecca's home.

The EMT assured her that he'd give the card to the nurse and have Anthony contacted once they reached the hospital.

Ellie sunk down into the darkness and let the pain medication float her away.

Chapter 29

Two days later

"Colton, I've got to take that phone back to the crazy cat lady. Billy keeps asking me about it." Mark returned home from a visitation with Billy.

"How is he?"

"Calmer than I expected. He likes the new case manager, Earl. Keeps asking when he's getting out, though." Mark shook his head. Seeing Billy in the institutional, minimalistic visiting room made his stomach turn. And the orange jumpsuit? Didn't fit him, not physically or mentally. Billy wasn't a killer. "Nothing can be done until the police have finished their investigation. And they seem to be taking their own sweet time."

"I know. We can go today, if you want. Let me shower and change clothes." Colton pushed the wheelbarrow past Mark and propped it inside the barn door.

If, hope on top of hope, Billy were ever allowed to return to the ranch, he'd be mucking out stalls for the rest of his life. He and Colton would make sure of it.

"Okay, I'll meet you at the house." Mark turned to leave. "You know, that kid lugged money all over creation and only spent a hundred dollars of it? And most of that was buying cat food for the crazy cat lady who let him stay with her."

"Huh. He had it on him? He didn't when we picked him up."

"He said once he realized what was in it, he stashed it by an old fence row, near a strip mall."

"Good grief. The things that kid's been through."

"I know. Meet you here in twenty."

"Yep."

They loaded up in Mark's truck in less than twenty minutes and headed out to talk to the crazy cat lady. Mark tried to remember how they'd gotten to the run-down apartment complex in the first place. Without Ellie's phone where they'd pulled up the address originally, Mark was running on recollection.

Mark's thoughts ran amuck, intertwined with conversations he wanted to have with Ellie, things he remembered from the last time they were together, Samson, ugh.

"I think it's here." Mark turned onto a street riddled with potholes. The small courtyard was ahead of them, only a corner visible due to the surrounding, equally run-down apartments.

"Wow, this is pretty." Colton got out and closed the door.

"And this is where Billy was supposedly holed up. Can you imagine?"

"Better than under a bridge."

"True." Mark walked up the cracked sidewalk, entered the overgrown courtyard and turned to the left. "Her apartment is in that corner. Billy's mom lived in the one to the right."

"Wow."

Mark knocked on the screen door. The curtain by the door raised slightly and then dropped back into place.

"What'd you want?" the voice behind the door yelled. "I gotta shotgun."

Mark and Colton eased away from the door and flanked either side. No one needed to get shot today.

"I was here a couple of weeks ago. Asking about Kitty. We're not police."

"Kitty's gone. And I don't have no cats. So go!"

Mark racked his brain for the name of her cat. "Ma'am, what happened to Tabitha?"

The curtain went up again.

"How do you know about my Tabitha? Who told you? That dirty old man across the way? He don't know nothing."

Mark shrugged his shoulders at Colton. She may be more than a little crazy.

"You did, ma'am. How nice Tabitha is. I even pet her when I was here last." He didn't think he did, but then she wouldn't remember anyways. "Ma'am, we're here about Billy. Do you remember Billy?"

"I think I do 'member you. You's with the kind pretty lady." They heard the bolts slide across and the peeling, veneer door opened a crack. "Who is you again?" The old lady squinted at them through the screen door, hunched over.

"Billy lived with me for a while, just like he did with you."

"I don't know no Billy."

"Ma'am, I know that's not true. You leant him your phone." Mark held up her small flip phone. "He asked us to return it to you."

Quick as lightning, the old woman opened the door wider, grabbed the phone with one hand, Mark's sleeve with the other and pulled him into the dark room. Colton stepped in behind him.

The room smelled of greasy food and something he couldn't place. The old woman moved several newspapers off a threadbare couch and offered them a seat.

Not a chance. Who knew what lurked in the cushions... dead mice, roaches, typhoid fever. No way.

"Oh, for Pete's sake. It's probably cleaner than your shoes." The old woman stood up straight, cracking her back. The old, crazy lady persona disappeared. "Billy, you say? Thanks for returning the phone. Wasn't sure I'd see it again, but it was worth it for Billy."

Mark's mouth dropped open. Colton paused inside the door.

The transformation from old, hunched back woman to this... this person standing in front of them was undefinable.

Mark narrowed his eyes at her.

"What? Do I have to spell it out to you?" She looked at Mark and then Colton, clear-eyed. "I guess I do. I'm a CI. You truly *aren't* cops. That means con-fi-den-tial in-form-ant."

Mark crossed his arms. "Could you have told us that before? Who do you report to? What do you report? Certainly not a runaway boy."

"With all the cops swarming the place? Uh, no. Mind yourself or I'll say nothing. And it's none of your business who I report to. I do good work in this community."

"Why are you talking to us, then?" Colton questioned.

"Duh. You brought the phone back. That means the boy trusted you."

"How long did you hide Billy?"

"Wasn't very long. No one needs to see their mother dead."

"Was she murdered?"

"What? No. I saw her shooting up in the courtyard, nobody around. That poor girl, she never caught any breaks. I wasn't about to let Billy see that, so I made him hide in the back bedroom until it was safe."

"Safe? Was he in trouble?" Mark used her words.

The lady cocked her head at him. "*He* told me he was in trouble. That not true?"

"No, it's true." Mark sighed.

She nodded her head. "Thought so."

"Who else knows you're a CI?" Colton injected.

"No one around here. None of the cops that were here that night you were here." The crazy cat lady slash CI sat down on the spot she'd cleared off for Mark and Colton. "They all think I'm crazy." She winked at Colton whose ears turned pink.

Mark looked at the room, magazines stacked

high, stained sheets covering the windows as curtains.

"Appearances, buddy. Gotta keep up appearances."

Mark nodded.

"Thanks again for returning the phone. Billy left something here that he may want. Or need." The old woman stood and disappeared into the back of the house. She carried Billy's dad's satchel out and handed it to Mark. "Figured he'd want it."

Mark looked at Colton. The backpack with all of the money? Billy said he'd buried it.

"It's all still there, if that's what you're wondering." she said.

"And you say he left it here?" Colton raised an eyebrow.

"Well, I may have found it."

"What does that mean?"

"He kept buying cat food for Tabitha and I didn't know where he was getting the money. I was concerned, so I followed him one night to where he'd stashed it."

"And where was that?"

"Near the hedgerow around the corner."

Confirmed what Billy told him.

"Why didn't he take it with him?"

"He said if I ever needed anything to go dig this bag up and help myself." She said. "I already knew where it was located, since I followed him, but I didn't need any of his money. The kid's sweet and all, but I could tell he'd had a rough go of it."

"Well, you obviously dug it up at some point."

"Yeah, I figured I could keep it safer here," she

pointed to the back room, "under the crazy lady's bed."

Made sense. There was no way anyone would request a look-see in this house for fear something, or someone, would reach out and bite them.

"Say, what happened to that pretty girl you were with that night?"

Ellie?

Mark cocked his head.

"She was by here the other night with the big guy, checking on all us crazies." The old woman chortled. "I hear she got shot."

What? Ellie? Shot? Mark felt his heart miss a step. Maybe the old woman was slightly touched in the head. He backed up, almost tripping over Colton.

"Here's her card. The one she dropped by." The woman pulled a business card off the rickety shelf next to a recliner.

Mark read out loud. "SAFE Ministries- Anthony - and a cell number."

"What made you think she got shot?" Colton asked, from behind him.

The woman pushed a stained doily off the next shelf down revealing a small box with an antennae and dials on the front. Clicking it on, the three could hear all sorts of chatter.

"A police scanner?" Mark asked.

"Yep. Helps to know what's going on, when the cops are coming, that sort of thing."

"Why do you think it was Ellie that got shot?" Mark stepped closer to the woman. His head was starting to pound. He wiped the sweat from his brow. It couldn't be Ellie. Could it? What was she doing in this neighborhood? And then it dawned on him. She was with a big guy, that had to be Samson. So, she was back at the club? But the card said SAFE Ministries. Didn't have her name on it, though. There had to be a mistake. Nothing added up.

"They described her. Tall, blonde hair, early 30's."

"That describes a lot of women."

"Said her name. Ellie Jenkins."

Oh no. No way. Mark turned, pushed Colton out the door.

"Do you know where that was? The shooting? Or where they took her?" Mark asked, letting the door slam behind him.

"No, no, but she shouldn't be hard to find. Call the hospitals close to here." The woman called after them. "Should have been on the news. There was a dead girl at the same location."

What in the world? Ellie? What happened? Why were you here? And who was the dead girl?

Mark and Colton ran for the truck, Billy's dad's backpack slung over Colton's shoulder.

"Call that number on the card first. Maybe they know where she's at." Colton grabbed the card.

"I'll look up hospitals in the area. When did she say this happened?"

"Within the last couple of days?"

Oh, Ellie. He'd been feeling sorry for himself for having to clean out stalls and wandering around like a lost puppy, and Ellie was lying in a hospital bed somewhere fighting a bullet wound. He'd been so much in his own head lately. *Please God, please let her be okay.*

The number on the business card rang and rang. Colton left a message and asked whoever was monitoring the phone to please call them back. None of the hospitals would confirm an Ellie Jenkins with a gunshot wound had been brought into their hospital, either.

Mark pounded the steering wheel.

Trust Me.

Oh, God! He tried that. Nothing seemed to come of it, this blind trust. Mark had fallen short. Again.

Colton reached across the seats and squeezed his shoulder. "We'll find her. Let's get rid of this bag at the police station. I don't know how much is in there, nor do I want to know."

Mark sniffed hard. "I can't- I don't know what- Jesus, please."

"I know, bro. Good call. Let's pray."

Mark had never really heard his brother pray out loud. He allowed Colton's words to soak into all of the places that had instantly frozen up with the thoughts of Ellie hurting and maybe worse.

He pulled out of the parking lot, narrowly missing an abandoned car. He let Colton's prayer wash over him. Turned blindly onto another road, and another. Going back the way they had come.

Trust Me.

"Uh, Mark. You've got lights behind you." Colton looked in the side mirror.

Oh, for the love of…! He couldn't catch a break.

Mark pulled over to the side, put the truck in Park, and thought about where his insurance card might be. "Dude, I wasn't speeding."

"I know." Colton put his hands on the dash.

Both of them turned to look at the backpack, in plain sight, in the back seat, holding how much money? That was stolen. Or at the very least, involved in a murder or two.

~

Ellie scooted off the kitchen chair and stiffly walked to the couch. The pain in her gut was overwhelming, but it could have been so much worse. She lifted her loose shirt. The stark white dressing would probably need to be changed today. This is certainly a lesson in depending on others for help. She couldn't change the dressing by herself and had to request Rebecca's help. Don't be a burden. But don't be an idiot, either. She just couldn't change it herself; the pain was too great. Who knew stomach wounds were the worst? The doctor told her it was just a deep graze, and she was lucky the bullet didn't penetrate any deeper into the muscle. From the amount of blood she'd lost, she'd thought she was a goner for sure. Luck had nothing to do with it. Only God could have prevented that from being much worse. Clara had lost her life. Ellie could have, too.

Clara. She'd just wanted to better herself. It was unfair. Samson had stopped by the first night she was released and explained what he'd heard on the street about Clara's death.

"Supposedly, she was one of their best dancers. When the boss caught wind of her planning to leave, they had to stop her. They couldn't afford for her to be picked up by another club." The big man confided.

"But she was getting out completely, not jumping to another club." Ellie shook her head.

"We may have known that, but the boss didn't."

"Are you safe, Samson? Does Clara's boss know about you?"

"I'm fine. It's you I'm worried about."

"Do they know about me?" Ellie blanched.

"They're asking questions. Who was Clara meeting with at the coffee shop, things like that. I really need you to stay low for a while. No more trips to the parking lot with Anthony until things calm down."

Ellie leaned her head back on the couch. That conversation with Samson had grounded her for the moment, as well as the pain of the wound. But restlessness was getting the best of her. She needed to be up and about, helping someone.

"I think it's time we changed that bandage." Rebecca came into the room with a tray full of ointment and gauze.

"I was thinking the same thing. I'm sorry I can't do it myself." Ellie blinked back tears. So frustrating.

"Girl, this ain't no thing. Pull up your shirt and let's get this done."

Ellie obliged, carefully peeling the tape around the bandage while Rebecca put on surgical gloves. The graze was deep enough to require stitches, but no punctures from shrapnel.

Rebecca leaned over to inspect it closer. "It looks pretty good, the skin around it is pink but doesn't look infected. And of course, you've got these deep bruises, which I suspect you'll have for a while. The good Lord was looking out for you." She took a cotton swab, added some antibiotic gel over the stitches, and taped new gauze over the wound.

"Truth."

"Do you want some pain meds?"

"I could use some, please. Thank you." Ellie shut her eyes. She felt so powerless to do anything. The prescribed resting was killing her, even though it'd only been days.

"Ellie? Are you okay?" Rebecca's kind voice brought fresh tears.

"I don't know." Ellie threw her arm over her face. "I thought I was doing what I was supposed to do, and someone died. I wish I'd never met Mark. Or Jason, for that matter. Everything got so complicated."

"Now I know you're not talking any sense. None of what happened was because of Jason or Mark. It happened because God has a plan for your life. Have you been reading Jason's Bible?"

"Still working through the things he underlined. They seem to speak to me the most." Ellie looked at her friend. She knew she was wallowing in self-pity; this wasn't about her. It was about doing something for the girls that she knew were caught in awful jobs. Honestly, what right did she have to speak into their lives when she's lost her own self confidence at the moment as well?

"I'll be right back." Rebecca went into Ellie's bedroom and brought out Jason's Bible. "I'm not sure you're seeing the truth in what's happened. I think you're in pain and forced to sit still and feeling guilty about Clara."

Check. All of the above.

"Let's read here. See, Jason underlined it, too. This is in Galatians, Chapter 5, 'At last we have freedom, for Christ has set us free! We must always cherish this truth and firmly refuse to go back into the bondage of our past.' There, He's talking about you not looking back. Back to the old you." Rebecca turned to another section. "Here in the Psalms, my favorite chapter 119, it says, 'Guide my steps by your word, so I will not be overcome by evil.'"

Ellie closed her eyes and let Rebecca's words flow over her.

"You know, Ellie? I've been praying and I think now's the right time to say this," Rebecca paused. "The good Lord told me, and this is for you, that you know the truth, sometimes you forget it, like I do, and need reminding."

"What truth are you talking about?"

"The truth that the woman out at Mark's ranch told you about, that scripture describing how nothing can separate you from God's love, not your past, especially."

Ellie nodded.

"And how much He loves you and how you've been set free from the bondage of sin."

"Yes."

"But I don't think you're walking in that freedom. It's like you know what the freedom brings. You've been set free by Jesus, and you should be ready to take the next step, one that only you can take. Walking in that freedom."

"I don't know what walking in freedom looks like." Ellie sighed.

"It's knowing that no matter what happens to you and around you, you have every confidence that the good Lord will walk with you. You can have peace knowing that God is with you. He didn't say you wouldn't have troubles or trials, but He did say you can be in step, walking beside, hiding under His wings of grace every day of your life on this earth." Rebecca smoothed the cover of the worn Bible. "It's a step and one that you have to be intentional about." Rebecca patted her on the arm and stood. "I best be getting back to fixin' lunch."

Peace, that's what she needed. The confidence that Jesus was walking beside her, that she wasn't alone. Comfort. She didn't have to answer to anyone but God for her shortcomings and failures. And that He accepted her just as she was, cracks and bruises and broken heart. All of it. Like a gentle rain washes away the stink of the world, He did this for her. Ellie slipped off into a deep, peaceful, sleep.

Chapter 30

Mark and Colton watched the two cops get out of their car behind them and slowly walk down each side of the truck.

"What do you think?" Mark kept his gaze forward with one eye on the rearview mirror.

"I don't know. If you weren't speeding and your tags are valid…." Colton whispered. "I have to wonder if it has to do with that backpack."

"Or we're being paranoid." Mark hoped as he rolled down the window. "Either way, we don't have time for this. I have to find Ellie." He rubbed his eyes, pain creeping over his shoulder, up his neck, into his jawline.

"Ellie is going to have to wait. We've got no choice." Colton eyed the officer approaching in the side mirror.

"License and registration, please." The officer on the driver's side asked. The other officer stood behind Colton's passenger window and looked in the back seat of the truck.

"Can I ask what this is about? Do I have a taillight out?" *God, please let it be a taillight.* Mark opened the console where his registration and insurance card were as well as his wallet.

The other officer motioned across the bed of the truck.

The first officer took Mark's license and registration card. "What's in the bag?"

"Um, what bag?" Mark looked at Colton.

"Don't play dumb." The other officer tapped his baton on Colton's window, indicating he should roll it down, too.

"Do I know you?" Mark craned his neck around to see the officer better.

The man frowned.

"I know, you were at the motel where all of this started. Where the two men were murdered. I recognize your voice."

"Where's the boy?" The officer shrugged off Mark's questions. "Never mind, we don't care. The bag. Hand it to my partner."

"Your partner. Who was also at the motel." Mark put two and two together. "Which is how you know about the backpack. Did you *follow* us?"

"Shut up. Give the bag to my partner."

"Hey, Sarge, what's he talking about?" The taller officer leaned in the window and spoke across Colton.

"Shut up. The bag. Now."

Mark reached into the back seat and handed it to Colton, who passed it out the window.

"Billy's at the police station now. We were taking the backpack to the detective on the case."

Colton nodded at the cop. "We know exactly how much money is in the bag. We called and told them we found it and were bringing it in. The bag and the money. All of it."

Mark prayed they would believe Colton's bluff.

The two officers took the bag back to their patrol car and talked for a minute.

Were these dirty cops that had been following them from the club when they'd first talked to Kitty? Did one of them break into Ellie's home looking for the cash? Had Mark and Colton wrecked the crazy cat lady's cover?

Trust Me.

Lord, when we get out of this mess, you and I need to have a serious conversation. I am failing in the trust department. Help me. Keep Ellie safe wherever she is. You're going to have to take over, because all my plans are sliding south.

The officers rejoined Mark and Colton, approaching on either side of the truck, minus the backpack.

"How much did you say was in the backpack?" The heavy-set officer asked Mark.

Mark tried to do a quick calculation in his head. Total amount minus the $100 bucks or so Billy spent on cat food and snacks, which was impossible, because he never heard how much the casino payout was to begin with. A very large sum, enough to draw the interest of several people including the cops on the take, but he had no idea.

"They don't know." The sergeant smiled at his partner. "Have a good day, gentlemen."

Mark pulled on the door handle and stepped out of the truck. Here goes nothing. "Honestly, officers, we don't care about the money." Mark paused. "If the money never shows up again, we're fine with that. No one seems to know how the money went missing from the motel. It was just assumed that the kid took it." It was a last-ditch effort and one that made him sick to his stomach. Totally ranking off-the-chart low on the integrity totem pole.

God? Any other way? I know you can make a way.

The sergeant turned back. "I thought you said you'd called ahead about the money and backpack coming into the station?"

"Well, we didn't. As far as we know, the money never turned up." Colton stepped out of the truck, followed Mark's train. Right over the cliff.

Great. And now your little brother's integrity matches your own. Congratulations.

"Who else knows you had it?"

"No one. The kid told us where to find it." No sense bringing crazy cat lady slash CI into the mix.

"Is he talking about the motel murders? And the robbery?" The officer looked at the one in charge and back at Mark. "A guy confessed. The third guy in the room. Right, Sarge?"

"Please shut up. That's an order."

Mark and Colton listened to their conversation. Maybe the young cop wasn't on the take? He didn't seem to know what the sergeant was talking about.

"So, the money in the bag is the casino payout that disappeared with the kid? And we're taking the money to the police station, right?"

"Uh, sure."

The officers walked back to their squad car, their conversation snatched away with a breeze. If the money walked out of there with Billy saying he had it last…that couldn't happen. Oh, what a complicated web we weave…

"We've got to do something." Mark whispered to Colton.

"I'm not going down for that." The younger officer shouted and pulled his gun.

The sergeant slowly turned. "What are you doing, you little snot. Five more minutes, and you could have been rich!"

"Sorry, Sarge, but I'm not going out this way. Get your hands up!" Into his mic, he yelled, "Officer needs assistance!"

Mark held his breath, watching the scene unfold.

"You." The officer gestured to Colton, tossed his handcuffs to him. "Cuff him."

Wide-eyed, Colton took the cuffs, placed them around the sergeant's wrists, and slipped his revolver out of its holster.

The sergeant began yelling obscenities at them. Turned to run, slipped in the gravel and landed down face first.

Mark carefully handed the gun to the officer. Opening the back door of the patrol car, the officer pulled the sergeant off the ground and shoved him into the barred seat. Spittle flew from the sergeant's lips onto his shirt front.

The three men stood at the corner of the cruiser until another officer joined them, swinging in behind them, lights blazing.

After a brief conversation between the officers, the tall one rejoined Mark and Colton.

"What just happened?" Mark ground out,

adrenaline pulsing through his core.

"I was tasked with riding with him for a while with the thought that he was shaking down businesses and strong-arming people. The higher-ups thought, since I was a peon on the force, that the sergeant may do something stupid, and we'd nail him for these allegations. Today was that lucky day."

"We may have more to add to that story." Colton shook the officer's hand.

"I'm sure. Why don't you follow me down to the station, and let's get this thing figured out with the boy you mentioned?"

"Are you taking the backpack?" Mark frowned as Colton walked back to the truck.

"I am. It's secured. After what just happened with the sergeant, you think I'm going to take the money and run?"

Mark shrugged.

"I'm not."

"We were truthful when we said we didn't care about the money, but it might just be the one thing that gets the kid released."

"Well, then, let's go see what we can do." The officer walked back to his patrol car.

Mark turned on his heel and beelined it back to the truck. He was not going to let the cop out of his sight.

This your way of working, Lord?

Trust Me.

And Ellie?

Trust.

Mark sucked in a deep breath. This is so convoluted. He felt drug along in a rip tide, barely able to breathe most days, tossed to and fro, waiting for the next big wave to sink him.

~

Ellie dreamt she was sitting at the top of the mountain, a slight breeze ruffled her hair. Interspersed among the rocky terrain were beautiful, tiny purple flowers with yellow centers, growing in clumps. She could sense a presence near her, a man silently enjoying the view with her. She felt protected, safe. Hidden from the cares of the world. She turned her face to the sun, let the warm rays calm the deep places in her. She wept with sheer gratefulness. When she stood, the man stood, too. Took her hand and led her down the mountain on a path she couldn't see, but she trusted him and followed where he stepped. Around boulders, through a tall stand of trees, into a valley, filled with wildflowers. Such beauty, all around her. The man gently let go of her hand and…

"Ellie?" Anthony's voice startled her awake.

Please no, don't go. Don't leave me.

Nothing can separate us…

Ellie blew out a breath and sat up, the dream vanishing. Only remnants of the peaceful, serene, safe feeling stayed.

"Sorry, I was going out for a walk before dinner and wondered if you wanted to join me?" Anthony's voice was soothing and matched the dream-like scene she'd come out of seconds before.

"Yes, I think that'd be good. Fresh air and all." Ellie pushed off the couch, used the restroom and grabbed a hat and light jacket.

"We're going out for a bit, sweetie. We'll be

back in time for dinner." Anthony called to Rebecca.

"Be careful." She called in return.

"Let's walk this way." Anthony took her good arm and guided her away from the street where the coffee shop sat.

"Is it safe to be out here? Maybe we should've stayed inside?" Ellie threw a worried look at him.

"We're fine, child." He patted her arm. "No one's looking for a white girl walking with an old black man. Now, if you were with Samson, you'd stick out like a sore thumb. That boy is big. I've got to go check on things at the church anyways, so we'll not be outside the whole time."

Her mind skipped along ahead, first with visions of Samson, standing tall above her, protective face in place, and then to the man in the mountain dream, who didn't have the same stature as Samson, but exuded safety as well. And then, Mark. She hadn't seen him for weeks, but her thoughts always trailed back to him. She missed him. If she thought about him too long, she would get down-right angry with him for being so self-righteous, thinking he was better than she. Then, something would gently remind her that people could change and be forgiven. She'd forgiven him, hadn't she? The old self wanted to hold onto that anger, it served as a protective wall around her heart and emotions. A memory of their time together would cause all of that anger to fall to pieces, so she prayed daily for him. Prayed his inner intellect would be softened, so he could see others like Jesus did, forgiven of their sins, a new creation. Ellie grimaced. The day may never come where she saw the results of her prayers. She may never see him again.

The church wasn't far and despite her whirling thoughts, Anthony's quiet demeanor and leisurely pace allowed her to enjoy the walk. Built rock solid in the late 1800's, the brick church was as steady as they came. It had weathered clashes of humanity and withstood the storms of life forever. Tall columns in the front with traditionally wide steps and beautiful doors welcomed generations. Only a few cracks and missing corners of steps indicated its age. Anthony led her on a steppingstone pathway to the back of the church, down steps that needed cement repair, and through a slightly askew oak door. The back looked completely different from the front of the church and was reserved for those less fortunate to pick up bags of food, get clean clothes, and eat a hot meal on Tuesdays, Thursdays, and Sundays.

Another one of Anthony's ventures. Ellie remembered the numerous times when she and Jason would serve in the basement. Whatever was needed, Anthony and Jason both tried to supply. Ellie would often stand in the kitchen or against the back wall, waiting for either of them to tell her how she could help. Jason would draw her into a warm embrace and then push her towards a young girl or elderly woman that looked like they could use a friend or even a shoulder to cry on.

"I'm going to go sit in the chapel for a bit," Ellie told Anthony while he spoke with a matronly woman counting cans of food in the pantry. He nodded at her.

The chapel, buried under the large church up top, was as intimate as the sanctuary was grand. Soft light flickered in smoky vases in the corner, the crucifixion hung in the middle of one wall. The roughhewn pews held thread-bare cushions, and probably multiple tears over the years from those seeking sanctum in the peaceful chapel. The small room seemed ancient with its rock walls and hardwood floors. She could almost imagine the people groups, slaves or not, congregating below the church, waiting for the cover of darkness to continue their journey to freedom. The SAFE ministry had formed with that thought in mind, freedom from all types of slavery. Sin, prostitution, human trafficking, all of it.

Ellie sunk down on the closest pew, dust rising from the cushion.

Reverence hung in the air, along with the smell of whatever was cooking in the kitchen for the Tuesday meal.

God, so much has happened in such a short period of time, and I got lost in the craziness. I know you love me as much as you loved Jason. I'm thankful for the time I had with Jason and for him bringing me into Your family. I know your word is true, that you will never leave me or allow anything to separate me from you. Not my past, not any stupid decision, not other's opinions of me. I'm sorry about Clara, I'm sorry about Mark.

What was she sorry about Mark for? Ellie shook her head. She was sorry she'd let his view of her shake her to the core. She should be more solid in her foundation than to allow a man to distract her from that truth. He was a distraction, a very handsome distraction, but one nonetheless. His feelings toward her after he'd discovered her past had not surprised her, rather he disappointed her. Rebecca had reminded her that she was a new creation, had thrown off the sin that held her captive, and that she only had to seek to please God. She'd be content with that. And if there ever was someone to follow Jason, she'd know for certain that God had brought her His best.

Ellie prayed, head bowed, until she heard a commotion at the chapel door.

"Son, leave her be." Anthony's voice overshadowed another voice.

A whispered conversation she couldn't hear.

The door creaked open.

Mark stood in the doorway.

Chapter 31

Mark glanced around the room, the object of his thoughts staring at him from a pew halfway down the aisle. Her baseball cap covered her glorious hair, making her eyes stand out even more, and he watched her slowly blink at him.

The older man, who tried to stop him earlier, came in behind him.

Ellie looked from Mark to the older man and nodded. The man stepped back out. His dismissal was encouraging.

Shyness washed over him, followed quickly by gratefulness and then shame. Would she hate him? Would she even talk to him?

He saw her now. The way God saw her, who she was now. Perfect, new, flawed like he was. He'd learned what grace meant, more for himself than her. He wasn't the one doling out grace. He needed grace. He was grateful to her for forcing him to really look at himself and to come out the other side a better man. Not worthy of her, for certain, but maybe…

Hesitantly, Mark walked down the narrow center aisle and stopped by her pew. Ellie faced the front, not making eye contact with him. Mark sat down in the pew opposite hers.

"How did you find me?" she asked, turning her eyes on him.

Had she been hiding? From him? The pain in her eyes was his undoing. So much to say. So much he wanted to know. So much to apologize for. And he couldn't open his mouth. He held eye contact with her as long as he was able and then put his arms on the pew in front of him, his head resting on his arms. *Lord, help me.*

In his peripheral vision, he saw her swipe her cheeks.

The pain he caused. He wouldn't be surprised if she never spoke to him again.

He cleared his throat. "Long story. We found Billy. Or rather he found us. Called a couple of days ago out of the blue and wanted to come back. I tried to call you, but your number had been disconnected, or at least the one I had. So, Colton went with me to pick him up. Had to turn him in, though. Too much has happened and there's multiple investigations going on… well, you know."

Ellie nodded.

"He had some crazy lady's phone that he borrowed and we, Colton and I, promised to return it to her. The lady, who we found out wasn't so crazy, also had the backpack with all of the money from the hotel and was holding it for him." He saw Ellie raise her eyebrows. "As we were leaving her house, she told us you'd been shot." Mark paused, took a deep breath. "I was worried. Out of my head worried. We didn't know where to go, which hospital you were at, or even exactly when it happened." Mark opened his palm and straightened out a SAFE Ministries business card on his jeans. "The crazy lady gave us the card you left with her. I called the number on the card and had to leave a message."

"We drove around a little, trying to decide where to look, when we were stopped by the cops. They had followed us from the lady's house and knew we had the backpack. The sergeant that stopped us was at the motel, maybe was one of the them that followed us to CATS, could have been the one who broke into your house and attacked us... I don't know. It's a crazy story, for sure. Anyway, the other cop who was with the sergeant was a good cop, arrested him in front of us. I was scared out of my mind by then, he asked us to come down to the station. Which was super frustrating because I needed to find you. But we did and when we collaborated Billy's story with what happened in the motel room and everywhere else, they let us walk. I really tried to reach you, you should have been with me when we picked up Billy. Colton suggested we check here at the address on the card. See if anyone here knew what had happened and where I could find you." Mark looked across the aisle at her. He was rambling like an idiot. Seeing no response from her, he put his elbows on his knees and his fists on his cheeks. He didn't know what to say. Maybe nothing would help this situation. Maybe Ellie was lost to him forever.

"Where's Billy now?" Ellie glanced at him and then away.

"He's still in lock up. For leaving the ranch. It's

considered another charge, but not as hefty a punishment as murder or stealing money. He's just labeled a flight risk now. He may have to sit there awhile. We'll go to bat for him since the money's turned in, and the third guy in the motel room is singing a different tune now that Billy's in jail and his story is ringing truer than that guy's. I'm sure there will be more fallout from all of this, and I don't know if they will ever fully solve the break-in at your house or find your rings, unless something comes of the gun we found. We haven't heard any more on that, so I'm guessing they stole the rings as a coverup for why they really broke in, which you and I know was to find the money. I'd hate to see him sit there for very long, but I don't know how to convince the court to do anything different, yet. And to be honest, through everything that's happened, I don't know if there's been a funeral or service for Kitty, but I can find out."

Mark's voice broke.

"Ellie, I am such a foolish man. I try very hard to be perfect, to be what everyone wants me to be. And all I seem to do is fail. I know there are things that I've said that were hurtful. I know that I've hurt *you*. I was so caught up in trying to make those around me perfect, too, that I forgot how God created each of us with a story to tell. Mine is littered with failures and many times, I wondered if it was in my genes to disregard others for my own selfish motives, like my father did. But I've come to realize that I have my mother's genes as well. The ones that rely on God when I can't change situations, that say I'm still worthy of God's love despite my shortcomings.

And in my attempt to be perfect, I was equally afraid to be around anyone who either unveiled my discrepancies or had failures of their own. I was so arrogant and ungodly. Can you ever forgive me?"

He looked up as Ellie eased her hand out of the pew and over the aisle.

Mark closed his eyes and wept, overjoyed that she was giving him a chance. He remembered the first time they'd held hands. She'd said it was a technique, holding hands during a hard conversation. He thought it was brilliant.

He wiped his hand on his jeans and reached out to touch hers.

"Mark, I'm called to forgive you." Ellie interlaced her fingers in his.

"But, Ellie, I want so much more. I was so wrong to judge you. You've been through more than I can imagine and me bringing judgment was so hurtful. I said once that your past doesn't mean anything to me. Words of a foolish man. What I know now is that your past shaped you to be the compassionate, kind person you are. Would I have preferred that you never knew Samson or endured the kind of treatment that you must have received? Of course. So many times, I wanted to protect you, save you from having nightmarish thoughts, be the person who shielded you from the ugly. What I didn't take into account from my own short-sightedness, was that was never my place. You'd already received that with Jesus. Who was I to come in and think I was God? I am so sorry."

"Mark, I'd forgotten who I was, if I ever really knew. All I saw was grief and condemnation."

"I didn't help that. If I'd been the man you needed-"

"Who are you now?" Ellie whispered.

Who was he now? A changed man, for certain.

"A man who's learned that God's grace has nothing to do with what I've done and everything to do with who He is. A man who's fallen hard for a lady who is wiser and kinder and more loving than he is. A lady, I might add, who has received the same grace as I, who isn't subject to things in her past, who, I hope, can forgive me." Mark moved over to her pew, regained her hand. "My prayer to the God who loves us equally is that you may, someday, have deeper feelings for me. If you'll let me, I want to prove to you that I have changed and how much I want you by my side. If you'll have me."

Ellie turned to him. "Mark, I'm far from perfect. I do forgive you. My own thoughts and feelings judged you, the perfect child, who didn't know heartache, who had the whole world by the tail. There could be nothing of substance between us. I was terrified you'd find out who I really was, and then-"

"I was a fool to let you believe I was better than you. That's not love." Mark interrupted.

"Love? Mark, I didn't love myself, how could you love me? I didn't even know who I was. And then, a friend, with the help of Jason's Bible, reminded me. If I kept my eyes on Jesus, trusted what He saw in me, He was all that mattered. Not my past, not my future, not anyone else. Just Him."

Mark squeezed her hand. "I love that. Love that we can walk in that freedom without the threat of being imperfect or failing." He brought her fingertips up to his lips and searched her face. Her blue eyes under the brim of the ball cap, so large, filled with tears. "I'm not Jason, though."

"I don't want Jason."

Mark looked at the floor, tears threatening again.

Ellie lifted his face with her hands on his cheeks, brought his eyes to hers again.

"You realize if it hadn't been for Jason, you and I may never have met," she said, softly.

He nodded and kept his eyes locked on hers.

Lifting the bill of her cap, he gently kissed her.

~

When their lips met, the rocks around her heart began to slide off, exposing a joy Ellie never thought she'd feel again. Rocks that had broken off with Jason, ones she'd picked up again after his death, fell for the second time. Rocks designed to protect her heart, rocks layered to shield her emotions, even impenetrable ones whose purpose was to keep people at bay, dropped and crashed to the ground.

Mark's arms came around her and she kept her lips pressed to his. The solidness of his body, his tears and hers intermingling, their hearts bonding with unspoken emotions.

They broke away from the kiss, only to rest their foreheads against each other's, the intensity of the moment continuing.

"Ellie, I love you. I think of you day in and day out. I can't imagine us not together."

Ellie leaned back, solemn, still within his embrace. "Love is such a big word, Mark. More than a feeling, you know. A commitment.”

“I know. I want that for us.”

“I do, too.”

Mark kissed her again, more soundly this time. His passion igniting small explosions of joy in the deep recesses of her heart, rocks of insecurity and self-preservation dropping away. She did love this man.

Epilogue

Six months later

Ellie sat in the bunkhouse and took a deep breath. The alluring fragrance of hydrangeas and roses filled the room. Never in her life could she have imagined wearing a beautiful champagne-colored dress with matching, heavy lace and a short headpiece that held her hair up. A short stool sat in the center of the bunkhouse, and the bunks had been scooted to one side to make room for a full-length mirror.

Unbelievable. God, you are so good.

A whirlwind, full of smiles and tears, hard conversations and joyful ones had followed Mark's declaration of love. They both had a lot of growing to do, but she was confident enough in her identity in Jesus to recognize what was true and the thoughts that ensnared her. True statements of commitment and love. She was free to walk in the freedom she knew was hers because of the truth.

Noisily, her bridesmaids came in and surrounded her with hugs. Selena and Brynleigh had become her closest girlfriends, something she'd never had before.

Brynleigh handed her an envelope.

"What's this?" Ellie asked her.

"You can read it now. Be ready to fix your makeup, though."

Oh boy.

Ellie opened it, expecting to see Mark's rounded penmanship. Instead, it held scratchy letters in a short note. From Billy. Ellie looked up at Brynleigh.

"I went to visit him and took some textbooks for him. Told him about you and Mark."

"Oh, my goodness."

Brynleigh handed her a tissue.

Mrs. Jenkins, I guess that won't be your name for long. I'm happy that you and Mr. Mark are getting married. I'm sorry I ran away. Please forgive me. Will you come visit me with Mr. Mark? Billy

Ellie nodded and patted her cheeks. "Please tell him I will, and with Mr. Mark."

What a perfect day, Lord.

Rebecca stepped up to the group. "It's almost time. Anthony will be here soon to get you. Let's pray really quick."

The other girls linked arms in a circle and bowed their heads. Ellie looked at the ceiling, afraid her tears would run down her face and ruin her makeup.

"Oh, Heavenly Father, we are so grateful for the works that you've done. Things that we could never have foretold, things that only you could put together through your faithfulness. Thank you for always working on our behalf to provide, to encourage, to comfort. For Ellie and Mark, we ask that you place protection over their mouths, so that only good and loving things will spring forth, protection over their marriage, as they walk hand in hand with you. Protection over their lives as they do Your will this side of Heaven. In your precious name, Amen."

All of the ladies said Amen in unison.

Rebecca ushered everyone out the door, except for Ellie. She blew a kiss to her and held the door open for Anthony to enter. Ellie hadn't even hesitated to ask him to walk her down the aisle. There wasn't a question of who should stand in that place.

"You look radiant, my dear." Anthony stooped to plant a kiss on her cheek. "Are you ready?"

"I think so. No, I know so." Ellie put cold fingers in his gnarled ones and stood from the chair. Rebecca bustled in and fixed her train and then held the door as they stepped into the bright sunlight.

Chairs were arranged in short rows facing an arbor lined with her cream-colored hydrangeas. Muted shades of ribbon attached to the chair backs swayed in a light breeze. Most of the chairs were filled with family and town people who knew Mark and Colton. Samson's tall frame stood above the rest.

The traditional wedding march began, and Ellie looked expectantly at Mark, standing in front of the arbor. Brynleigh and Selena had already gone before her and waited with tears on their faces.

Ellie smiled and glided with Anthony to the front, listening to the swell of the music. When Mark took her hands in his, she couldn't tear her eyes from him. The people in attendance faded away and only she and Mark remained. His thumbs rubbing the back of her hands in gentle circles spoke of his nervousness, but also his love.

"Ellie, I vow to be the man you can grow with, the one who sees you as Jesus does, the one who puts you before myself. I vow to protect you in all ways. I promise to hold your hand in mine through the good and the bad and to show my affection for you always. I promise to seek wisdom and direction from the One who loved you first, Jesus, so that I can lead us through this marriage journey. I am so desperately in love with you and will remain so for the rest of my days."

Ellie lifted a gloved hand and wiped the tears freely flowing down Mark's face.

"Mark," Ellie blew out a breath, caught his hand in hers again. "Mark, I never believed in second chances. Never believed I was worthy of a first chance. I now know that the God we serve sees me as more than worthy of love. He brought you into my life, and we've grown in our own understanding of how God sees us. I promise to walk beside you as we discover who God wants us to be as a couple now. I respect you, Mark, for being vulnerable, for being strong, for seeking after God. I promise to always hold your hand even when the footpath is steep, but also when the journey is light and fun. I am deeply in love with you, too, and will be so for the rest of my days."

Ellie's heart soared as the minister pronounced them man and wife. Turning to face the crowd in attendance, she took Mark's arm and started down the aisle. One guest after another stepped into their path and handed her a Tootsie Pop.

"What is this?" She looked at him, puzzled.

Mark kissed her on the cheek. "Stick with me, babe, and you'll never run out of these," he whispered.

Oh my. So thoughtful, so romantic. And he planned it under the radar, without her knowledge. Such a sweet surprise.

Beaming at Mark, she accepted them all until her free hand held a bouquet of multi-colored lollipops.

As they took their place in the receiving line, Ellie rejoiced. This is what freedom looked like. Second chances. Joy. Opportunities to love and be loved. And the freedom that can only be found in the grounding goodness of God's love.

The Tootsie Pops addition to the story is not fictional. It's a part of my parent's story and a brilliant, romantic gesture by my dad. After 62 years of marriage, they are a Godly example for my siblings and I. I love seeing the bowl of Tootsie Pops on the table in their home!

ACKNOWLEDGEMENTS

Cora- You are the best crit partner! I love our Thursday dinners, our brainstorming vacations, and our sisters in Christ friendship.

Brianne- Thank you for reading my story, making suggestions, loving my characters!

Matt and Gary- Thank you for your firefighter and EMT knowledge, you were both so helpful!

Hannah and Angie- Blessings to you both for helping the movie in my head make it onto the page.

Kari- you are one of the strongest people I know! Thank you for your encouragement, sarcasm, and wisdom!

My Family- You have supported me from day 1 of this journey. Love you all.

Thank you always to my publisher, Cynthia Hickey of Winged Publications. If Cynthia hadn't taken a chance on me, I may never have graduated from being a writer to a published author.

To My Heavenly Father- words will never be able to describe how grateful I am to have this creativity gift- I am blessed beyond expectation or measure.

Questions to Ponder

1. Reread the main verse- Romans 8:35-39. Which part of this verse trips you up?

2. Do you have friends in your life that can ask the hard questions?

3. Have you ever found yourself judging someone for what they've done in the past?

4. Have you ever been afraid if people knew the real you, they wouldn't like you?

5. Do you ever feel like you don't deserve some things?

6. Do you live for the expectations of others?

7. How often do we allow other people to define us?

8. What do the voices in your head say?

9. In Chapter 27, Brynleigh remarks that the boys think differently about Mark than he does himself. Ellie has been told the same. Why do we believe those things?

10. The Word says in John 10:10 that the enemy comes to steal, kill, and destroy. Ephesians 6:12 says "For we wrestle not against flesh and blood,

but against principalities, against powers, against the rulers of the darkness of this world, against spiritual wickedness in high places." As someone who understands the difficulty in shutting out the whispers of the enemy, I encourage you to surround yourself with good friends who are willing to ask the hard questions and love you enough to gently say what you are listening to is not truth. Mark had Colton and Brandon, Ellie had Anthony and Rebekkah. Who do you have?

You can always contact me at julie@juliebrown-author.com and tell me your story. I love to hear from readers! My website is also a great place to connect! juliebrown-author.com

May you always find freedom when you walk in truth and may you always feel His pleasure for you in His life-giving Word.

Julie Brown

Other Titles by Julie Brown

Truth=Freedom series
Christian Romantic Suspense

EVEN WHEN series
Christian Inspirational